THE

SERENITY

OF

WHITENESS

THE
SERENITY
OF
WHITENESS

Stories By and About Women

in Contemporary China

TRANSLATED BY

Zhu Hong

BALLANTINE BOOKS   NEW YORK

An Available Press Book
Published by Ballantine Books

Translation and notes
copyright © 1991 by Zhu Hong
Foreword copyright © 1991 by Catherine Vance Yeh

All rights reserved under International and Pan-
American Copyright Conventions. Published in the
United States by Ballantine Books, a division of Ran-
dom House, Inc., New York, and simultaneously in
Canada by Random House of Canada Limited, Toronto.

Library of Congress Catalog Card Number: 91-92143
ISBN: 0-345-37097-X

Cover design by Barbara Leff

Text design by Holly Johnson

Manufactured in the United States of America

First Edition: January 1992
10 9 8 7 6 5 4 3 2 1

CONTENTS

FOREWORD

As early as the 1930s, the legitimacy of depicting women was a point of contention among leftist writers in China. Women writers like Ding Ling, who had created the modern female voice in fiction during the 1920s and wanted to continue to deal with women's issues beyond general political interpretations, were writing within narrow confines. To depict women as authentic individuals was regarded by Communist party authorities as an expression of petit-bourgeois sentiments incongruent with the basic tenet that literature was to serve class struggle.

As a consequence, women characters in Chinese fiction functioned only as symbols and metaphors. A woman might stand for the Chinese nation—weak and trampled by powerful Western and Japanese imperialism. She might represent the weak and oppressed, whose liberation was the main task of socialist revolution. Or she might stand for the intellectual class, inherently weak, but with the potential to see the light, transform herself, and become a force in the revolution. As a result, women as genuine characters with their own concerns and voices were altogether eliminated from literature after the Communists took power in 1949.

But when Chinese fiction, after long years under rigid

controls, made a comeback with the reforms of 1979, women writers as well as women characters showed their resilience and were among the first to reemerge; they challenged the traditions of a literature defining its characters by class status, and spearheaded a movement committed to humanism.

Women characters have since come alive, interacting in authentic situations. They once again speak with distinctness. Within a very short time, this voice has become lively, self-assured, and diverse. Works written by women have begun to explore and redefine the meaning of being a woman. There has been a revival of literary subjects long ostracized by established political conventions, such as love; marriage; ambition; the duty of being a wife, a mother, or a daughter.

The stories in *The Serenity of Whiteness* record this awakening and show its potential. The authors, all women, have many common links. They are from the same generation, being born during the 1930s and 1940s. They share the experience of both traditional and socialist China as socialism became its own tradition. Their concerns and burdens, as well as their understanding of the role of fiction, set them off against some of the more radically feminist authors, many of whom are younger. This younger generation endorses the process of writing as a re-creation of their identity by using strong autobiographical elements—and they are in this sense, more westernized in their approach.

The stories in this anthology primarily present women as a group with a collective experience; the social aspect of their existence is more essential than their individual dimension. The characters' experiences are representative rather than unique. These characters move in an environment harsher than just a patriarchal system. In the name of communism, a political doctrine ostensibly committed to progress and women's liberation, many of these women have been deprived of even the minimum of human dignity and social leeway.

The women in these stories paid for communism with the absence of romantic love. Love, as depicted here, often constitutes the subtext of a woman's life; her joys and sorrows are not linked directly or exclusively to loving a man but instead to its consequences, such as pregnancy, childbirth, or family sacrifice. The absence of romantic love highlights the overwhelmingly social nature and social burdens of their lives.

The stories in the volume belong to two different time periods. Those published in the early 1980s share in the humanistic concerns of the era and depict "women as human beings" rather than as women. In Chen Ruiqing's "Guessie Grows Up" and Niu Zhenghuan's "Lost in the Wind and the Snow" the sad state of the human condition is evoked and epitomized by the suffering of women. In Bao Chuan's "The Loudspeaker" and in Gu Ying's "Jingjing Is Born," the dehumanizing effects of the political battles during the Cultural Revolution are felt. In the story on her mother, Wen Bin reflects on herself and her sisters actually being part of the traditional forces that denied her mother the freedom of love and self-fulfillment; their blind insensitivity fosters the cruelty exhibited during the Cultural Revolution. These stories treat the fate of the women as the epitome of injustice and dehumanization.

Zong Pu's "The Tragedy of the Walnut Tree" marks the transition from depicting women as human beings to depicting women as women. In the story, the aged and ill woman finally decides to cut down her silent companion, the walnut tree in her yard, after coming to terms with her husband's abandonment of her. The story centers on the interior of a woman's emotional world. Although the significance of the tree is largely defined by its social meaning, the narrative remains private and personal.

The later stories from the mid-1980s evoke more self-conscious female protagonists, who struggle against the fate of always being the victim, and in the process redefine their own worth. Their central concern is the question of what it means to be a woman. This enables these authors to focus on the individuals and their response to the world at large. They are written with a different kind of sensibility, and the characters in these stories in most cases actively confront their fate. Dai Qing's "The Unexpected Tide," Gu Ying's "The Serenity of Whiteness" and Lu Xin'er's "The Sun Is Not Out Today" are all stories of confrontation. Women brought up by traditional values struggle for a new self-understanding and eventually create new responses rather than yield to the familiar old. Their struggle is intensely personal and private; there is no acceptable norm as a guideline; the decision ultimately depends on their capacity to realize their own strength. Counteracting this upbeat and idealistic vision of women's fate, Lu Xin'er's "The One and the Other" and Hu Xin's "Four Women of Forty" remind the reader of the price women have paid and might have to pay for this new self and of the deceptive potential inherent in this new vision.

The stories brought together here and translated with much sympathy by Zhu Hong, who herself belongs to the generation of these authors and shares their concerns and sensibility, stand as a testimony to the vitality and growing self-awareness of the woman's voice in contemporary Chinese literature. Writings by other women writers, who themselves are more westernized and write for a more westernized public might have had a more familiar ring to Western readers. The stories collected in Zhu Hong's volume, however, find their interest, strength, and authenticity in their very link to a strong and still pervasive tradition among both modern Chinese women writers and the Chinese reading public.

Catherine Vance Yeh
Harvard University
August 1991

THE
SERENITY
OF
WHITENESS

GUESSIE GROWS UP

CHEN RUIQING

CHEN RUIQING, born in 1932, is currently a scriptwriter for the Beijing Film Studio. Chen joined the Revolution in 1947, but she was labeled a rightist (enemy category) in 1957 and remained a political outcast for twenty-two years. Since rehabilitation in 1979, she has published steadily. The Call of the Great Northern Wilds, *her best-known work to date, is a semiautobiographical series of episodes about political exile.*

"Guessie Grows Up," one of the episodes in the series, is a fresh and tender treatment of a young woman's initiation into the strange conditions of a labor camp for thought reform.

It was clear from the very beginning that she was different.

I first met Guessie on the train that was taking us to the Great Northern Wilds. She had round rosy cheeks that dimpled when she laughed. Her short hair was worn in two little pigtails held together by rubber bands. Her figure was slight, as if she had not yet grown to her full height. But she was full of vigor as she rushed to and fro. She hummed snatches of song as she bustled about, mostly songs from Soviet films: "Red Roses Blooming," "As I Was, I Always Will Be," "Joyful are the Steppes of Kur-

3

ban," "In the Dusk, A Young Man." Almost everyone else was dozing. She alone seemed tireless.

She took out her map to locate our destination. Her questions were endless. Are there mountains over there? Rivers? Is it true that the frost will bite our noses off? Is it true that the ice figures on the windowpanes are like giant paintings? Is it true that dogs are used to draw the plow? She sounded like a toddler on a pleasure trip with her parents. People looked at her pityingly and shook their heads. How can she be so lighthearted? they wondered. The leading cadres from the various work units to which we respectively belong, and who were supervising our transport, looked her up and down curiously, as if saying to themselves: *Cheerful, are you? The tears will flow by and by. . . .*

But Guessie was totally unaware.

Soon it was night. The train rumbled through the darkness like a huge cradle rocking. Most of us slept in our seats, huddled against each other.

Guessie, however, was wide-awake, staring into the darkness, as if reading her future. Suddenly she turned and shook her companion. "Hey, Sister Liu, tell me, will we be *unhatted* after a year of reform-through-labor in the Great Northern Wilds?"

Little Liu muttered through her sleep. "I suppose so. Even landlords are unhatted after three years. Aren't we better than landlords?"

"Of course! How can we let ourselves be compared to landlords and capitalists?" Guessie was indignant.

"Don't be so sure!" exclaimed an older man sitting behind them. "Didn't you read the editorials? Now that private ownership of the means of production has been eliminated, we rightists are considered the most dangerous enemies—because we are private owners of knowledge."

"We dangerous!? I should think such talk as yours more dangerous!" Guessie retorted.

Elder Sister Shang came over from her seat and gave Guessie's head a friendly push. "Stop chattering! Get some sleep!"

"But I mean it!" Guessie insisted. "How can we be more dangerous than landlords and capitalists?"

"Shut up." Elder Sister Shang again gave Guessie's head a push as if she were an intractable child.

"But Elder Sister Shang, please tell me. Shall we or shall we not be unhatted in a year's time?"

"This girl is impossible," Sister Shang exclaimed. "Why does she have to get to the bottom of everything? Get some sleep now and we'll discuss this tomorrow. Then we'll all make a guess."

Guessie laughed and closed her eyes. She opened her eyes again and tugged at Shang's sleeve. "Even if we are unhatted after three years, I will still be only twenty-one."

"That's the right spirit! Guessie has a great future ahead!" Shang patted the girl's hand.

Guessie was finally satisfied and dozed off. Elder Sister Shang moved back to her own seat, sighed, and lit a cigarette. Now it was *her* turn to be sleepless.

The train gave a long hoot, startling the people out of their sleep. *Wake up comrades! We're approaching Mishan. We get off there.*

People scrambled to their feet, looking for their belongings. They put on fur coats and padded cotton pants, arming themselves against the icy chillness of early spring in the Great Northern Wilds. One veteran actor had arthritis of the knees. His trousers were padded with three-and-a-half-*jin* of cotton; they could stand up on their own. When he put them on, he could hardly move—a comical sight.

But Guessie didn't join in the laughter at the old man's expense. She had her eyes glued to the window.

It was around three o'clock in the morning. The sky was already turning a creamy white, the first sign of sunrise. In Beijing it would still be the darkest hour before dawn, but here on the northeastern border, daylight was an hour earlier.

"Look, everybody! It is morning here!" Guessie cried out in the joy of discovery. *It Is Morning Here* was the title of a Soviet novel about the lives of fishermen on the Kureli Islands. It was not for nothing that Guessie was a typist in Russian. She had read a lot of Soviet novels.

By now the travelers had collected their possessions, but Guessie was still crouched before the window. Finally, several of us helped her get ready. She was the little sister. All she had was a knee-length coat with artificial fur lining and a red wool cap. Smart, but not properly fitted out for severe weather. After much arguing, Guessie was persuaded to borrow a coat, a dog-fur hat, a pair of knee-high padded boots, and an unlined fur jacket without sleeves, which she draped over her own coat. She began to enjoy her new outfit and pranced up and down the compartments asking everybody, "Do I look like a hunter? What fun! Now I am a real northeasterner!"

The train eased into the station. We formed a line and stepped off the train—to be greeted by a piercing cold blast.

We stood waiting in line on the platform, crunching the snow under our feet. Just then a sound of clanking irons reached us from the end of the train. We turned and made a discreet glance in that direction.

The last compartment of the train carried the labor-gang convicts. It was not light enough to see their faces, only their bowed heads. But the clanking of the irons on their hands and feet gripped our hearts. They reminded us of our own situation. We held our breath and marched away in silence. The clanking of the irons resounded clearly in the chilly silence.

Suddenly a voice cried out: "Look, comrades, Venus!"

It was Guessie's voice, breaking the silence.

People at the head of the line looked back, not at the star, but at the speaker. Who could it be, to say such a thing, in such a place, at such a time? The people behind, however, followed the direction of Guessie's finger and looked up at the sky—what a star, so big, so bright, glittering against the blue velvet of the sky. Guessie's cry of delight lifted our spirits out of the depression caused by the clanking irons. Many faces broke into smiles.

"What a star!"

"So bright!"

"It can't be seen in Beijing."

"The stars here in the north are bigger than anywhere else."

"We should be proud of this place."

Guessie spoke again. "There is a song that goes 'Star of victory shining over us . . .' Does anybody remember?"

"It is the Soviet Comsomol Song," I said.

Somebody started singing and we young people in the ranks joined in:

"Goodbye, Mama,
Do not cry for me,
Wish us good luck all the way.
Goodbye, dear homeland,
The star of victory will shine over us. . . ."

The song evoked our memories of the Fifties, when our country was in its first phase of reconstruction. It evoked our longing for our own Youth League. Though we had been expelled from its ranks, our hearts remain unchanged. We sang as we marched, tears streaming down our faces. More and more voices joined in. We marched to the beat of the tune as if we were indeed soldiers marching off to war. Thus we marched on and sang on, an army of convicts without irons on our hands and feet. We finally stopped at a primary school—the first stop on the trek to our destination: the labor reform state farm. As we reached the school the sun was blazing over our heads in all its glory.

Guessie was like a cheerful chirping little sparrow among us. Her song and her laughter were everywhere—in the fields, in our dorms. Even her name was a happy symbol. She said that her mother, while carrying her, would always say: "Guess! Will it be a boy or a girl? Guess!" She had wished for a daughter, and when she got her wish, she named the child Guessie.

In school, Guessie's teachers and classmates used to tease her. "What a name you have!" they would say. When Guessie told her mother that people laughed at her name, her mother had said, "Your name is made up specially to call forth laughter. Guessie is a symbol for happiness. Don't you see? People say 'Guess what?' only when there is something good coming." Guessie had laughed. Now that she grasped the meaning of her name, she began to like it. She was even proud of it.

Out in the fields the month of May was the most exhausting.

After work, as we marched back with the tools on our shoulders, most of us fell asleep on our feet. But not Guessie. No matter how tired she was, she would run about, sometimes to gather wildflowers to decorate her window. Or she would make a crown of flowers and wear it over her head or around her neck as she worked, attracting butterflies and bees to herself. After work, she would look down at her own image in the water as she washed her hands in the river. She would make faces at herself, or throw a stone into the water and break her own image into rippling fragments. Once, while kneeling by the riverbank, she sang to herself snatches from a Polish folk song:

"I want to marry a rich man—oh oh oh,
I want to ride in a six-horse wagon—oh oh oh,
But if I truly love you—
I'd follow you barefoot 'round the world—oh oh oh!"

"So Guessie wants to marry?"

Guessie raised her head toward the voice. She saw several male comrades standing on the opposite bank looking at her. She blushed and ran away.

She ran all the way back to the women's dorm. Several comrades were hovering around Elder Sister Shang, who was reclining in bed.

"What's the matter with Elder Sister Shang?"

"She has a headache," we told her.

"Let me have a look." Guessie clambered up the bed to examine Shang's head. "Where's the wound?"

"It's a headache," we told her.

"But there is no wound," she insisted.

Sister Shang smiled in spite of herself. "Silly girl. The hurt's inside. It's nerves." She pulled Guessie's pigtails and sighed. "You're so young, you don't know what a headache is."

Guessie looked around dumbly.

A twenty-one-year-old girl spoke up. "To tell the truth, it's only lately, after I was labeled a rightist and I cried for three days, that *I* suddenly discovered what a headache is!"

Even Guessie had her fleeting moments of sadness. One of those times stemmed from a joke.

That was when we women were sent to work along with the men to weed peas. The men liked to tease Guessie as we were hoeing.

"Guessie," said one of the men, "with all the good luck you bring, tell me. Shall I get a letter today? Can you guess?"

"Guessie, tomorrow is a holiday, will it rain or shine? Give it a guess!"

"Guessie, how many pieces of meat shall we get for our dinner today? Give it a guess!"

"Guessie, which part of the country is your bridegroom coming from? East or west? Give it a guess!"

"East, of course," one of the men shouted. "The West is decadent!"

Guessie laughed and joined in the fun. Then someone blurted out: "What's the use of all that guessing? You never even guessed you would be labeled a rightist."

Guessie's smile vanished in a flash. That was touching a sore point indeed. She worked silently all afternoon, her tears dropping over the weeds.

After work, I walked back with her. I tried to change the subject. "Look, how beautiful!" I said, pointing to the sunset.

The rays of the setting sun pierced through chinks in the western sky, casting a network of light over the earth. We felt as if we were walking into a fairyland.

Guessie raised her head and broke into a smile. "If I could fly, I'd disappear behind the clouds. Nobody could put a label on me anymore."

Then Guessie told the story of how she was labeled rightist.

In Beijing Guessie had been a typist for a research institute. She was especially valued because of her facility with Russian. She was elected model worker by popular vote. That didn't please a notoriously bossy busybody, who goes by the sobriquet of Always Right. "Why should the honor go to someone who is not a party member?" asked the quarrelsome woman. "She's not even a Youth Leaguer! Just a chit of a girl! I covered more distance crossing bridges than she ever walked in her whole life!"

In a rage, Guessie tore up the certificate of honor and gave the woman a piece of her mind. After all, she *was* but a child. However, this little fit of temper sealed her fate. It was the evidence for her antiparty activities. Guessie was the youngest in the institute. All the people who joined in denouncing her were considerably older than she was. The denouncements took the form of a mass ritual. Poor little Guessie was cast in the middle of a ring, while her detractors each had a tilt at her. Even a borrowed songbook that she damaged, even one occasion when she threw down the cards after being accused of cheating in the game—all were traced to her reactionary nature, analyzed in the light of basic principles and party lines. During the lengthy denunciation sessions, she was compared to Cao Cao, the scheming minister of the Three Kingdoms period two thousand years ago. It didn't matter if Guessie understood the accusations or not. The more obtuse the argument, the better.

"It was a nightmare," she said agitatedly. "The faces around me were frightful, like a pack of mad dogs, ready to sink their teeth in me. To this day, I don't understand what really happened."

My eyes filled with tears. This was so like my own experience. Elder Brother Su had caught up with us by then, and the two of us listened in silent indignation as Guessie went on.

One engineer in the institute had raised an objection. He maintained that Guessie was childish, that she needed education, not political labeling. For his pains, the engineer was promptly attacked as leaning toward the right. After that, all attacks on Guessie concentrated on refuting his view.

"Age has nothing to do with it," one detractor said. "There is no dividing line by age between revolutionary and antirevolutionary. Guessie is young in years, but an old hand at antiparty activities."

Another proclaimed: "Young as she is, she dared to trample under her feet the honor bequeathed to her by the party! If we don't rise up as one to denounce this crime, where is our loyalty to the party?"

Elder Brother Su gave a snort. "Don't repeat this to anyone!" he said to Guessie as we reached our dorms.

"Why?" she asked.

"People will say that you are not properly repentant." Elder Brother Su put his hand protectively over Guessie's shoulder.

"But I am not guilty. Why should I repent? Should I be labeled just because I stood up to that shrew? Always Right doesn't do a spot of work! And then she's jealous if others perform better. What nonsense! She is always singling out people for attack. That's what she did better than anybody else!"

"What is her position in your institute?" Elder Brother asked.

"In charge of documents and data."

"I mean her social connections."

"Social connections?" Guessie stopped to consider. "Her *social* connection is the secretary of the Party Committee. He is her husband." Elder Brother Su and I looked at each other significantly, but Guessie added, "To be fair, he had nothing to do with it."

"Did his busybody wife conduct your case single-handedly?"

"No. She didn't handle my case. She was away when I was denounced at those meetings. It was those others— friends one day, enemies the next. They changed overnight."

Elder Brother Su was lost in contemplation. As for me, it was a dozen years later that I learned what really happened.

———

The store at the branch state farm where we rightists were made to work kept hours to match our own. The store opened each day when we went out to the fields. It was closed again before we got back. These office hours were very inconvenient. We conveyed our complaints through the proper channels from the group section upward, through the brigade level right to the top command. But nothing happened. The fact is, the regular staff on the farm just lumped us together with the labor-gang convicts.

Once at the end of a day's work, Elder Sister Shang began to have a vomiting seizure. The coarse corn that serves as our staple food did not agree with her. Guessie suggested that we get some pastry from the store. But we all knew we'd never arrive there before closing time. Guessie said she would run. She usually lingered in the fields after work—to gather flowers or catch a grasshopper. But on that occasion she ran like a rabbit.

Her breath completely spent, Guessie reached the store just seconds before closing time. But even so, she was too late. A big lock hanging on the door stared at her. A few men were also standing in front of the locked door, thwarted like Guessie.

"We should erect protest posters!" somebody suggested.

"Yes," Guessie responded. "Big-character posters. That will make them sit up!"

That same night, Guessie took up pen and paper and wrote out a big-character poster criticizing the opening hours of the store.

"Guessie," Elder Sister Shang remonstrated, "they are not shutting us out on purpose. They are just thoughtless."

"Well, this will make them think!"

"Please, not on my account."

"Certainly not! This is for everybody!"

"Please listen to me, Guessie," Elder Sister pleaded. "I am older than you are."

"Don't worry. There are many other people who suggested these posters. We are together in this!" Guessie's mind was made up. Nothing anybody said could stop her.

The next day, she took her poster to the men she had met the day before. She showed them her handiwork. They looked at her with open mouths. "We were just saying it to let off steam," one of them muttered.

"Guessie, haven't you had enough of big-character posters?"

"Guessie, how can you be so naive?"

"Guessie, have you forgotten? It is our duty to reform *ourselves*, not others?"

Most of the men seemed bitter, but one of them spoke sympathetically to her. "Guessie, it is hard to change anything, even a small matter like this. We must be patient." He rolled her poster into a ball and threw it away. "Guessie," he added kindly, "Don't be such a child."

Guessie had been all aflame. Now, drenched in this cold shower, she stood there dazed, looking at the man without comprehension.

We had worked nonstop for nearly three months. The May the First Reservoir, which we had built with our own hands, was finished, and the top command finally announced a holiday. We were wild with joy.

But how were we going to spend the day? There was so much to do: our cotton-padded clothing needed to be taken apart, washed, and stitched together again; our blankets, which had gone damp during the winter, needed to be shaken out in the sun; our clothes and stockings needed patching and darning; we needed to go to the post office to mail letters or retrieve parcels; we needed to do some shopping. We didn't know where to begin.

As we were puzzling over the matter Guessie took out from her trunk a skirt and tried it on. It was a knee-length skirt in bright orange with a pattern of white flowers. To this she added a sporty white blouse. She looked stunning. We couldn't keep our eyes off her. Bent over backbreaking labor from day to day, we had long laid aside any interest in life. Guessie in a pretty outfit, turning this way and that in the middle of the room, was such a refreshing sight.

"How pretty! Where did you get it?"

"It's a bit short. How many years did you have it?"

Guessie said the skirt was five years old, from her high-school days. Her mother had made it. "It is a bit short," she conceded, "but looks all right."

Following Guessie's example, we all rummaged in our own trunks and brought out our finery.

One woman, shaking out a flowery patterned skirt, said, "This is the so-called symbol of my degradation. I nearly sold it off to a secondhand store."

"I never thought I'd look at this again," said another.

Our old clothes hung loosely over us. The observations came thick and furious: "I've slimmed down!" "Lost ten *jin*!" "Your old man wouldn't recognize you!"

There is the saying that three women is enough to start a show, let alone a dozen of us. We chattered and giggled as we tried on our long-forgotten clothes.

"Tomorrow is our only free day," Guessie reminded

us. "We can't do everything, so why don't we put on our skirts and enjoy ourselves in town?"

We young ones decided on the spot to promenade along Tiger Forest Street. Tiger Forest Street was the main street in the county town.

Our deputy group leader opposed the idea. "There is no harm wearing your good clothes indoors. Nobody can see you. But showing yourselves in the streets—people will say we are not devoting our attention to reform."

"We've already built a reservoir, haven't we?" I retorted. "We should enjoy ourselves for one day! I have no patience with this kind of overscrupulousness."

"This is voluntary," Guessie said. "Nobody is forcing you to go!"

"Don't let yourselves be carried away," the deputy group leader cautioned us.

"What harm can there be?" I asked.

"People will say you're not reforming properly."

"Ha-ha-ha!" Guessie laughed defiantly. "Are we supposed to cry all day? I won't oblige!" She gave a twirl and her skirt ballooned out like a big flowered lamp shade.

The next day, the holiday, was clear and bright and sunny. We sallied forth in our holiday best, like so many butterflies. I was in a short-sleeved white shirt and a dark blue skirt with white flowers. Little Zhang was in a brown-and-yellow dress, to match her brownish hair. Little Liu was in a purple skirt and a black silk top. Little Ding was in a tight woolen skirt of dark green and a checkered yellow-and-green shirt. Xia Caihong came out in a dress with scarlet stripes over a white background. We were tastefully decked out in all the colors of the rainbow. We went off very pleased with ourselves.

———

We had a great time in town, laughing and singing as we walked down the road joining the state farm to the county center. Soon we found ourselves on Tiger Forest Street. We went window shopping in the department store, did our business at the post office, enjoyed a dinner of stuffed dumplings, and made a tour of the town. We came back happily to Base 754.

We had just set foot in our courtyard when we saw Elder Sister Shang walk out of the political director's room. She made a sign to us to keep silent. "Shh! Stop chattering! The political director has reprimanded us."

"How did the news get about? Somebody has reported on us." I gave the deputy group leader a hard look. She was sitting on her bed patching clothes.

"People who spy and report are called Judas," said the deputy group leader composedly. "I know my Bible." She should; she was there for being a Christian.

Elder Sister Shang didn't want the incident to go any further. "Don't say anything. Take off your skirts, wash yourselves, and get some rest. We have a rush job tomorrow, on a new project."

Our tour of Tiger Forest Street had become a major incident! Only then did I remember that in the county town people had stopped and stared, just as they used to stare at foreigners in the main street in Beijing. We had overheard some of the whispers:

"Where did this bunch come from?"

"Female rightists from Base 754."

"Look at the way they deck themselves out!"

"And their waists! My two hands could go around them."

18

"Don't underestimate these people. They've got a thing or two up their sleeves. All children of landlords and capitalists."

"Yes, the men are reckless and the women shameless."

"Indeed, look at them. Just like witches."

"Now, are they here to reform themselves or to enjoy themselves?"

"Look at the way they laugh. Does that look like repentance?"

As I learned later, those were the comments from people who saw us with their own eyes. As for those who judged us on hearsay—and the news spread like wildfire—it was much worse:

"These people are full of evil!"

"A woman stood up and made a speech right on the steps of the post office."

"She said she could cover the whole length of our Tiger Forest Street with one stride!"

"They downed half a bottle of vinegar at the dumpling shop, just for one meal! Something about protecting against contamination."

"Heavens, they are chockful of poison! Half a bottle of vinegar for one meal? Won't that make a bottleful every day? Who can afford to keep them?"

These comments passed around by the locals were heard by some of the men from our group who also happened to be in town. And that started another round of disapprobation, this time straight from the rightist regiment itself. Our fellow rightists were indignant.

"Gallivanting about, as if we are not notorious enough!"

"Is this the place to show off?"

"Don't know their place!"

"If the local reaction is negative, we will never be un-hatted."

"They just want a fling, and to hell with the future. But we have our wives and children to think of!"

Thus they got themselves all worked up and decided to report the matter to the political director so that they themselves would not be implicated in the event of a reprimand. "Don't know what those women were up to in town today. But the local reaction was negative."

Were our clothes too showy? No. Some of the local women we saw on Tiger Forest Street were gorgeously dressed—in red and green and ribbons and flowers and what not—and nobody gave them a second glance. Was it because we were rightists? Not likely. There were many rightists up and down the street—there were thousands in the area. There were no labels on their foreheads, but you could tell at a glance who they were. They looked stricken—hangdog. What marked *us* was that our expressions did not match our status as rightists. That was our offense.

Later, we learned that Elder Sister Shang claimed responsibility for the whole affair. She said she had encouraged us to wear our lightweight skirts, thinking only of the heat, that in her concern for our comfort, she overlooked the demands of our thought reform. She made a pledge that this would never happen again, and thus the matter was allowed to drop.

Midsummer, even in this northern country, could bring excruciating heat. For those working in the fields, there was absolutely no shelter from the sun—no trees, no buildings.

It was always a joy to find a creek in which to immerse ourselves—but for the most part, we just bore the discomfort until sunset.

There was a patch of corn that needed weeding. The main army of the rightist labor force was wanted elsewhere, and this work was assigned to us women. We were to keep going until the whole patch was weeded.

The corn was but two inches high. Weeding out the grass between the young sprouts was a delicate job, like embroidery. At the beginning of the day, we bent over the ground as we worked. After a little while we squatted. We couldn't keep that up for long either, and finally we just sprawled down on all fours and moved forward as best we could.

When the sun was at its most intense, we stripped. In the morning when we first set out, we kept on our shirts, pants, and knee-high boots to protect us against the mosquitoes and other insects that buzzed around us. By eight o'clock, it would be unbearable, and we would take off the shirt and boots. After nine, we would remove the pants. By ten, we would be down to a pair of shorts and a vest. Anyway there was nobody around. We enjoyed thorough liberation.

One day during the noon break, Xia Caihong led us to a little creek several *li* away, a tributary of the Muling River.

The creek was very clear. We could see the little fishes and frogs that were disporting themselves in the water, and the plants and seaweeds down below. It was a lovely refuge from the heat. We jumped down and stood in the water, splashing each other. It was shallow on the edge and about a man's height in the middle.

"How I wish I could swim!" someone exclaimed.

"A pity we didn't bring our bathing suits," I said.

We watched the fishes with longing eyes. As we were talking I turned and saw Guessie doff her clothes in a flash and dive into the water.

Her figure was perfect, the ideal of youth and beauty, making one think of all the goddesses in art and legend. What will her fate be like? My thoughts wandered as I stood and gazed at her swimming easily with breaststrokes.

"Guessie!" Little Zhang shouted at her from the bank. "For heaven's sake, people will call us witches again! How can you!"

"This is a free world. This is not Tiger Forest Street!" So saying, Guessie ducked her head, plunged forward, and emerged thirty feet away. "Come and join me. This is wonderful."

Just as I was hesitating, Xia Caihong also undressed and plopped down. "Come on, you witches. Come and enjoy the water! Unless the fishes can talk, who's going to report us?" She did a somersault in the water and followed Guessie.

The rest of us could not resist the temptation. We threw aside our clothes and jumped into the water. All except for Little Liu, who could not swim. The water was warm and cleaner than any swimming pool. There was only the sky above and the green riverbed below. We were at one with nature and delirious with joy. It was the single most memorable experience of my life. Since then, my youth has gone forever.

We swam up and down the stream. Only Little Liu sat by the bank washing her feet. We called to her to join us.

"Let's drag her down and teach her swimming," Xia Caihong said. Xia was always a bit wild. She swam up to

Little Liu and, catching her unaware, dragged her into the water.

"Oh, heavens!" Little Liu screamed. She laughed as she struggled. We helped her out of her clothes and threw them on the grass to dry. We proceeded to teach her to float. Little Zhang stood in front and held her hands. Xia held her feet. I stood in the middle and held up her belly with my palms. By and by she managed to keep floating and we released our hold. She kept afloat with eyes tightly shut, arms stretched rigidly, her feet beating water. When she discovered that we had released our hold, she shrieked and promptly fell into the water. So we tried it all over again, laughing and clapping our hands in delight.

We went back and told the story to Elder Sister Shang. She put her finger to her lips and signaled us to keep our voices down. "I'll join you tomorrow, you bunch of mermaids."

The next day Elder Sister Shang went with us. I swam for a while and then scrambled to where Elder Sister Shang sat on the bank watching us.

"Elder Sister, what are you thinking of?"

"I'm thinking: what a pity I don't have my paints here. You would make a beautiful picture." She sounded heavy-hearted.

"Can't you look hard and store everything in your memory? You can paint it later when you're back in Beijing."

She didn't answer but continued to gaze at Guessie and Xia Caihong as they played in the water.

"There is a famous photograph from the Second World War," Elder Sister said with her eyes still on the group in the water. "A group of children on a truck, being taken to

23

a concentration camp. They were standing at the rear of the truck, feeding pigeons from their hands, and they were laughing."

"What about it?"

"Nothing. Except that the sight of Guessie out there reminds me of that picture. I know I shouldn't think like that. There's no connection, none."

Again, it was a dozen years later that I understood what she meant.

It began to snow. Our first snow of the year, right after October 1—National Day. The world was one whirling mass of white. Our windowpanes were frosted over with a thousand shapes and designs, some like a forest of pines, some like garlands of flowers, some like petals of chrysanthemums. Beautiful.

At dusk, Guessie sat in front of the window and made little footmarks on the windowpanes. She used the heel of her palm to make a print of the heel and sole of the foot, and then added the toes with the tips of her fingers. They were cute little footprints, smaller than a child's. She sang snatches from the Cuban folk song "La Paloma" as she worked.

We stayed indoors.

Whenever the telephone rang in the political director's room, Guessie would prick up her ears. "Listen! It might be directives to unhat us!"

All of the older ones would smile at her. "Guessie is homesick?" one of them asked.

"Yes, a little," she admitted. "It will soon be New Year. I can see my mother getting fish for New Year dinner. I love sweet-sour fish."

As New Year got closer Guessie's questions multiplied.

"When *will* we be unhatted anyway?" Her inquiries were met by shakes of the head.

"Do you have any information?"
None.

"What do you think, then. Will we soon be unhatted?"
No idea.

"Why are we still not unhatted?"

"Perhaps soon," someone would say. And Guessie's eyes would sparkle with hope.

One day, we went into the mountains to gather firewood. We met a hunter, a local man. Guessie mistook him for one of our own people who were cutting timber in the mountains. "Comrade, do you people up in the mountains have any news about our unhatting?"

The man was perplexed. "Unhatting? Oh, no. Always keep your hat on. It's cold out here, not like your south." We all laughed at Guessie's embarrassment.

May came around again. Guessie was suddenly taken ill. She felt drained of all energy. Her face was flushed with fever and she had a severe ache on one side of her head. We took her to the clinic and they gave her some pills.

The fever raged on for another two days. On the morning of the third, Guessie got up and found her right jaw painfully swollen. She said the right-side half of her face, up to her right temple and down to her tonsils, was one mass of hurt. We were alarmed and summoned the doctor. He turned his flashlight into her open mouth for a moment and laughed.

"It's just her wisdom tooth," he said.

We all gave a sigh of relief.

"It's a happy event," I said. "Guessie is now an adult."

The wisdom tooth, which usually appears between the ages of eighteen and twenty-five, is taken as a sign of initiation into adulthood. Sometimes the symptoms are light, sometimes severe. Guessie's wisdom tooth had a hard time fighting its way out.

The doctor gave her some medicine to relieve the pain. "There's a little bump already. In a day or two, the new tooth will appear."

Some of the male comrades came to visit.

"Is Guessie better?" one inquired.

"What is Guessie's complaint?" asked another.

"My complaint?" Guessie held one hand to her jaw and looked at them unsmilingly. "I am all grown up."

First published in Harbin Literature and Art, *No. 11, 1980. Translation completed at the Bunting Institute, Radcliffe-Harvard, December 1990.*

THE LOUDSPEAKER

BAO CHUAN

BAO CHUAN, born in 1942, is currently on the editorial staff of Sichuan Literature *magazine. She graduated from a teachers' college in 1966 and worked at various jobs, writing in her spare time, before becoming a professional writer of short fiction. Her stories—including "Before the Wedding," "Maternal Love," "Toast to Our Bicycles!," and "The Loudspeaker"—focus primarily on the day-to-day frustrations of the underprivileged in a presumably egalitarian society.*

"The Loudspeaker," ironically, is about people *power. Here, downtrodden citizens are empowered by the Cultural Revolution to lash out—but only at each other—while the emblematic loudspeaker, spouting slogans, towers above them all.*

We live in one of those square courtyards that are quite common in our town. There are five families altogether and we have been neighbors for over fifteen years. We moved there in 1954. At that time, we were a friendly community. If someone was away on business, the neighbors would keep an eye on the children. If one of us became ill, there was always a neighbor to lend a hand with getting the herbal medicine and stewing it. If one household made some special treat, like sticky rice dumplings, not only would the smell pervade the courtyard but every family would get a taste. Even we guys who were in our teens at the time rarely quarreled, much less got into fistfights.

But today, fifteen or so years later, everything is changed. I don't know what happened. Is it something in the metabolism? Or a genetic deviation? Or has human nature entered into a new stage of evolution? Whatever it is, neighborly relationships have sadly deteriorated. Actually, we see more of each other, now that all normal work is stopped with this ongoing Cultural Revolution. In the space of the little courtyard, we stumble into each other whichever way we move. But we don't so much as bat an eyelid when we meet face-to-face; we might as well be staring into thin air. The fact is, to spit, or cough, or even sigh in the presence of another might be construed as provocation. It might easily be the spark that sets off a blazing fire. We keep our voices down even when speaking behind doors.

One morning, I sat on a stool on the step outside our front door (all the rooms open directly into the common courtyard) and stared listlessly at the loudspeaker jutting out from the top of the Economic Committee building. I was bored and wished for some kind of distraction, anything to break the silence. Even the loudspeaker with its deafening roar and abusive screeches. Anything.

Bang! Something hit hard against the wall in the room next to ours. Was a battle about to begin? Every nerve in my body tensed in expectation.

Boom! Boom! Boom! Whatever it was that hit the wall now bumped over the floor. Following the sound, Little Ming, our neighbor's teenage son, shot out into the yard. He stood in the middle of the yard, his neck stiff, his head lifted at an angle. He glared at the door to his family's rooms and cursed under his breath. His eyes were slits and his chin pointed, like a mouse's. I'm not prejudiced, even though his elder brother and his gang of Red Guards did beat me up three years ago at the beginning of the Cultural Revolution—just because I was a member of the Workers' Vigilance, a different faction. No, I'm not prejudiced. The fact is he does look like a mouse. He's even nicknamed Mouse.

His father, the blacksmith Guo Shun, appeared at the door, naked from the waist up.

"So your wings are strong, are they?" His broad bronze face was twitching and the muscles on his shoulders rippled as he waved his arms angrily. "Get out of here. Go and rot in jail. Go get stuck by a knife. Get hit by a bullet! I don't give a damn!"

Little Ming rolled his eyes and shouted back. "I'm telling you, it's my turn at sentinel duty, headquarters' orders. It's to defend Chairman Mao's revolutionary line. How dare you interfere!"

Blacksmith Guo Shun snorted, but for the moment he was silenced. Then he stuck his head out of the door and broke out again. "Right! Then you needn't come back to eat!"

"Want to get rid of me?" Little Ming now spoke slowly and deliberately, shaking his head from left to right. "Not so easy."

"Why not? I support your revolutionary acts!" Guo Shun also changed tactics. "Just pretend you never had a father. . . . "

"You want to have it all your way, do you?" Little Ming squinted. "I'm not eighteen yet. Not for another year and nine months. Have you forgotten?"

"So what?" The blacksmith was, after all, just a lump of iron and couldn't follow his son's arguments. "Do you mean you can go crooked just because you're not eighteen?"

"Ha!" Little Ming laughed dryly. "And do you mean you can just go and breed children and not do your duty?"

"Oh, you've got me, have you?" The blacksmith was furious. His nostrils quivered and he shouted at the top of his voice. "Okay, I've made a mistake. I shouldn't have spawned you in the first place! Then I give up being your father! Let's settle accounts at once and sever relations. I'll publish a statement in the papers." There were steps behind him. He wavered for a moment and diminished his tirade. "Two hundred *yuan* yearly for your keep. Sixteen years altogether. How much does that add up to? Make it out yourself."

"Are you saying that *you* kept me all these years?" Unlike his father, Little Ming raised his voice as he saw his mother approaching. His mother doted on him, the youngest. Besides, mother and son were attached to the same faction—the Battalion. He drew out his chest and curled his lips in a smile. "*You* kept me! By what right do you say that?"

"Didn't I feed you? Didn't I clothe you? Didn't I pay your school fees?"

Little Ming threw back his head and laughed, drowning out his father's words. Then he pursed his mouth and started to deliver a lecture. "Well, let me tell you I don't mind settling accounts, but don't think you are getting any credits! I am indebted to Chairman Mao! If it weren't for the chairman, where would you be yourself? Probably a starving corpse on some street corner. Think again. Who should get the credit? Don't forget what you owe to Chairman Mao!"

Little Ming had really outdone himself. I didn't know what to think—whether to cheer or to spit. I ended up saving my saliva.

The middle-school teacher Zhong Kaiwen was squatting outside his own door cleaning his bike. He, too, was shocked. He raised his head and stared at Little Ming, openmouthed.

"You!" the blacksmith was no match for his son at argument. He wasn't a debater, but he knew how to use his fists. He made a lunge at his son.

Mother Guo was alarmed. She held back her husband with both hands while her stare penetrated the schoolteacher until he lowered his gaze. Then she pointed to the loudspeaker towering above us all. "Day in and day out," she said, dragging out each word significantly, "it reminds us to be on the alert, to beware of class enemies making rifts among ourselves. Have you forgotten?" She put on her best manner, trying to sound amiable, but her words were enough to draw a little crowd, some from our own courtyard, some from our neighbors next door who stood in the entrance. They smacked their lips in happy anticipation.

Mother Guo was well-known for her piercing voice. She was a saleswoman at a vegetable stand. She hawked stale vegetables all the year round. In spring it was "tender shoots, ten *fen* for a pile"; in summer it was "red tomatoes, ten *jin* for one *yuan*"; in the fall it was "cabbages, twenty *fen* for a bunch, your money back if they are rotten"; in winter it was "celery cabbages, eight *fen* for one *jin*, buy one get one free." When Mother Guo sold her vegetables at the main crossroad, her voice could be heard down the streets in all four directions. It was certainly not a musical voice, but the bargains it offered somewhat neutralized its unpleasantness. The true demonstration of Mother Guo's talents occurred during the contest of the two factions seeking supremacy at the inauguration of the so-called Committee of United Workers of the Fresh Produce Department. On that occasion, Mother Guo, loudspeaker in hand, represented the Battalion and entered into a shouting contest with the representative of the Red City faction. She drowned out the bleatings of the other woman in less than half an hour. Later, when the Battalion got the upper hand, Mother Guo was honored with the title of Loudspeaker. At the inauguration of the Provincial Revolutionary Committee, Mother Guo was invited to stand in the stadium with a plastic red badge over her breast.

Mother Guo now made sure that the insinuation of her words was not lost on the schoolteacher. Zhong Kaiwen kept his eyes studiously lowered. Mother Guo rubbed her chin complacently, making the pockmarks stand out one by one under the pressure of her fingers. She drew herself to her full height and strode over to her son, who was still in the yard. "Go back home. Quarrels between people mustn't allow cousins to get hurt. Conflict only makes classes and conserves happy."

I knew, of course, that she was trying to quote from Chairman Mao about peaceably resolving contradictions between the people. She was also trying to use a set phrase about refraining from internecine fights that hurt loved ones and gratify the enemy.

I was not the only one who got the message. A woman who had been scrubbing clothes in a tub outside her door caught the thrust of Mother Guo's words and took personal offense. She was Wang Lei, cashier at the Sechuan Cotton Mill. The word *conserve* stung her, as she had joined the Industrial Army faction, which was labeled conservative. She had ample experience of Mother Guo's verbal darts and was always on the alert. Now she flung the soppy clothes into the tub with a splash and shouted in the direction of her own room, though raising her voice for our benefit. "Hey, you, cursed with a short life, get me another tub. Stuffing yourself and doing nothing all day long! Want me to leave a *mark* on your face?" She gave Mother Guo a hard look.

Mother Guo bridled and smiled contemptuously. She clapped her son on the shoulder. "Well, the mother's not much to look at, but the son's not bad," she exclaimed. "Get a pretty wife for yourself, my son, anytime you like."

The people standing at the entrance to our courtyard burst out laughing. Little Ming was embarrassed. He growled something at his mother and pushed her away, nearly tipping her off balance.

"Your mother followed the correct line," Mother Guo announced to no one in particular. "I've stood in the stadium, shaken hands with officials big and small." She glowered and gave Little Ming another clap on the back.

"A warning, though, my son. Don't get involved with shameless hussies. Remember, your uncle spent a pot of money and got smeared and slandered into the bargain."

"Slander yourself!" Wang Lei's face was crimson, and for a moment she was at a loss for words. More than ten years ago, Mother Guo had introduced Wang Lei to her own brother. They met several times, but nothing lasting came of it. Both parties married elsewhere and the matter was forgotten. But later, during the antirightist movement, Mother Guo's brother was implicated, and officers on his case interrogated Wang Lei. Wang Lei never said anything untrue, but even so, whatever she revealed was used to build up the case against Mother Guo's brother. Since then the two women had been deadly enemies.

Wang Lei protested her innocence throughout. Now she again pointed upward with her finger. "By the heavens above and the earth below, whoever made a false statement will die an instant death, and that goes for those who make unjust accusations, too!"

"Has anybody been naming names? Well, if the cap fits . . . *Instant death* indeed! Go kill yourself, you shameless slut!"

"Slut yourself," Wang Lei retorted. "Put yourself on sale like your rotten tomatoes!"

The people watching by the entrance now joined in the fun. A young fellow sporting a military uniform with a broad belt across his waist snapped his fingers. "Go at her," he cried. "Go at her!" The crowd roared with laughter.

"So what if I sell rotten tomatoes! You sell your rotten—a pity my brother wouldn't buy!"

"You're disgusting. You're beneath me!" Wang Lei,

unnerved by the laughter of the crowd, lost control. And anyway, how could her voice hold out against Mother Guo's loudspeaker? As always, she turned lamely to the defensive. "Oh, well, what can one say to the likes of you? Demons and monsters . . ."

Schoolteacher Zhong's wife had been in the backyard all this time. The minute she heard Loudspeaker, she picked up a stool and swiftly took up position at her own front door, as if answering a battle cry. Her husband signaled to her with his eyes to keep away, but she ignored him, stoutly maintaining her position on the stool, a glass of water in her hands. She worked behind the registration desk at the local clinic. It meant daily confrontations with angry patients. On top of that, she was tempered by faction wars, which she joined with zest and fervor. Taken altogether, Mrs. Zhong was a seasoned verbal combatant; a tiff in this little backyard was just child's play to her. She and her husband subscribed to the rebel August 26 faction. During the February suppression of the year before, they had seen some hard times while Wang Lei and her conservative faction had had the upper hand. Thank goodness, they had managed to reverse the situation, but not before verbal bricks had been flung about and hard knocks exchanged.

Now she pricked up her ears at the words *demons and monsters*, terms usually applied to class enemies singled out during the Cultural Revolution. Having missed the prelude, she thought Wang Lei's words were directed at her. So she remarked: "Why give up like a whining dog? If you are in the right, why don't you go and eat the sesame-seed cakes that Li Jingquan has thrown to you?" Now Li was the toppled provincial party chief and it was the accepted thing to taunt the so-called conservative faction with their connections to him, as if they were in his pay.

The minute Mrs. Zhong opened her mouth, I knew that a sparring melee involving many combatants had begun. I sneaked back into my room, leaving a gap in the door to keep track of developments.

Just as I had foreseen, the term *sesame-seed cake* (*ma bing*) had struck a chord. The term shared one ideogram with the term *pockmark* (*ma zi*) and the pockmarked Mother Guo took up the challenge. She assumed that Mrs. Zhong was retaliating on her for alluding to her husband as the class enemy. She put Wang Lei aside for the moment and trained her guns on Mrs. Zhong, directing her words ostensibly at her own husband: "What are you standing there for like a lamppost? Take care you don't fart, or someone will make a case of it and report you!" This was a thrust at the Zhong couple: at the beginning of the Cultural Revolution, schoolteacher Zhong had created a poster accusing the blacksmith of holding a private job for extra gain. "Hum," Mother Guo continued, "we eat by the sweat of our labor. What is it to you? Did it snuff out the joss sticks at your ancestors' graves?"

Mrs. Zhong had originally directed her attack at Wang Lei of the hated conservative faction, but since Mother Guo picked up the gauntlet, she was just as ready. "So what! Tit for tat! Worthless trash! As if I had eaten chicken over her ancestors' graves!" This was an allusion to an earlier grudge dating back to 1964, when Mother Guo herself had accused Mrs. Zhong of pocketing the registration fees to treat herself to chicken. There had been an investigation, but nothing came of it except damaged relationships.

"Serves you right! Come full circle! You evil thug! Spy! Can't change your nature!" Mother Guo reverted to her favorite tactic: shout down your enemy; never mind whether the words are relevant or not, so long as they hurt.

Schoolteacher Zhong reacted as if he had been hit, and the container of bicycle grease that he was holding spilled over. He raised his tired eyes and signaled his wife to stop. He was afraid to rake up that painful episode in his past. But with the word *spy* that raw nerve was touched and the memories came flooding back. Those memories harkened back to 1947, when he was graduated from high school and spent a whole year looking for a job. Finally he became a traffic policeman. He was on the job a mere three months, when in an accident involving a private rickshaw owner who had hit a beggar, he gave an honest account—and got a slap in the face and the sack. Little did he dream that this humiliation would be a blemish on his file and a blight on his whole career. It was raked up during every campaign of the last thirty years—the campaign to suppress counter-revolutionaries; the antirightist campaign; the socialist education campaign—all the way down to this so-called unprecedented great Cultural Revolution. There were endless interrogations and unending confessions. Even to this day, he had to be prepared against anything and everything—to have his home ransacked, to have a black carbon board hung over his neck advertising his crime, to be paraded down the streets with a piece of straw between his lips. Now he tried to explain for the nth time. "Traffic p-police directing traffic," he stammered, "is n-not the s-same as spies." In spite of all his explanations, however, isn't it true that his sons were barred from senior high school, excluded from jobs in state-owned enterprises? For a moment he was overcome. His legs shook. His head throbbed. He began to sway where he stood.

Mrs. Zhong was alarmed. She smashed the glass in her hand onto the ground and rushed to her husband. She helped him to a stool. "Come, come, old man," she said. "Don't bother about the bike. Here! I've got ten *yuan* in my purse. Go to the teahouse and enjoy yourself. The little singsong harlot will sing on order, and you can even hold her hand for an extra *yuan*!"

"Oh, you!" Zhong stamped his feet in exasperation. He gave a deep sigh and sat down speechless.

Mother Guo had lost her mother when still a child. Her father was blind, and father and daughter had once been reduced to singing in a teahouse for a living. It was a dark moment in Mother Guo's life. Life is not an easy thing after all, we all have a page or two that we would rather not turn back to. Nobody with a sense of decency would probe these wounds. But Mrs. Zhong had forgotten herself in her anger.

Mother Guo was deeply wounded, wounded to her innermost being. Her eyes bloodshot, her face pale, she became demented. "Okay," she screamed, placing her hands on her hips. "I'm selling, right here. Come and get me if you have the guts! Why one *yuan*? Ten *fen* will do! Like turnips and cabbages!" She twisted her body frantically and headed in the Zhongs' direction. "Gutless creatures! Here, I'm delivering myself!"

The crowd at the entrance to the courtyard laughed mirthlessly. Some made sounds of disapproval or cried "Shame." The chap in the military outfit said to his companion, "Come on, let's go. We don't want to be splattered with blood."

Meanwhile schoolteacher Zhong had shrunk into his own room, his knees still shaking. Fortunately, blacksmith Guo picked up his wife by the waist and shoved her back into their quarters, thus concluding—for the moment—this phase of the battle. Each side had used the most degrading language possible, and each had paid the price in the utmost measure of personal pain.

As a final stab, Mother Guo screamed at the top of her voice: "Spy! Secret agent! Low-life creep!" The strain of her effort produced a fit of coughing. The schoolteacher, provoked beyond endurance, took advantage of her coughing and poked his head from behind his door. Quivering with anger, he raised his index finger. "You, you, you *square* low-life creep!"

Square? What is this newfangled term that the bookworm has cooked up? The contending parties and the onlookers were silenced for a moment, savoring the flavor of the term. Even the returning section head, Mr. Zhu, stopped in his tracks, with one foot across the threshold.

"You! Square yourself!" Mother Guo was the first to regain her wits and gave him as good as she got. A smile stole across the tired face of Mr. Zhu, which he converted into a dry cough as soon as he saw Mother Guo catch him in the act.

"Smile, do you?" Mother Guo thought she had somehow lost out in the exchange of *squares* and moved to surer ground. "Smile on your mother's fucking feet, you capitalist roader. You deserve a thousand cuts!"

At that time *capitalist roader* was the extreme form of opprobrium. The section head being denominated in this manner was too stunned to reply. Wasn't he made to clean the latrines every day at his workplace? He gave Mother Guo a look of contempt and dived into his room.

Immediately the blaring of *Dragon River Eulogy* (one of the eight model operas) from his radio effectively drowned out all the sounds of battle in the little courtyard. When the section head had first rigged up an amplifier, I had been mystified by his sudden interest in the radio programs. Only now did I begin to understand.

The sounds were drowned out, but the faces were still there before my eyes—livid faces, tearful, furious, vicious, pained, desperate, heartrending.

I shut the door and leaned against it in anguish.

My deaf old mother came in from the backdoor. How lucky she is, I thought. She is above and beyond all this sordidness. She can dismiss everything. But now she cocked her ears and tried to catch what was going on. She crept up to me on tiptoe and shouted into my ears. "Now, who is it who started the row?"

I gave her a look of disapproval. Then I was struck by the question. Who indeed!

Suddenly the loudspeaker at the top of the Economic Committee building was turned on full blast, drowning out the radio, literally enveloping us with its sound. The air around me seemed to quiver with the vibration. My nerves could not stand it anymore. My head began to swim. A humming assaulted my ears.

I knew that in a minute the racking pain would return. I lay down quickly and put my fingers to my ears.

Heavens, when will all this end?

First published in People's Literature, *No. 2, 1981. Translation completed at the Bunting Institute, Radcliffe-Harvard, December 1990.*

THE UNEXPECTED TIDE

DAI QING

Born in 1941, DAI QING graduated from the Harbin Insti-tute of Military Technology in 1966 and first worked as a technician before becoming a professional journalist and writer of fiction. Her first short story, "Anticipation" (1979), de-scribes the trampling of talent and disregard for human values through the tragedy of one middle-aged couple. Readers' re-sponse was so strong that it elicited the greatest number of letters in the history of the national daily (Guangming Ribao) in which it was published. Continuing to write through the Eight-ies, Dai Qing again won attention for her series of interviews of noted intellectuals, among them the physicist and political dissident Fang Lizhi. Her reportage on controversial issues such as the Yangtze River Three Gorges Hydroelectric Project se-cured her fame. Her investigative report on contemporary Chi-nese women, from prostitutes to political prisoners, titled Series on Women, *is the first of its kind in China. Dai Qing was arrested in July following the June crackdown in 1989 and re-leased ten months later.*

"The Unexpected Tide" celebrates a woman who crosses the line between letting herself rise and fall with the tide and taking her fate into her own hands.

One might well say that human life is like a ship sailing on the sea. Who can tell how many perils she faces once she leaves port and launches into the surging waves of the open water? Who can tell what treacherous rocks, what hidden shoals lie unblinking under the placid waves? Without doubt, there are buoys to guide her path. But who can tell when an evil wind might blow from nowhere and sweep everything away, snapping in two the rudder?

Anyway, *her* ship of life is stranded. Perhaps it may even overturn. But then, if she sticks to her resolve to sail on, who knows? Perhaps her boat may one day sail again into the tide rushing to meet her. Perhaps . . .

"Ready to go! Ready to go!" Old Zhang's voice boomed from somewhere, loud and assertive. Old Zhang had a trick of imitating the famous Peking opera actor Hou Xirei's unique exclamation: *Wa-ya-ya!* He also had some pretense at spotting sports talent. ("See that young fellow? He's cut out to be champion at the hundred-meter dash" was one of his oft-repeated lines.) That was the extent of his accomplishments as far as culture and sports were concerned. But in our sedate research academy, anyone who had the slightest interest in anything beyond his own specialty was a rare bird, and thus Old Zhang had been honored with the chairmanship of the Sports and Culture Department for twenty years running.

But perhaps the tide did not know the limits of its own strength? It surged upward and then retreated. And the boat riding on its crest? It had high hopes one moment, only to see them dashed in the next.

"Little Wei, why are you still dawdling? It's late!" The aforementioned chief of sports and culture—who doubled as an amateur Chinese-opera singer—pushed open the door to my office and hollered at me. "Wei, you are the only one missing in the show."

I put aside my ships and tides and fished for my running shoes behind the wastepaper basket.

"She's not going!" Old Mother Liu, whose desk was across from mine, butted in. She kept her eyes on the knitting in her hand.

"Not going? But wasn't everything agreed on ages ago?" Zhang was alarmed; he turned his sweaty unshaved face toward me and searched my face.

This was the eve of the lunar New Year in Beijing, the day for the championship marathon race for government workers. Certainly there was no lack of girls at our academy to take part. But they were so delicate, like swaying reeds as they minced along in their high-heeled shoes. Besides, the significance of the annual marathon was way down the scale of priorities, lumped together with such items as sanitation, birth control, and fire prevention during the holidays. Thus, the task of striving for the championship on behalf of our academy devolved on me, as it had always done in the past.

During morning and afternoon breaks, right in the corridors of our office building, I practiced monkey shadowboxing, which I had learned as a child. That helped keep me in shape. The marathon is no joking matter.

This, I thought to myself, was the one important event under Old Zhang's jurisdiction. He was nearing retirement age, and had finally gotten himself a department chair, even though it was the least noteworthy account, mainly in charge of ordering train tickets or booking hotel rooms. I vowed not to let him down. Yet today . . .

"Little Wei, please!" Zhang pleaded as I stood undecided, my running shoes in my hands.

"You silly old man, why don't you take a hint?" Old Mother Liu declaimed. "Didn't I tell you that she's not running today? What do you know about girls' affairs?" The old woman stood up from her chair with its battered old cotton-padded cushion and waddled over to us. She always calls me *girl*, although she knows that I am thirty-three. Once she even knitted a little red cap for my six-year-old daughter.

Old Zhang didn't mind Old Mother Liu, but kept working on me. "Little Wei, if you let us down, it will be over for our academy."

I hesitated for a split second and began to put on my running shoes.

"Foolish girl," Mother Wei scolded, "you are playing with your own life." She was alluding to my having donated blood a week or so ago. If she had known that I had not slept a wink last night . . .

"If I must, I must!" I steeled myself to put on the other shoe and pulled out an old army pullover. The way I see it, my ship is stranded. I must resort to the heavenly oracles to decide on my next step.

Old Zhang was not bluffing. We were indeed late. A host of women decked out in all the colors of the rainbow were assembled at the starting line, the starting gun gleaming over their heads.

"We're coming!" Zhang shouted in his eighty-decibel voice. "Wait a sec. . . . "

I saw a wisp of smoke emit from the pistol, followed by a muffled sound.

It is all over, I thought to myself. *I have failed, Wu Guo. It's no use striving. Don't you see the smoke dissolving? So it is with everything else in life. . . .*

"What's gotten into you?! Run!" croaked Old Zhang as he gave me a shove on the back. What's the use of running under such circumstances? I turned to answer back. As I turned I noticed that there was still a crowd huddled at the starting line. With two or three hundred people in the race, not all the entrants would start off at the sound of the gun. I quickly pinned on my number and joined the back of the pack. So, Wu Guo! The moon had swerved from its course and decided to give the tide full play.

I found myself running with a few girls taller than myself by a head. I let my legs swing and was careful that I kept my shoulders relaxed. I inhaled every four steps and exhaled every four steps. My sports instructor in middle school had repeated this rule a hundred times. I trained under her for six years and went through twelve pairs of running shoes.

Before we had put five hundred meters behind us, several girls dropped out. They turned green round the gills and collapsed into the arms of their attending beaux. Poor girls, they knew hundreds of knitting patterns, knew how to pile their hair atop their heads without showing a seam, but what did they know of the trick of controlling the soles of the feet and the muscles of the shoulders? Did they know that one must not wear turtleneck tops and tight underwear when running? Did they know about setting your teeth and surviving the first stage of exhaustion and then distributing energy according to a mysterious formula known only to the initiated? All these I knew—I who was their senior by ten years, I who was educated under teachers who were not beaten as theirs had been during the Cultural Revolution. So what if I was thirty-three?

Unobstrusively, I made my way forward—from the three-hundredth to around the one-hundred-and-fiftieth. I still had to force myself to overtake another hundred. That would be devilishly hard, as exhausting as tying the mast in a hundred-mile wind. But I had no choice. I wanted the marathon itself to resolve my dilemmas.

I overtook another dozen. I had my eyes on a girl in white sportswear. She had elasticity, but her movements were too showy, like an underrehearsed amateur actor. I knew she wouldn't last—that once we turned into the Avenue of Eternal Peace, I could dispose of her.

My boat was not really stranded in treacherous sands, after all. One way or another, I had always made it. Like the time when I had meningitis and was at death's door. I survived that. Then I had been cheated when I was working as an office temp; someone cheated me so thoroughly that I had no money left to buy a meal. I had also been labeled a counterrevolutionary—and then became a hero on the same grounds—for copying and clandestinely printing verses in the momentous year of 1976. Looking back, I wondered if it was worth all the passion spent on it. But all these were nothing compared with the last ordeal—just as I was happily feeling my baby kicking inside me, news arrived that my husband and his comrades were caught in the Tangshan earthquake and buried under the barracks they had erected with their own hands. And this on the anniversary of our marriage! But I came through everything. No wavering, no need to seek advice. I knew what I had to do and did it.

———

How long had I known him? Twenty years? One week?

He lived in the building behind us and was in the same class in primary school as my little sister. The two of them shared a desk; the desk was cut by several dividing lines, the exact line of demarcation never having been decided. Whoever's elbow happened to stray over the line would be immediately pushed back. Yes, I knew him as the child who often played in our garden, who would often sit on the wall and count the passing cars or spend hours in our backyard digging holes in the soft soil.

Then I joined the army and forgot about him. Once I came home for a visit and saw a young fellow at the gate to our compound, tall and thin with stiff black hair standing up on his head like a brush. He stopped in his tracks to give way to me, saw who I was, and blushed.

"Sister Liming," he mumbled, and slunk away by the wall.

"Who was that?" I asked my sister.

"From the apartment building behind ours," came the reply. "Don't you remember? His name is Wu Guo. He's now a blacksmith. A little blacksmith. Such a joke."

I didn't see him again until 1975, after I was demobbed. It was a hot day and I was pregnant. I had two sets of china in one hand and with the other I was pushing a pram I had just purchased. I was exhausted and could barely keep on my feet. Suddenly a hand relieved me from behind.

"Oh, you, little blacksmith." I gazed at his thick hair and equally thick eyebrows, helplessly fishing for his name in my memory. "Are you going to work?"

He didn't specify. The parcels that had weighed me

down were like playthings in his hands. He accompanied me upstairs. Just as I was fumbling about for a teacup, he vanished.

When my daughter, Xinxin, grew up, she often came back from play with trophies from a mysterious source. Balloons, chocolates, comic books. When asked, she would say that they were from her little uncle. I did not pay attention at the time. My fatherless daughter was always spoiled by many uncles and aunties among my acquaintances, and I never associated these trophies with Wu Guo.

Even less did I imagine that the shy little blacksmith would accomplish in seven days what conventional people never dreamed of doing in a lifetime. Anyway, my little ship was stranded, and I saw no way of setting sail again. This was why I decided in spite of everything to join the marathon. This race, like all momentous events—the launching of a space missile, for example—was counted backward: "Four-three-two-one Go!" So it was with my ship waiting to set sail.

7

I was barely in my office when Little Sister rang. She said that Wu Guo rang up a friend of hers, inquiring through that friend to ask me if he could take a few photographs of my little Xinxin. There's not a mother on earth who could resist having her darling's picture taken. So what were all these convoluted negotiations about? And who was Wu Guo?

"Don't tell me you don't remember Wu Guo! The little blacksmith in the apartment building behind ours!"

"The blacksmith? Is he an amateur photographer?"

"Not amateur anymore. On the upward move, I'd say. He's working as decor artist for a big enterprise. He wants to photograph Xinxin for their print-ad campaign!"

"Oh, him!"

"Come on, what do you say?" Little Sister was losing patience. "She can wear the one-piece woolen dress I just gave her."

"All right, all right."

"Don't fob me off with your *all rights.* If it's yes, phone him immediately. Number 553864. Have you got it? Immediately!"

"All right, all right."

So I dialed the little blacksmith's—rather, the little decor artist's—number to settle this momentous business. The phone barely rang before someone picked it up. It was Wu Guo himself.

6

It was Sunday. Xinxin was still in bed when he arrived. He had a lot of odds and ends with him, strips of cotton cloth and pieces of cardboard.

"Didn't you bring your camera?" Little Sister loved anything trendy and couldn't wait to have a look at his camera.

He didn't say anything. Just put down the paraphernalia in his hands and fished out of a ragged bag a camera worthy of the status of his enterprise, an Olympus OM-10.

"This trash . . ." Sister touched his cardboard and cotton strips with the tip of her shoe.

"Oh, no!" Wu Guo put down his camera to protect his treasures. "These are for the light adjustment. And I'll need your help with them."

We were busy with the photo session for two hours, but Wu Guo spent another four hours because Xinxin insisted on being taken to the zoo.

I saw the two of them off. They had not gone a few steps before Wu Guo stooped to pick up Xinxin and put her on his shoulders. The tears leaped to my eyes. Xinxin had never had a father and never knew the luxury of riding on a father's shoulders. She had to use her own feet as soon as she could walk.

5

That same night, Wu Guo called on me. You know, of course, that our academy has a resounding reputation but no housing to match. For four years we have had to make do in prefabricated shacks. As for me, having no family, I became the Permanent Officer for fetching hot water mornings and afternoons and for security duty on holidays. That was Old Zhang's title for me. I had one corner of the office room screened off. There, I set up a plank over two benches and that was my bedroom.

Wu Guo brought the package of barely dried photos, the edges not yet trimmed. There was Xinxin laughing, Xinxin dancing on one foot, Xinxin contemplating the camera with a serious look, Xinxin making faces. . . . She was six years old, yet it seemed that this was the first time I saw my child so closely. How like her father she was, especially the restless eyes twinkling in the shadow of the heavy lashes. My mother gave me a pair of eyes that are perfect as far as vision is concerned, to the satisfaction of doctors and reconnaissance commanders, but they were just narrow slits in shape, not to the taste of artists or photographers. I sometimes regret, but mainly am relieved, that Xinxin's eyes are not like mine.

"Let's use this one. What do you think?" Wu picked out one picture among the lot. It was Xinxin bundled up like a ball at the moment of stepping on ice. Her arms were stretched out and her little coat was going to burst at any moment. As I looked at the picture it flashed across my mind that Xinxin's eyes are similar to Wu Guo's, too. The thought made me blush.

"You see, everything depends on this button. And that's the ad for our company," Wu explained.

"I'd say it's thanks to the thread that holds the button," I retorted. "It seems more like advertising for the thread factory."

"But only high-quality buttons stay sewed. Otherwise, they will be gnawed through in a couple of days. Didn't you know that?"

"Gnawed through?"

He smiled and drew out of his pocket a handful of buttons of all shapes and sizes. He told me which designs were pressed, which were drilled, where they should be rounded and where back-angled. Then he told me about air traffic accidents in Pakistan: "On average, one pilot crashes down every year because there is a back-angle missing on the shoulder of the main axle of the generator." He told me this in all seriousness.

"So what if the back-angle is missing?"

"Lack of balance in internal stress." Wu blew some warmth into his freezing hands and proceeded to demonstrate on a piece of paper the distribution of internal stress. I looked at him, a tousle-headed young fellow. He was twenty-eight, one year older than my little sister. Under normal circumstances, he should have been five years out of the university with five years of work experience behind him. Nowadays, people like Wu Guo were often written off as heady youths who can't be trusted. But of course, the generation of Wu Guo had only had primary-school education.

"Where did you get all this information?"

"Do you mean all this about internal stress? Well, that's the essential of a blacksmith's job, internal stress. Of course, there's also the problem of hardening by quenching. . . ." Thus, sitting on the corner of my desk, he began to tell me about the ancient practice of hardening iron by pissing into the fire. He wanted to know whether it was just an ancient hoax or had some basis in chemistry.

"Hardening by quenching is a physical operation, I'm afraid," I reminded him softly.

"Is that so?" He raised that pair of burning eyes and blushed.

Suddenly I saw myself in one of the photos. I was holding up Wu Guo's self-made contraption for light adjustment and doubled up with laughter.

He snatched it away. He blushed as he rubbed the picture against his trousers and tried to fold it up and stuff it into his pocket.

"Come on." I tried to stop him. "It's very nice. Give it to me. I never had such a flattering picture taken of myself."

"Is that so?" He handed me the picture hesitantly. "You are not angry? You were lost in laughter and I couldn't resist clicking. All these years, I had so wanted you to laugh like that. Of course, according to the rules of our profession, it is rude to take your picture without asking permission."

"What rubbish! Who cares about these fine points? Give it to me."

"Certainly. I still have the negative." He took up the photo to have a close look. "In the future, if we need an ad on equipment for light adjustment, we'll use this."

Thus we chatted until eleven o'clock. He was on the point of leaving when he saw the stamps under the glass top of my desk.

"Elder Sister, do you collect stamps?"

"I used to, just for fun. Take these if you like them."

"Oh, no, I can't do that," he said as he bent over my stamps with interest. "But we can exchange. I've got lots. I'll bring them tomorrow."

"All right, all right, but you must go now."

4

"Wu Guo, how did you come by such a name?" I asked him the next day. *No fault*—who would name a child that?

Wu Guo sniffed. "I didn't name myself. Don't blame me!"

I laughed and with a movement of my foot overturned a thermos flask that was on the floor.

He took out a hot-water bottle from his greasy bag. "I spent three hours here yesterday and went back with a

54

vicious cold. Elder Sister, how can you bear it, night after night, in this place?"

How? Something stuck in my throat. In the old days, when I was in the army, I had been through marches and campaigns and untold hardships. But that was nothing compared with the last several years. Nobody could imagine the difficulties of a woman bringing up a child on her own. If Wu Guo had said, "It's so cold here, let's go somewhere else to look at the stamps," or "It's disgraceful, how can they turn off the heat at night! Talk to the chief tomorrow," it wouldn't have hurt so much. After six years I had grown used to having nobody care for me. But Wu Guo was just a young friend. How could I accept anything from him?

"If you refuse, I'll cut it into pieces. Now you decide." Thereupon he reached into his pocket. I was sure that he had brought the scissors.

"All right, all right," I said, and picked up another thermos flask to fill the bottle.

I slept very well that night.

3

The next day, Wu Guo was on the night shift. It was seven o'clock in the evening. I had just finished my supper. I spread out a sheet of paper and prepared to copy a manuscript for a friend. The telephone rang.

"Sister, guess what I am doing."

"What?"

"Listen, can you hear it?"

I put my ear to the receiver. There was a medley of

sound, but I could still make out the strains. "The Fifth Symphony! Fate!"

I put down the receiver. How can there be such a co-incidence?

Seven years ago, when Husheng and I decided to join our lives together, we were sitting on a little knoll outside the barracks and the moon was shining brightly. Husheng turned on his radio and the strains of this very same Fifth Symphony nearly took our breaths away. At the time, I felt that the sails of my ship of life were full and heading for unknown waters. "Husheng!" I cried, grasping his big rough hands, a man's hands. And he had said deliriously, "Yes, fate is knocking."

At the time, I did not recognize that these were not Husheng's own words. Far less would I have foreseen that I was to hold the fatherless Xinxin on many a chilly night and immerse myself in that refrain for solace. It was a vital and lasting fount of memory that Husheng had left with me, a unique mysterious knot tying us together. Except for the even more mysterious link between us: our daughter Xinxin. She grew up with this symphony in her ears. I remember the time when she was watching the Japanese cartoon series *Atumu* on my mother's TV. When the little mechanical figure leaped into the air to the strains of the Fifth Symphony, Xinxin turned to me in surprise. "Mummy, how did he know . . . ?" How did Atumu know her own music? she wondered.

"Heh, Sister Liming, do you hear it? It is thus that fate knocks at the door." Wu Guo was still at the other end.

"Stop it, Little Wu. The telephone company is going to interfere."

"But do you hear it?"

"No, there's too much noise in the background. I'm going to hang up."

"Sister Liming, what's wrong with you today?"

"Nothing. I'll hang up." I did not leave myself any time for hesitation, but put the receiver firmly back into its cradle.

It was very quiet, except for the wind and the occasional sounds of laughter from a TV somewhere. Only my own heart was pounding wildly.

I put my hands, stiff with cold, under the hot-water bottle and felt a hot spring bubble up under the placid surface of my river of life. Six years had passed! Xinxin, from a pink-faced infant, was now ready for primary school. And with time, I had found my place in life. It was not that I lacked suitors. Only the other day, a good friend had talked to me long into the night about her brother's offer. And there were many more before that. Six years was a long time. I could have gone through a dozen suitors—but I had refused them all. I couldn't step into the role. We were too cool and calm, going over the terms rationally, according to conventional standards. It was literally looking for a partner. Is that love? No.

That was not how I and Husheng had grown together. We were like two fighting cocks, squabbling all through the three years that we had known each other, and suddenly we couldn't tell how it happened, but we realized we couldn't do without each other. After that, everything was like a dream: writing applications for permission to marry, waiting for approval, getting the use of a little room, putting two wooden planks together to make a bed. And then being together as man and wife three or four times, even though we were in the same regiment. We were not like a couple at all in the usual sense of the word. No pillowcases and tea set. Just a burning love. We figured the rest could wait, commonplace occurrences like going to restaurants or taking long walks together. We had all the time in the world. Who could have foreseen the earthquake that snatched away Husheng in one swoop?

I had Husheng. How could I love anybody else? Besides, Xinxin is vitally important to me. My poor fatherless daughter. I could not bear to think of someone being my husband and indifferent to Xinxin.

"This is fate knocking at the door," Wu Guo had shouted to me from the other end of the phone. Could it be that there was an invisible link between our two souls?

I knew that Wu Guo was born to a cultured family, but we never discussed music. And anyway I barely knew any tune except the one Husheng had brought into my life. Wu Guo was so young. I wondered if he could also love this kind of music? Could he understand its heartrending impasse and then its cascading overflow into the joy of victory? Perhaps he was just showing off. More likely, though, he just wanted to share his understanding of the world. I should not let my fancies run away with me.

My mother had long said that Wu Guo and my little sister would make a pair. As a matter of fact, they have known each other for twenty years. Wu Guo had been over to my place for several days running. Was his presence merely camouflage for paying attentions to my sister? I was the big sister, after all—big sister to both of them. Should I step aside, I wondered, and benignly supervise the affairs of these two young people? But I felt instinctively that that was not the point. I could sacrifice everything—my time, my little corner, my meager salary—but that was not the point. Wu Guo had already announced on the telephone that fate was knocking at the door. I knew that if this situation continued, I was going to lose the peace of mind I had acquired so dearly. I decided that on the following day I would bring matters out into the open. I would channel this stream of disaster, or perhaps of happiness—depending on the outcome—into the port of my little sister. Healthy and lively at twenty-seven, she was a flower waiting to be plucked.

2

I had considered a hundred ways of activating my plan. Eat out? Hepatitis was rampant. Meet at my mother's? Mother was sometimes in the way. Get together at my own corner here? That would send all the wrong signals, making me the center of attention. And anyway it would be too cold. Little Sister is delicate. Go to a park? That wouldn't do. The park with all those couples in it, the women in middle-length coats of the same cut and pattern and hair clasps with the same kind of eight-ring embellishments, accompanied by men in corduroy jackets of the same design, walking in the same listless way while keeping an eye open for a spare bench . . . It gave you the feeling of being packed off wholesale. Now what was to be done? As I was about to fill my hot-water bottle for the fifth time from the office thermos flask—over the protests of my fellow workers—Old Zhang remarked, "Very likely you are feverish. Just as well. There are not enough tickets to go around for tonight's ball anyway."

My hand caught his in a vise. "Yours and Old Mother Liu's and my own. Don't say no. I must have all three for tonight. It's an emergency."

The three of us went together. Little Sister, decked out like a flower in full bloom, was invited to every dance. Her face was streaming but she kept on dancing. I had many acquaintances, so I flitted in and out of the crowd, chatting, drinking soda water, introducing my sister and Wu Guo to everybody. "This is my young friend. That is my sister, the one in the purple sweater. She has style, hasn't she?"

Wu Guo got tired of being shepherded around and edged himself toward the sound equipment. At first he just stood by silently. Then he lent a hand changing the cassettes and helped with the tuning. Later, when I stole over to the group, I saw him in deep conversation in technical jargon.

I was at a loss. Now, I had set up this meeting. Was it going to end up like the countless times they had met in the last twenty years? I had brought them together, like hundreds of thousands of matchmakers from time immemorial. I had done it unthinkingly, following old established practice. But if they had not felt a ripple of emotion toward each other for the last twenty years, could an outsider's meddling fingers stir up those dormant waters? Well, I decided to give up and go home. The manuscript I had promised to copy was still on my desk. As far as I was concerned, she could go on with her dancing and he could stick to his machines.

It was a moonless night. I was trying to locate my battered Flying Pigeon among a sea of bicycles.

"Sis, ours are right here."

He had followed me out! All my surreptitious maneuvers to put on my hat and coat and sneak out didn't work.

"If you don't like dancing, why didn't you say so?"

"I came for the music and to watch the dancing. It's quite fun. And anyway, if I'm not here, who's to see you back?"

"I don't need anyone to see me back. I've walked on darker nights than this, alone, in the country. If you are not interested, you might as well go home. Or you could wait for Little Sister."

"Little Sister?" He smiled. In the darkness, his smile seemed to exude warmth. "She doesn't need me to worry about her."

Did I need him to worry about *me*?

We rode our bikes shoulder to shoulder in the silent streets.

"Sis, why?" he asked. "Why?" That was his question. It could mean several things. Why did you maneuver this threesome dance party? Why did you not dance yourself? Why did you leave so early? Why rush back to your freezing shack? Why live like this? He could mean any of the above questions. Or any one of them could include all the rest.

"Wu Guo, you are very young. There are matters that are beyond explanation."

"No. They can be explained. You just don't want to talk." He pressed hard on his bicycle horn for no special reason; the streets were empty. "You think that even if you do explain, no one will understand you."

"Is that what you think?" I countered, feeling that this was treading on dangerous grounds.

"But supposing there is someone who understands. Supposing there is someone who is sick and tired of being misunderstood, who one day discovers that he understands you and that you understand him . . . ?"

"But . . ."

"Are you willing? Are you willing to give up going it alone, hiding your bitterness from everybody—friends, relatives, colleagues?"

"That's not true!"

"Your cheerfulness is forced," He jumped down from his bike and caught hold of my handlebars. "Now don't rush to deny it. To put it another way, there's something missing in your life. Of course nothing on earth is perfect, but supposing we have the power to make it better?" His eyes were piercing, forcing me to face the question.

"It's not worth the try. Think of all the inhibitions, enough to suffocate."

"But supposing there is someone who doesn't give a damn, who is above it all."

"Wu Guo, my mother has asked me to approach you, about you and Little Sister. . . ."

"Sis, is this what you really think?"

Perhaps I should have told him that I have put my own brains aside. I was just following ancient patterns. . . .

"And the heart. What does your heart say?"

"Wu Guo!"

"Sister Liming, perhaps this is neither the time nor the place to say this. Perhaps my speaking out now is offensive to you. But what I want to say is: the weather will always turn warm, flowers will bloom, and the waters of the stream are bound to flow. How can one cold blast freeze up a whole river? Why should we let ourselves be bandied about like puppets? Why don't we take our affairs into our own hands? Sis, last night the truth suddenly dawned on me. Isn't the whole situation as clear as daylight? What are we waiting for?"

He grasped my hand across the bicycle. I felt a strange warmth suffuse my body. I raised my head and saw his somewhat childish eyes looking at me earnestly. No! It was precisely on this account that I must protect him. I extricated my hands slowly.

"Wu Guo, it is impossible. Think of the difference in our ages, my young friend. And my child. I am no beauty. And I am not a good housekeeper. You can see for yourself. I've never had a home, my salary is very small, and I've squandered it all."

"Sis, is this all you have to say to me?" His voice was constrained.

"What will the people around you say? Won't you be ashamed to be seen with me in public? What about your parents? Can you do this to them? I'm used to living alone. I don't need sympathy, much less sympathy at another's expense. . . ." I got on my bike and rode off, leaving him under a solitary street lamp swaying in the wind.

"Wei Liming," he shouted after me, "you place idle gossip above the treasure of your own heart?"

I flew on my bike. My refusal was weak and unconvincing. If he had caught up with me and caught hold of my hands, I might have risked everything just for the happiness of a few years, a few months, or even for the moment, in gratitude for his understanding.

He did not catch up with me, although he could easily have done so.

1

"It is a dream," I kept saying to myself the next morning. "See, now the sun is out and I am awake." I emptied the hot-water bottle and put it away in a drawer.

In the afternoon, the porter rang to say there was a letter for me. I ran. It was in an official envelope printed over with BEIJING HOUSEHOLD WARES FACTORY BRANCH 2. I ripped it open. Inside was an official letter stamped over with a red seal:

> To the East District Public Security Office:
> This is to certify that Wu Guo, male, twenty-eight years old, unmarried, staff of our factory, has our approval to register for marriage with Wei Liming, female, thirty-three years old, widow, staff of the Art Institute. Sincerely,
> Beijing Household Wares Factory Branch 2
> January 24, 1982

The calligraphy was beautiful, probably from the hand of an elderly person who had received proper training. Was that all? I shook out the envelope and a note fell out: "I'll cum over agin tonight." No name of addressee, no signature of sender. Of course, it could only be my young friend who would scrawl such a misspelled note.

I didn't want to see him. I was awake and didn't want to lapse into dreams.

I asked Mother Liu to give him a ring, telling him not to come, that I was away.

My poor little ship had endured so much buffeting, I wanted to dock her for a while, to spread my net under the sun, to dry my sails as I greeted passing boats on their way. Who would have thought that the tide would turn unexpectedly and carry me into open waters, to start again on a soul-stirring, perilous new journey!

The problem came upon me so suddenly it was too brain racking. I was always quick to act—not a thinker. But it was then and there that I decided to compete in the marathon. And I bargained my own terms: if I succeeded in the race, I would ask for a letter of approval to match his; if I dropped out, I would never see him again.

I kept on running. By an optimistic estimate, there were probably two hundred behind me, but somehow I seemed further away than ever from the goal. It was like the prospect of communism. It seemed closer in 1921 than in 1971. The more distance you cover, the further away it seems.

I was out of breath, dizzy. I wanted to throw up. My stomach ached first in one place, then in another. Omens. I knew that these aches and pains were illusory, not physical but psychological, a test of will. They were always there to meddle with one's life.

I had long ago announced that I was an atheist, like thousands of good, bad, or mediocre people before me. But only now, through every inhalation, through every movement of my legs did I truly realize that God does not help. Of course he might have been off on holiday. This dilemma came upon me so suddenly, I gave him very short notice.

The crowd of bystanders was getting thicker. They were so relaxed standing there, laughing and chatting. Some shouted out: "Step on the gas." I dragged a pair of legs that felt like logs. Suddenly it occurred to me that though we all lived on the same planet, how different were our burdens. If I had decided not to participate in the marathon, I, too, could stand idly by, eating big chunks of ice cream. Yes, that would be pleasant. But what about the joy of hitting the ribbon at the end? That sensation could last a lifetime. And the doggedness of sticking it out to the end, that was also something that could last a lifetime. Not to mention Wu Guo, riding over and above worldly conventions. In my life from now on, I would need all the confidence and persistence I could command to deal with all that might descend on my head. Or perhaps we would need it for all that might descend on *our* heads. Suddenly I realized that the bet I made was not just a bet like any other. I thought I was leaving it all to chance. Actually I was testing myself: can you deal with it or can't you?

A sea of multicolored flags greeted me on the way. And a sea of faces. The air seemed so thin. Had the crowds sucked it all up? The sun was so bright, as always during winter in Beijing. It was then I knew I had to make a dash for the finish line!

"Little Wei!" Old Zhang shouted at me, his voice ringing above the noise.

"Eighteen! Nineteen!" The timekeeper, a little flag in his hand, was keeping count of the runners who hit the line.

At that moment I knew that Wu Guo and I had made it. We had won. Our flouting of convention, our search for something better had prevailed. But I wanted it to be still better. I swung my arms as I swept on. I panted as I overtook four or five girls. One more step and . . .

"Thirty-three!" I had crossed the line. I was the thirty-third, exactly my own age. What a pity I had not dashed forward seconds earlier and made it to twenty-eight, Wu Guo's age.

Suddenly I realized someone was holding me. Strong manly hands. Wu Guo!

"I've never seen the likes of you. Look around, see for yourself. Is there anybody running as desperately as you are?"

I shook the sweat from my eyes and looked around me. So many pretty girls. Laughing, jumping, eating cream cakes offered by the boys. My throat was burning. I could not bear the thought of food.

All the others had apparently run purely for fun. Suddenly I wanted to cry. Nobody else was like me, so desperate. Life for them was such a lighthearted affair.

0

Wu Guo stuffed the marriage certificate into his greasy bag. He disposed of it as casually as if it were a piece of wrapping paper. When he saw my alarm, he laughed.

"This is just the people's acknowledgment. Or to put it more grandly, the acknowledgment of the state organ. What I want is you. You have given yourself to me this morning at the marathon. Although you looked quite knocked out and can't be put in a bag."

I was still wearing that pair of running shoes and that old pullover. Two hours earlier we had gone to Hongbin-lou Restaurant for lunch. Wu Guo treated, and invited Old Zhang to join us. After the meal, the two of us hijacked Old Zhang to his office to make out the certificate of approval for me to register for marriage. Only then did Old

Zhang savor the full implications of his succulent roast beef sirloin. He looked at the two of us by turns and suddenly gave his best imitation to date of Hou Xirei: "*Wa-ya-ya!* Your humble servant . . . has wielded the seal of authority for twenty years. And finally the day has come . . . when it is put to a worthy use!"

"Well, I suppose we can start practicing the love talk now," I joked. I felt as if I had just lost in a battle to repel the enemy. The battlefield was deadly quiet.

"Why so conventional? It doesn't sound like you." He frowned in a mock imitation of a political-affairs officer. "Considering your performance this morning, we'll withhold the label for the moment. You get washed and join your husband this evening."

"And what about the thirty-five legs due to a bride?"

"Can't afford them. If you had mentioned it earlier, I would have gotten out of this, but now it's too late to back out. Let's settle for two legs, and they are for Xinxin."

I went to my mother's house. Mother was wiping the spotless tables in the room. "I know everything. Last night, the Wu couple came over. They told me not to worry. They said they always had absolute confidence in Wu Guo." Mother wiped her eyes. "Your father always said not to worry about you. He said Liming is not the kind to end up unhappy."

"Where's Little Sister?"

"She's off to buy candy. She said you had always spent your money on us. Now we won't let you skimp for your wedding."

I spotted Xinxin's overcoat. "Where's Xinxin?"

"The Wu family took her away this morning. At first she said she wanted to wait for Mommy, but later she changed her mind and left with them."

So everything was true?

I took a bath. Soon it got dark. The children in the courtyard had started to set off firecrackers in anticipation of the New Year. I looked at myself in the mirror. My face was smooth and radiant like the evening sunset. I wonder if Husheng, from where he was, was looking at me at that moment. My thoughts were interrupted by a patter of footsteps.

"Mommy!" Xinxin rushed in, followed by two younger boys. Xinxin had a big doll in her hands. Was that Wu Guo's contribution of the *two* legs? The other children, Wu Guo's nephews by his sister and his brother, brought up the rear with a music box, building blocks, and comic books. They made a pile of these objects on the bed. They were her devoted slaves.

"This is from Aunty; this is from Uncle; this is from Granddad; this is from Granny. . . ."

My darling daughter, she had joined the family before her mother!

"Aunty says you must hurry and go over. Aunty knocked on Little Uncle's head. . . ." Her name for Wu was Little Uncle.

"Why did Aunty knock on his head?"

"Aunty said—"

One of the nephews volunteered a reply. "My mommy says, you've done a smart thing after all."

I cried and held the three children in my embrace.

Wu Guo came over. He was dressed in a new suit, which made him look slightly comic. "Weren't you told to deliver your message and go back? Off with you all!" He shooed the children away and sat down next to me.

"Liming, you are crying. Are you thinking of Hu-sheng? Next year, we'll go and bring back his ashes. Xinxin must keep his name. . . ." My tears continued to flow. He took out a crumpled handkerchief. "I announced to them this morning at the factory—I'm not Little Wu anymore. I won't be ordered around anymore with Little Wu this and Little Wu that. I announced that I am a father. Not the diaper-swashing kind. My daughter will start primary school next year. Come on, don't cry. I've asked every-body to come over next Sunday. I told them, now Wu Guo is closer to the party than ever. After all, my wife has twelve years' party membership and that's not a joking matter!"

I picked up the doll. "Two legs?"

He laughed as he put his arms around me and led me to our bridal chamber in his parents' house, a room the whole family had readied at a day's notice. In one corner stood a Xinhai brand piano, its two legs gleaming in the lamplight. It was the only new object in the room.

"I've thought it over. We'll just have this one child. And she doesn't have to be a pianist. The piano is there just to give a sparkle to life."

The moon dipped to the west. Only the stars were in the sky. Wu was deep in slumber.

"It's just seven days," I whispered in his ear.

"Seven days is long enough. God created the world and Adam and Eve, all in seven days. While I had just married a wife, the best wife in the world, unlike any other . . ." He murmured as he kissed me.

I realized that he was still young. Earlier, Mother Liu

had said as she dragged me to a quiet corner: "Don't let yourself get carried away for the moment. Right now I'd say you are both young. But what about ten years later? He'll still be young, while you'll be an old woman."

I knew that day would come. But even if one day he decides that he has made a mistake, I'm prepared to pay the price of a lifetime for sharing a slice of his life. It will be my way of thanking him for his kindness now. If that moment arrives, I will be very calm. I will allow him to correct his mistake, just as I am abetting his mistake right now. Life would be so drab if one could not afford one glorious mistake. That's not living. That's just hiding under a mask.

Wasn't this stupid? But stupider things were to follow. I was pregnant. I let myself become pregnant on purpose and then I went and had an abortion. I did this because I heard the whispers. People had gone through the genealogy of three generations on both sides and decided "There must be something wrong with Wu Guo. Isn't it as clear as day?" I let myself be pregnant and had an abortion. I can't bear to have anyone cast dirt on pure marble.

My little ship sets sail again. Oh, you unexpected tide!

From The Last Elliptic Circle, *October Publishing House, Beijing, 1985. Translation completed at the Bunting Institute, Radcliffe-Harvard, February 1991.*

JINGJING IS BORN

GU YING

GU YING, born in 1945, first studied art in her native Yunnan in southwest China. She worked for many years in museums and as an art teacher before becoming a professional writer, whose chief concerns are issues relating to women and children.

"Jingjing Is Born" is about the horrendous experience of giving birth under a system that sets no value on human life.

"The Serenity of Whiteness," using a hospital ward as background, describes how a terminally ill young woman ponders divorce—when divorce still carries a stigma for women.

It was a snowy day in winter. Two men and a woman were sitting in a warm restaurant near the railway station. On the table before them were dishes of sliced ham sausage and smoked fish. There was also a small platter of dried fruits and tri-colored nuts, as well as a kettle of the strong *erguodou*, just heated in a pot. The men's collars were loosened and their faces flushed. The glass in front of the woman was empty. She did not drink, but merely nibbled at the apricot kernels in the platter.

The tall, thin man with a square forehead and a straight nose seemed to be the host. And the woman, clear-skinned and lively in her general demeanor, was evidently his wife.

The two of them kept plying the other man with food and wine. The guest looked travel-stained, with two bags behind his seat. More likely an old friend who had suddenly turned up.

"Take your time," said the woman. "The steamed dumplings will take at least half an hour to arrive. We have two hours and ten minutes. It's a shame you are so rushed. We can't even leave the railway station."

"What can I do? This is a business trip. But I see you two, that's something. Though I'll have to miss your precious Jingjing. She must be grown?"

"Thirteen already," the man answered proudly.

"No, four more days to her thirteenth birthday," the woman corrected him. Her face took on that expression peculiar to mothers when they talk about their children. "She's nearly as tall as I am. A big girl altogether. She has Lao Xu's nose and forehead, but her skin is like mine. And her temperament as well. With that combination, she is better than either of us. A couple of years ago, a teacher from the ballet school pestered me to allow her to learn dancing, but I resisted." The woman stopped, and then added earnestly: "If I had a choice, I would rather Jingjing grow up to be an obstetrician."

"Obstetrician?" the guest asked. "Why?"

The couple exchanged glances and told the following story.

AS EXPECTED, THE WOMAN BEGINS THE TALE

Lao Xu and I were married nine years, and we still didn't have a child. Injections, pills, medicine made from secret prescriptions—I'd tried everything. But no matter how hard I tried, I did not conceive. We finally decided to adopt a child. And just as we were about to take steps, I became pregnant. We were up in the clouds, as you can imagine. But there was one drawback. The timing was bad. I became pregnant in the middle of March in 1967. That meant my delivery would be in late December—a winter birth. But worse, Jingjing decided to enter the world on December 16. Later, I often wondered how Jingjing could have made such a bad choice. If I had the choice of my birthday, I would never have chosen that wretched day. You see, December 16 was the beginning of the great faction war in our city.

On the morning of December 15, Lao Xu was in a hurry to get to his plant. Zhang, our upstairs neighbor, and Wang, our downstairs neighbor, both masters at their craft, were staying home with their flowers and their goldfish. Why, I asked him, should you give a damn for the plant? But he had an important conference and had to attend, even if the skies were raining knives and daggers. But supposing I must go to the hospital today, I asked him. He laughed and said, "It's still ten days to the projected date. My precious baby would not play nasty tricks with its daddy."

Unfortunately, the precious baby had a mind of its own. Lao Xu was barely out the door before I started feeling ill. I thought: it's far too early, it can't be the baby coming. So I ate a bowl of noodles and took a little nap. When it grew dark, I felt bad again. Our neighbor old Mrs. Wei came over for a chat. She was immediately alarmed. "With all this faction war and commotion around us, how can you wait for Lao Xu? If he is not back by now, it means he has decided to stay through the night. That is their style, the rebels, as they call themselves. They strike at night. I'd say that you needn't wait for your husband. Anyway the municipal hospital is just at the corner of the alley. I'll take you there and we can call your husband afterward."

Old Mother Wei wrapped some food for me and helped me down the stairs. Our alley is straight as an arrow. We can see the main road where the alley intersects, people and bicycles and cars going back and forth, and the little shoe shop guarding the mouth of the alley.

It was a long time since I had been outdoors. Lao Xu would not let me go to the neighborhood dressmaking cooperative where I work, and he never mentions what's going on outside. So when I first stepped outdoors, I had a real shock. I was not prepared for the change. All the little stores were tightly shut and locked up. What's more, they were all plastered with big-character posters and slogans, right up to the chimney. And then to see the men and women rushing about, as if there was a fire. Others advanced in columns, carrying guns and clubs across their shoulders. They all looked so grim, as if out for blood. I had always been timid. I clutched Mother Wei's arms. "Good heavens, what are they doing?" I asked.

"Out for a fight," Mother Wei said casually. Evidently she had encountered scenes like these.

"Who's fighting whom?"

"It's United Headquarters against the Battalion. The two sides had a go at it yesterday. The Battalion surrounded one of the fortifications of the United. The United sent reinforcements. See there! Look eastward! That's where it happened." Old Mother Wei pointed to a building about ten stories high. The top of the building was swarming with people, like so many ants.

"What are they fighting for?"

"Heaven knows. They all call themselves the revolutionary rebels. All claim to be upholding this and defending that. All to the death, too."

I tried to calm my anxieties. Let them do their worst, the hospital was right at the corner from the alley. Nobody could stop me going to the hospital to have my baby.

Who would have thought that the minute we were out of the alley, we couldn't move. The crowd was so dense. Someone at the back shouted, "Give way, give way!" A stretcher borne by two young men surged forward from behind and nearly knocked me down. Then another stretcher. Followed by pushcarts. People were piled pell-mell on the carts with bandages around their heads. I trembled all over and just wanted to go home. Mother Wei clutched me tightly and steered through the crowd, pushing, cursing, begging her way through. Finally we made it to the door of the hospital. We were just about to step in when two figures with red armbands leveled a wooden pole across the door.

"What's your business?"

"Please, please make way, we must get into the hospital." Mother Wei pointed to me with great assuredness.

The two revolutionary rebels stood their ground. "The hospital has an emergency revolutionary task. No patients whatever will be admitted." They were so cocksure of themselves.

"There is nothing so urgent as a woman giving birth!" Mother Wei had worked for the neighborhood committee.

She was ready with words. "Please, please make way for us. Babies are the future of the Revolution, you know!"

"Nothing doing. All the patients at this hospital have been sent back."

"We are going to the obstetrics unit. Do you hear me? Obstetrics!"

"Obstetrics no exception. All patients sent back. Those that have had their babies, and those that didn't get around to having them yet, all sent back."

"Oh, no, you must be joking. She is assigned to this hospital. She's always had her examinations here. Look, here are her records." And Mother Wei handed over my prenatal examination files. "She's thirty-three, and this is her first baby. Where can she go?"

"That's your own concern. Now move on. It's dangerous here. If you get hurt, you've yourselves to blame."

Mother Wei and I were paralyzed. I felt my head spinning. I couldn't think at all. Luckily Mother Wei regained her presence of mind and led me to Aunty Zhao, who runs the shoe store. "Don't worry," Mother Wei said. "I'll ask Lao Xu to take you on his bike to Pingan Hospital. It's a specialized maternity hospital in a quiet area. They can't drive out all their patients. I'm going to phone Lao Xu right away."

So I sat in the shoe store and listened to the howling of the crowd outside. The sky was murky, as if it was going to snow. My tears dropped as I cursed Lao Xu in my heart. "You son of a bitch, why don't you show up?"

Why the hell didn't he show up?

THE MAN CONTINUES THE NARRATIVE

While Gui Zhi was sitting in that shoe store in an agony of waiting, I was at my plant, listening to our chief relaying orders from headquarters. Headquarters announced that very same night that the decisive battle between the two lines was launched and that every soldier of the United Headquarters had to be ready to fight and to fall for the glorious cause.

Many comrades formed ranks immediately and made ready for battle. I was a member of the Red Pen Brigade and our task was to print two thousand campaign leaflets and draw a large-scale poster. Everything had to be finished before dawn.

My job was to do the poster. I had already drawn up a sketch. It was a huge caricature of all the leaders of the Battalion faction. I pictured them as a convoluted mass of crawling creatures with human heads and reptile bodies. The next step was to pick out the outlines in white against a pitch-black background. When Mother Wei's call came through, I was just halfway through with the background. I put down my brush immediately and requested to leave.

The chief was disgusted. "Perfect timing, isn't it? Don't you know that this is the crucial hour? A matter of life or death? We may all have to reinforce the front lines any minute. Go and be damned. There's no relying on the likes of you."

I felt as if I had swallowed a fly. I, Xu Guoliang, have always stuck to the revolutionary left. I had borne the whiplashes of the conservatives without a flinch. I never whispered a word of it to my wife, in case she might hold me back from fighting for the cause. Can anyone say that

I am a coward? But my wife was going to give birth. What could I do? I put on my cotton-padded overcoat and made my way out. I hunched my back, keeping my head low as I got on my bike, looking furtively around, as if I were a deserter. As I made my way back I felt more and more justified. Was it my fault? Here I was nine years married, and still childless. I was thirty-four, my wife thirty-three. Who would have thought that she was going to be pregnant at such an unprecedented moment in history? And who could have seen that she was going to give birth just at the moment of the decisive battle between the two lines? If we had had a child eight years earlier, my son would be in primary school right now, and a little revolutionary rebel, too, like his father!

The shoe store was easy to locate and I quickly put Gui Zhi on the backseat of my bike.

"Be careful," Mother Wei reminded me. "The streets are so unsafe. Don't worry about things back home. I'll put the chickens in the pot when she is ready to come back."

Pingan Hospital was about eight *li* away. Not far. All we had to do was to cross three streets and two alleys. But luck was against us that wretched night. We were barely out of the first alley before the snowflakes came floating down around us. The ground slipped under my feet and I could only move inch by inch. I was soaking in sweat.

Then, as soon as we emerged into the second street, we saw a huge black shape in the distance lumbering toward us. I was petrified. There were no street lamps, of course. In the darkness, the gigantic shape appeared to have tentacles shooting out of its forehead, like some mythological creature. How did such a thing ever get here, into our town center, in the middle of civilization? I watched it with dread as it approached. Finally, the rim of tires showing underneath gave away its secret and I saw through the mystery. It was a homemade tank! A truck covered with plates of iron welded together, with a few holes drilled in front for firing, and there you have the basics of a tank. It crawled forward slowly and ponderously, like a giant snail, totally oblivious to my anxiety. At last, it moved out of sight. I quickly steered my bike through the next alley and emerged into the last street. But bad luck stuck to me, it seemed. As we passed a building a few bricks fell out from the wall above and scraped the tip of my nose before they crashed to the ground in front of me. I looked up and saw gun barrels poking out of holes made in the wall. In the darkness, they cast a menacing, cold reflection on the snow beneath. I am as brave as the next man, but who likes to walk under the barrel of a gun? I took a look at Gui Zhi and hastened my step. By the light of a passing car, I could see that she was deadly pale and her eyes were full of fright. "Don't mind it," I assured her. "We are getting there."

Gui Zhi began to groan. "It hurts," she cried. Her hands trembled as they grasped the seat of my bike. Good heavens, suppose she delivers the baby now—in this cruel and deadly street! I began to curse under my breath. I cursed the unlighted streets. The columns of people rushing about madly. The homemade tank. The holes in the wall. The gathering snow. They were all in my way. All working against me. Why won't they let us have our baby in peace? These reflections, of course, were not worthy of a leftist revolutionary rebel. They smacked of betrayal. But I couldn't help it. They keep cropping up in my head. After all, my wife was sitting at the back of my bike and going to deliver our baby!

I finally let out a sigh of relief. We were at Pingan Hospital.

The walls of the hospital were very high. All the buildings were hidden behind trees. Not a flicker of light anywhere. I began to panic. In the momentous hour of the decisive battle between the two factions, work units would be likely to close down and disperse its members. And even if the work units didn't close down, people were likely to stay home. Who would have the heart to work, anyway? If Pingan Hospital were really closed down, my poor wife would be left in the streets, in the snow! The blood rushed to my head, and I pounded the gates with my fists, shouting desperately. "Open! Open!"

The sound of footsteps! Footsteps actually approaching! A woman's voice, shrill with impatience, came from the other side of the gate. "What do you want?"

"My wife is going into labor! Please open! Quick! I beg you!"

The gates opened a crack. A hand stretched out. "I must inspect the medical files."

I handed over my wife's booklet of medical records. It was shown on her records that she was assigned to the municipal hospital. I hoped that the person on the other side of the gate would not notice.

But that was exactly what she was checking on.

"This is not her assigned hospital. Go to the municipal hospital."

"That's where we come from! They have an emergency task, and the doors are closed to patients!"

"Then go and talk to whoever is responsible. What right do they have to saddle us with their patients?"

"Doctor, please . . ." Through the gap between the gates, I saw that she wore her front hair in a frill beneath her white cap. A typical trainee from the nursing school, I decided. I called her *doctor*, hoping that this promotion would put her in a good humor. "The streets are so unsafe, we had such a hard time getting here. Please stretch a point. Do us a favor, please."

"A favor! A favor! You all want a favor! But who's going to do us a favor? The two of us have been here over fifty hours! No heating! No hot water! No food! And no one to take over the shift! Nothing! Who cares if we die of fatigue! Let me tell you, it's *no*. You can shout yourself hoarse, but let me tell you, it's *no*!"

"Please, have some pity, doctor."

"And who's going to pity us?" She started to shut the gates.

"No, no. Don't, don't!" I edged my body between the gates. "Doctor, can you stand by and watch her die?"

For a minute she stood irresolute. Perhaps my plea struck a chord. But when I tried to pry open the gates, her anger erupted.

"Hey! What, what are you doing?!"

"My wife must go in! She must!"

"*She must.* Is that it!"

"Yes, she must. that's it!"

I tried to force my way in. She was no match for me. "Your grand-aunt has said no!" she screamed. "Go in if you dare!"

I threw caution to the winds and screamed back. "We will! And right under your nose!"

Thus we started this shouting match, our voices getting higher, our tempers getting hotter. All this time, Gui Zhi stood by helplessly, drenched in her own tears. I don't know how this would have ended if a voice had not intervened. "Let them in!"

It is strange, the effect of a soft voice in the middle of loud and angry shouting. I calmed down immediately. The voice was indeed unusual. Perhaps it was because the voice came from behind a gauze mask. It was not what you would call a sweet voice. But it was soothing. Like the rays of the sun in winter.

"You always let them in," the nurse complained. "There's six of them already who are not from our beat."

"They can't help it," the voice replied. "They have gone through a lot of suffering. Don't make it worse for them."

"And we, don't we suffer, too?" the nurse complained, though her anger had abated. "One after another, they all come here. As if we were the Temple of the Goddess of Birth."

"Come in," the voice behind the mask directed us. The door opened halfway.

"Thank you, doctor! Thank you, doctor!" I mumbled as I hustled Gui Zhi through the threshold, afraid that somehow the gates might close before we got through. Before they could change their minds, I dragged Gui Zhi toward the main building.

"Don't rush her like that," the voice behind me warned. "She's about to give birth. Support her properly. She is stiff with cold."

"Oh, thank you." We stopped in front of the building,

brushing off the snow from our clothes. Only then did we have a chance to see the person who had let us in.

She was a slightly plump woman of medium height, the kind of plumpness that bespeaks a heart condition. A white cap covered her head down to the forehead. The big gauze mask hid the lower half of her face. Only a pair of narrow eyes was visible between the edge of the cap and the top of the mask. Mind you, they were not what you would describe as beautifully chiseled shapes or of burning brightness. They were quite plain, but they were black and clear. Coupled with eyebrows that were lightly sketched in a straight line, they conveyed a sense of gentleness. One would imagine that the contours of her nose and mouth beneath the mask would also be soft. She was no longer young, judging from the little wrinkles creeping beneath her eyes and on her forehead. And her slightly puffed eyelids and bloodshot eyes certainly denoted fatigue.

She made me register in the lounge and then led Gui Zhi into a door on the right. I noticed that she dragged her left leg as she walked.

I finished registering and had time to look around. The little cubbyholes with REGISTRATION, PRESCRIPTIONS, and CASHIER printed on the glass panes were all shut. A door leading to the right carried many signs: DELIVERY ROOM, NURSERY, WAITING ROOM, NO ADMITTANCE. The door leading to the left carried the signs: WARDS, VISITING HOURS EVERY-DAY 5:00–7:00 P.M. and SILENCE. The whole corridor was deserted. There was a hole in the door of the building, and the wind crept through, bringing flakes of snow.

After a little while Gui Zhi appeared. She had changed into the hospital's baggy striped pyjamas. She came over and stood close to me. I knew something was wrong, so I took her hand. "Gui Zhi, do you need some food?"

She shook her head and sniffed.

"Is something the matter?"

"Doctor says that the water is out. And the position of the baby is not right. . . ."

"But wasn't the position all right before?"

"The stupid municipal hospital! All the doctors are chased away and made to clean the latrines. That wretched girl who examined me got everything wrong. She took the baby's bottom for the head!"

I wanted to reassure her but didn't know what to say. Her eyes were swimming with tears. "The doctor says that after the water is out, I mustn't walk about. I must go in." She looked at me piteously, like a hurt little lamb, with no one to protect her.

"Gui Zhi," I exclaimed after her, my voice quavering, "courage! Don't panic! Take those cakes with you."

Suddenly a moan drifted through the freezing atmosphere. It was contagious. Immediately, more moans, some loud some soft, coming from behind the door on the right, seemed to fill the air.

We stood petrified. Gui Zhi's lips were white. She leaned against me as if she was going to fall. "I'm scared, I'm scared," she cried.

THE WOMAN ADDS A WORD

I was really scared to death. I daresay all women in labor for the first time must have the same feeling of dread, so hard to define. And on top of that, the pain. I could neither sleep nor eat for the pain. It was horrible. There were four of us in the waiting room and we were all moaning, sometimes singly, sometimes in chorus. We just couldn't bear up any longer. The room was so cold. Our towels were frozen into stiff icy sheets. The blankets and bed paddings felt cold and slimy to the touch. And the light bulbs in the room were all broken. Outside, through the windows, the snow on the ground was reflected in an unearthly bluish gleam. It seemed the whole place was haunted. How could we help moaning?

Our moanings finally managed to wake up the nurse, who was dozing at the table with her head on her arms. She got up to her feet and scolded us. "Stop it! Have some control! Women bear children all the time, but I've never seen the likes of you! Just listen to this grunting! Do you all have pigs for your zodiac animal?" She went out for a moment, then came back and said, "You three, your numbers are ten, eleven, and twelve. Your babies aren't due before midnight. Now you, number two"—she turned to a short young woman with freckles on her face—"follow me to the delivery room for observation!" She banged the door behind her and left. Number two followed meekly.

THE MAN TAKES UP THE NARRATIVE

I can hear the trio in the waiting room. Gui Zhi was the alto. The words she sang were "Oh, oh, oh . . ." What a tune it was! It made my hair stand on end. I am thirty-four years old, but I had never imagined that women giving birth had to go through such a hell.

"Go into the corridor, there are benches inside." The doctor was pushing a flatbed wheeler from the right door into the left. She added: "It's warmer in there. There's no wind." I suppose I must have been a sight, wretched with anxiety and shivering in the cold, because she smiled at me, a kindly smile. "Don't be so tense, young fellow. Relax. I'll let you know when the time comes."

Behind the door on the right was a long corridor. The delivery room, the nursery, and the waiting room were all in there. Benches lined one wall along the corridor. I sat down on a bench.

Not far from me, on another bench, was a young fellow. He was wrapped in an army overcoat, very fashionable at the time, and was fast asleep and snoring. I looked at my watch: 11:40.

I lay down, but I couldn't sleep. Once I was just about to doze off when the sound of an infant's yowl pulled me up. The wail came from the direction of the delivery room. The sleeping young fellow shot up as if he had been pricked by a needle. He glared at me. "The baby has come?" he asked.

"Whose baby?"

"Mine! My wife is number two. Short and plump, with freckles on her face."

"Someone like that was wheeled in a little while ago."

"Oh, is that so?" He cocked his ears and listened.

Piercing cries of pain arose from the delivery room. Then the doctor's voice: "Try to be quiet, you are taking too long. You mustn't exhaust yourself. Give her the drip. Continue observation."

"No, the baby has not come, after all." The young fellow held his head in his hands dejectedly. I looked at him. He looked like a bull. Low forehead, protruding eyes, short neck. All he needed was a pair of horns.

We sat next to each other on the bench, each lost in thought. From the sound of the cries, the newborn was being transferred to the nursery. Evidently its cries were catching, for very soon there was a chorus of infants' cries.

"Have a smoke." The young fellow tossed over a Battle brand cigarette. As he held his lighter I glanced at the red armband on his sleeve: Battalion of Mao Zedong Thought! The Battalion! So this bull is from the detested Battalion! Suddenly I was consumed by faction loyalty and cursed under my breath: "Wretched conservative."

"Say that again!" He turned toward me menacingly. A livid scar under one eyebrow began twitching. His eyes shot out like a pair of bronze bell ringers. He was ready to pounce on me—just like a bull. Of course he had seen my armband, too.

It was absolutely ridiculous. The only explanation was that we were bewitched. There we were, two grown men, by pure accident passing the time in the same room, exchanging a word now and then. And suddenly we discovered we belong to different factions—warring factions, actually. And lo! We are gripped by the deadliest hate for each other, as if caught in a vendetta. The bull and I eyed each other. The screech of loudspeakers far and near, with their mutual denunciations, seemed to egg us on. Just at that moment, however, his wife's cries from the delivery room joined my wife's cries from the waiting room. *"Oh! Oh! Oh! Ah! Ah! Ah!"*

Those cries brought us back to reality. Our militancy was completely deflated. The bull and I sighed in the same breath. We would not fight. But we did not have anything to say to each other, either. We just sat there—smoking, waiting, and miserable.

It was 4:55 in the morning.

The door to the delivery room opened and a woman was wheeled out. The same flatbed wheeler. The woman's hair was all disheveled; she looked utterly exhausted, but at peace. She had done her job.

Bull threw down his cigarette and stood in the middle of the corridor, blocking the way of the doctor who was pushing the flatbed wheeler.

"My wife has agonized for two days and two nights. Why can't she deliver?" His voice was harsh and belligerent.

The doctor answered quietly under her mask. "Her contractions are very weak."

"This won't do! Two days and two nights running. This won't do!" The fellow stopped. Then, as if catching hold of an idea, he struck his arms akimbo. "Mind you," he spluttered, "me and my wife, we are workers, third-generation true-blue workers. You stuck-up city doctors, you better take care how you treat our proletarian offspring!"

The doctor's eyes registered a bitter smile of helplessness. She tried to control her voice as she replied. "The facilities here are very poor. But we do our best for all mothers and infants with no exception. Let us observe your wife for another two hours. If she still cannot deliver, we will use forceps."

"Forceps?" The young fellow lowered his head as he looked hard at the doctor. If he had horns growing over his forehead, he would have gored her with pleasure. "If anything goes wrong, you must answer! We are true-blue workers."

A soft sigh was emitted from under the mask. The doctor closed her eyes without saying anything.

I pulled bull out of the doctor's path. "She is so tired. Can't you be polite?" I said to him softly.

"Polite! The old hag is probably from an evil background."

"Why do you say that? Did you investigate?"

"Why bother? She's a doctor, isn't she? She's been to a university. Now you tell me: before the Liberation, could you attend a university and *not* be from an evil background?"

"You can't make sweeping statements like that. Besides, she's staying at her post to help your wife. You should be grateful to her."

"Grateful! Two days and two nights!"

"If you don't like her, why don't you take your wife someplace else?"

"Go stuff yourself!"

I did not respond because the doctor now emerged from the waiting room with Gui Zhi on the flatbed wheeler.

"The baby's coming?" My heart pounded wildly.

"Soon." The doctor's eyes twinkled at me kindly. Her smile penetrated me like a ray of sunshine. And from the bottom of my heart, the words sang out. *Soon! Soon you'll be a father!*

The screams coming out of the delivery room rang loud and clear. It was Gui Zhi's voice. It was unbearable. "Oh, oh, I'm dying!" she screamed.

The screaming was like a whip lashing at me as I walked up and down the corridor. Finally I couldn't bear it anymore and turned into the courtyard, leaving the bull in the corridor, smoking away.

Outside, snow covered everything—the ground underfoot and the roofs of buildings overhead—bringing a measure of charm even to the dirty courtyard. The trees, which had hitherto gone unnoticed, now stood out in snow-clad elegance, the flakes lingering on their branches looking like so many blossoming white flowers.

Sounds of commotion were still coming from the streets outside, but they seemed to come from another world, totally irrelevant, totally incompatible with this courtyard shimmering in silvery light.

THE WOMAN INTERRUPTS

The delivery room was just as cold as the waiting room. The delivery packet was icy to the touch. The pains were getting worse by the minute. And the two loudspeakers outside gave us no peace. One screeched: "You worms of the Battalion, surrender! Stand behind the revolutionary line! Surrender, or death!" The other loudspeaker droned on the two lines of a battle song: "Upright stands the everlasting pine! Stalwart stands the invincible Battalion!" Both factions kept it up through the night. If I had died that night, believe me, it would have been that loudspeaker that was responsible.

"Some people are just more fussy than others," the nurse complained, meaning me evidently, but perhaps also including number two in her condemnation. "Eh, what's your name?" she asked me.

"Gui Zhi"

"Family name Gui?"

"Yes."

"Where do you work?"

"The Chestnut Lane Neighborhood Dressmaking Co-operative—*oh*!"

"Stop whining! Don't tell me that dressmakers are more sensitive than others. Your husband's name."

"Xu Guoliang."

"Work unit?"

"Weaving and Dyeing Factory—oh, I'm freezing."

"What do you expect me to do about the weather?"

The doctor came over to check the baby's heartbeat: 124.

"A bit slow," she murmured. "Give her oxygen, and calamin injections." She patted my arm, then shook her head as she sighed. "It's hopeless. The normal temperature of a delivery room is twenty-four-point-six-degrees Celsius. You walk around in a shirt. But here"—she glanced at the barometer on the wall—"it's five degrees below zero!"

The doctor mused to herself for a moment, then resumed with spirit. "You should all be honored with the title of heroic mother—to deliver your babies under such conditions. Yes, heroic mothers." Evidently she was just trying to cheer us up, but the words were warming to my heart. "You must deliver your baby properly, to deserve that title!" she added.

I looked at her and nodded weakly. Her eyes were kind and warm, but also tired. My heart trembled. Suddenly I felt I had seen those eyes before. Yes, it was when I was small and had pneumonia. Under an oil lamp my mother sat by me through the night and she had looked at me just that way.

"The conditions are not too good, but that's no reason to lose confidence. And now"—she inserted the oxygen tube into my nostrils—"you must cooperate." She smoothed my hair as if I were a child. "Now you are all set to become a mother!"

The doctor washed and disinfected her hands and put on a sterile gown. The nurse put a platter of delivery instruments near where I lay.

There was a knocking at the door, a timid soft knocking. The nurse went out for a moment. "It's little Wei," she told the doctor when she returned.

"What does he want?"

"Something happened at home, it seems."

"Oh!" The light suddenly went out of the doctor's eyes. She fixed her eyes on the rubber gloves over her hands and remained silent. But she did not go away. She walked over to me. Her arm was pressed against my leg. I felt a warmth where she touched me, as if she instilled some strength into me.

"Very good, very good." The sound came from behind her mask, soft and steady.

I had no idea how the baby was born, but born it was. I heard it crying.

"A chubby daughter," the doctor announced happily. "What a pretty girl, just born and already you can make out her features. Here, have a look." She lifted the baby and I saw a pink little bundle of flesh, and next to it the tired and loving eyes of the doctor.

"Thank you, doctor," I managed to say as I felt an ice-cold drop of water trickle from my jaw into my hair.

THE MAN TAKES UP THE STORY AND ENDS IT

The minute I heard the baby's cries, I rushed into the corridor, sat plump next to the bull, and gave him a nudge with my shoulder. "Hey, can you hear the cries? Such a strong voice!"

The bull's face was clouded with anger. "What number is your wife?"

"Twelve."

"Fuck!" he spat. "If my baby doesn't get here soon, I'll bash that hag!"

The doctor poked her head out of the delivery room and called out: "Family member of Gui Zhi." I hastened to respond.

"Your wife is all right. She just gave birth to a girl—seven *jin* and two *liang*."

"Thank you, thank you!"

She was about to say something else when a boy rushed up to her. I had seen that boy before, when I was walking in the yard. Actually I had opened the door to him.

"Mommy!" He tried to grasp her hands.

"Don't touch my hands. They are disinfected!"

The boy lifted himself on tiptoe and said something in his mother's ear. The doctor had her back to me, but from the way she swayed in shock and held on to the door frame to support herself, I could tell that some calamity had occurred. So I dashed forward and prevented her from falling. She opened her eyes slowly. Her eyes were so red, so dry and dull.

"Let's go, Mommy." The boy tugged at her clothes. She pushed me aside and passed by the waiting room as if sleepwalking. The groans coming from inside the room held her like a magnet. She leaned against the door of the waiting room weakly, her two hands crossed together. What could be seen of her face was as white as her gauze mask and the cap on her head. Her eyes were downcast.

"Doctor! Doctor!"

"Oh, coming." The doctor answered in a quavering voice and walked mechanically into the waiting room.

The boy slid into a corner and wiped his tears.

Bull went over and punched the boy in the shoulder. "Hey, little fellow, why the tears?"

"My daddy . . . beaten . . . wounded."

"Why?"

"He wouldn't let the Fight to the Death Brigade take away his books."

"What does your father do?"

"He teaches history at the Duofu Road Middle School."

"Where do you live?"

"Duofu Lane number seven."

There was a strange expression in bull's eyes. I asked him in a low voice, "Have you been to ransack their home?"

"Not I personally. But someone in our battalion had mentioned that house number, someone whose brother is a student in that school." There was a nasty taste in my mouth. I myself had taken part in those ransack-and-search parties. Sometimes on the trail of an incriminating letter, a notebook. Sometimes just for the sense of power that they confer. We never thought of the pain that these searches caused to the victims, the parents, the spouses, the children.

I hung down my head. I did not know how to pursue the subject, but was overcome by a deep sense of guilt. How I wish I had never taken part in those lawless searches.

Who knows what bull was thinking. He also hung his head dejectedly. "Oh," he groaned as he shook back his matted hair. "Another forty minutes observation period—it is hard." He looked at his watch helplessly. Compared with that bully who threatened the doctor a while ago, he was a changed man.

The doctor appeared, helping another expectant mother from the waiting room to the delivery room. Both bull and I stood up and walked over to the doctor as if propelled by a hand from behind us.

"Doctor, about my wife—number two . . ." Bull said ingratiatingly.

"I'm afraid we have to use forceps."

"Mommy!" The child stood up from the corner and cried out.

"Wait a little while—there're only three more," the doctor said to the child softly, and then turned back to bull, anticipating his protests.

"It is as you say, doctor," bull said humbly. "Is there . . . is there any danger?"

"Of course there is danger. The child's heartbeat is too fast, while the mother's contractions are so weak. This is a case for a caesarean birth, but that is out of the question now. I'll do my best."

"Yes, yes. Whatever you say, doctor. Thank you so much for the trouble, doctor." Bull was very tense but tried to put a brave face to the situation.

"Don't mention it," the doctor said lightly, and turned to me. "Your wife is leaving the delivery room soon, young fellow. Go and get her some breakfast. There is nothing here—no hot water, no milk. You have to get everything yourself."

"Mommy . . ." the child called to her again.

"Little Wei." She was on the point of saying something, looked at the child, and held back the words. Finally she just said: "You go back first." And she continued on her way to the delivery room with the expectant mother.

"Doctor!" I cried in spite of myself. "Please go back and have a look."

"Thank you." She nodded to me gratefully and added softly, "There are just three more."

As I came back carrying millet porridge in brown sugar and boiled eggs the doctor was just wheeling Gui Zhi from the delivery room into the ward.

Generally speaking, hospital wards conveyed a vision of whitewashed neatness, especially maternity wards, which also carried associations of mystery and joyful celebration. But the ward that Gui Zhi was wheeled into was more like a refugee center. The bloodstained bedclothes, the greasy pillows, and the people occupying all the space between the sickbeds, some lying, some sitting, some moving about—a perfect picture of a refugee center.

All these people were in the suite of the women who had just given birth. Among them were male and female, old and young. The floor was covered, here with dry hay, there with furry blankets. Old women squatted on the floor and gossiped. Bored old men, tucked away in a corner of the room, smoked and played cards. The children drew squares with pieces of chalk in the free space on the floor—whatever there was of it—and played hopscotch. Chicken bones and fish bones were piled behind the door, while crumpled sheets of wrapping paper were scattered all over. The whole place gave out a strange smell.

Gui Zhi was barely installed in bed by the window when the doctor who came with her was besieged by the relatives from the various suites.

"About the mother of our child, could her stitches be taken out tonight?"

"Doctor, my daughter seems to be running a fever."

"Doctor, my aunt has no appetite, why?"

The doctor looked at everybody by turn, giving one an injection, feeding some medicine to a second, and giving advice to a third. She often had to stop to clear her voice.

"Doctor, when is your next shift?"

What a stupid question! Of the one thousand and more work units in this city, could you find one that was operating normally?

So I butted in. "Doctor, try to get a moment to yourself and get some sleep." I then realized that my advice was equally stupid. The doctor barely had time to sit. But I wanted to say something, so I asked: "And your child, doctor, where is he?"

"He is gone," she answered shortly, evidently reluctant to pursue the subject. "You should also get some sleep, young fellow." And with that she left the room.

Gui Zhi ate some breakfast and slept. She slept so soundly a cannon would not wake her. My poor little wife was completely exhausted.

For the next four days, my job was clear-cut and simple. Mother Wei cooked and all I had to do was bring food to the hospital on my bike.

Back at the hospital the next night, I spread two sheets of newspapers on the floor next to Gui Zhi's bed and spread a rug over that. And that was my bed. After tucking everything into place, I curled up and tried—unsuccessfully—to get some sleep.

I suddenly thought of bull. Why had he still not turned up? As I couldn't sleep anyway, I got up to look for him.

Two women were sitting on the bench in the corridor, probably family members of numbers ten and eleven. But there was no sign of bull.

It turned out that he was in the yard, by the wall. He was pacing restlessly backward and forward with his head in his hands. As he saw me he cried out in agony, "My wife! She's still in there, and she hasn't delivered yet!"

There were tears in his eyes. Poor bull.

The doctor's son was also in the yard. His head was bare and his ears raw with the cold. He rubbed his hands and stamped his feet. He was not crying anymore. He kept his eyes on one window of the building, the window of the delivery room. The blue curtains could be seen through the windowpanes glazed with ice.

"Why are you still here?"

"Waiting for my mommy. When the aunty in there has her baby, my mommy will go home to look after daddy."

I devoutly wished that number two would deliver her baby quickly. For the sake of bull. And for the sake of the doctor's child.

It was not until noon of the next day when I came back with Gui Zhi's lunch that I heard bull's shout of joy. "Born! Born! Eight *jin*, three *liang*! A big fat son!" When he saw me he grabbed me and wheeled me around in a circle. "Oh, a big fat son. Eight *jin*, three *liang*!"

I could hardly breathe in his delirious grip. I could understand how he was feeling, though. We faced each other with smiles, smiling from our hearts. If our comrades from the United Headquarters and the Battalion could have seen us, no doubt they would discipline us for betraying the cause. Surprisingly, at that moment, I didn't give a damn. I had changed overnight. I had become a stranger to the cause. The cries of my comrades leaping into the fray held no appeal for me. All I felt now was that they interfered with my child's birth, interfered with my wife's sleep and meals, as well as the peaceful daily lives of many families like mine. I'd had enough. And I suspect bull felt the same.

"Has the doctor gone back home?"

"Not yet, but soon," said bull confidently. "There is nobody else in the waiting room. She should go home."

"It would be indecent to keep her away from home anymore," I answered.

Half an hour later, number two was shifted to the ward. Bull fussed around her clumsily. "How scary! The umbilical cord was wrapped in a double knot around our son's neck. Both of you nearly lost your lives. We owe everything to her."

I knew who he meant by *her* and I asked again: "Has she gone home now?"

"Probably."

But just as he spoke, there was a noisy disturbance from the direction of the yard. From the window, we could see two men both pushing their bikes, and on the two bikes were two women both wrapped up in huge blanket rolls. The two men were in loud argument with the nurse. Their voices were drowned out by the loudspeakers, which were still blaring. But from their gestures and facial expressions, I determined that—like me on the night before— these men had brought their expectant wives. And, as before, the nurse refused to admit them. And the women wrapped in blanket rolls were suffering the same fright and pain as Gui Zhi had been suffering. The two couples had my full sympathy. I had gone through it all. But now the nurse also had my sympathy.

The argument rose in a crescendo. Everybody in the ward gathered at the windows out of curiosity. Even the mothers who had just given birth tried to sit up in bed to have a look. Just as the argument was at its height, somebody said softly: "Look! The doctor!" Then we all saw the doctor emerge from the building. She had put on a dark blue padded overcoat with a gray scarf wrapped around her neck. She still had her mask on. The little boy was walking beside her. Evidently she was headed for home.

From the window we could see that when she was five or six feet from the group, she stopped in her tracks. She looked silently at the two women in blanket rolls and her eyes were full of sorrow. She went to the nurse and spoke to her. The nurse looked up in shocked surprise. I guessed what it meant, of course. The nurse could not believe that the doctor had again decided to accept the newcomers. The doctor did not explain. She just waved the two men in. The two men were all grateful smiles as they helped their wives into the building. The nurse followed slowly.

Only the doctor and her son were left in the yard. The boy's clear-cut features were all twisted as he fought back his tears. The doctor drew him to her side, and with her delicate soft white hands, a doctor's hands, she smoothed his hair. Her eyes looked far away. The child kept his head against his mother's breast, waiting, hoping. They stood like that for half a minute. The doctor lifted the boy's face slowly and forced a smile out of her puffy eyes. That smile carried apology, sorrow, and a deep love. I knew that it was precisely that kind of love that made her stretch out to others when in deep distress herself. She took out a carefully folded white handkerchief and wiped away the dirt on the child's chin. She could not remove the stain on his forehead. *That* was not dirt, but the mark of a blow. She said something to the boy, who then bit his lips and nodded. She gave one last lingering look at the child, then turned and walked swiftly into the building.

As soon as the doors of the building were shut the boy leaned against a tree and burst into tears. His thin shoulders shook so that the snowflakes dropped from the branches of the tree he was leaning against and settled on his head and shoulders.

Suddenly the sound of shots rang out from the east end of town. With the shots, all the loudspeakers and shouts fell dead, so that the shots rang clearer than ever. Soon the shooting swallowed all other sounds and filled the air.

The bull and I exchanged glances. We both knew that the decisive battle between the two factions had started. Our feelings were mixed. If not for the birth of our babies, the two of us would be on opposite sides at the front lines. But now we were both standing shoulder to shoulder at the window of the ward looking at the weeping boy. In the far distance, a column of brown smoke rose. Bright flames broke out from the smoke.

The three of them ate and drank and talked. The guest seemed lost in thought. Suddenly he remembered himself and looked at his wristwatch. It was twenty minutes before his departure time. He turned to pick up his bags, then suddenly asked, "What was the name of that doctor?"

"We are ashamed to say that we found our conscience very late," the husband replied. "When we finally realized we should seek her out and thank her, we couldn't find her. The hospital was disbanded. The doctors were sent down to the country."

"But she had an address in town, Duofu Lane number seven."

"We went," said the wife, "but somebody else was living there."

"Wherever she goes, a doctor like that will always be respected."

The married couple nodded in agreement.

"We are very sad that we neglected her," said the husband. "She was a good woman."

The guest was borne away by his thoughts, but he didn't know how to form them into words. With another glance at his watch, he bade goodbye to his hosts and fled toward the track where his train awaited.

First published in Beijing Literature and Art, *No. 3, 1980. Translation completed at the Bunting Institute, Radcliffe-Harvard, December 1990.*

THE SERENITY OF
WHITENESS

GU YING

I heard the cry of the cranes.

"Look!" I shouted, pointing up to the clouds. "The cranes are coming!"

"They are flying from the north," said Yan Pin, who was standing with me beside the lake. "You used to spend only the summers here, so you never met them. Now that you're here permanently, you'll see them through the winter."

The flock of birds continued to emit their long-drawn-out squawk. Their spreading wings shimmered in the light of the sun.

"But why did the cranes at the hospital never make sounds like these?" I asked.

"Because, my dear, they were in the hospital." Yan Pin smiled. "That's my guess."

"I wonder if she's still in that ward? How she loved the sound of the cranes!"

"Let's hope she's had her operation by now—and that she has recuperated."

"She has. I *know* she has." I was confident.

My painting of her, *The Serenity of Whiteness*, is completed and ready for exhibition. How I wish she could see it.

I'm sure she will some day.

1

As an art teacher, I was immediately overwhelmed by her beauty. She would be the perfect subject for a color portrait, I thought to myself. Imagine a young woman reclining in bed with a piece of knitting in her hands, a dainty bit of fancywork in light green. More yarn of the same color scattered about her pillow. Imagine white pillows, a white bedspread, white sheets, white walls. The woman herself dressed in white . . .

Against the slanting rays of the sun, the varying shades of white blended into a rich variety, faintly yellow under the light, purply bluish in the shade, while the white dress and white pillow reflected a faint gray green against the soft green of the yarn. The background brought forth the elegance and charm of the woman. Or was it the figure of the woman that lent charm to the background?

I gazed at her steadily.

She was slender, her cheekbones somewhat high, her lips rather on the thin side. But the pair of soft phoenix eyes under the straight jet-black eyebrows atoned for all and blended all her features into harmony. Hers is an Oriental kind of beauty, which is best revealed in white. Two spots of red on each cheek just about completed the picture.

The portrait as I first visualized it was to be called *Spring in the Sick Ward*. Or *The Passing of Winter*. No, I quickly decided. *The Serenity of Whiteness*—that was the proper title.

Subtler, it invited more contemplation. I had an impulse to take up my paints immediately, but then remembered that I was tied to a sickbed.

How long had I been lying here? I had no idea. I only remembered that I was seized with faintness while in front of an ironware repair store, and passersby had taken me to the emergency ward of a hospital on a flatbed tricycle. It was afternoon, I remember. And to tell by the slanting rays of the sun, it was afternoon again as I awoke and found myself in a sickbed. Had I been in the hospital for an entire day and night?

Never mind how many days and nights, I decided. I must paint *The Serenity of Whiteness*.

"Oh! You're awake?" Apparently my staring had caught her attention. The figure in my painting lifted her head and smiled at me. Her eyes were bright and her voice slightly husky. She went on: "You gave everybody a fright when you were first wheeled in. The nurse said you fainted in the streets." She sat up in her bed.

"Yes, and I don't remember anything after that."

"Of course. They gave you injections and medication, all to make you sleep. Since your arrival you've had several batches of visitors. When they saw you sleeping, they didn't stay long. They left notes and food."

Yes, indeed. On my bedside table were pastries, fruits, and get-well notes—left by my colleagues and the secretary of the art department at my school. One note indicated that my friends had wired my husband, Yan Pin, and that my daughter Xiao Yan was staying with a neighbor, Granny Zhu. I was not to worry.

I suddenly remembered that Xiao Yan was in a singing competition and needed a white shirt. That the coal store would soon be sending in our winter supply. That the grocery store would soon be selling each family's allotment of cabbages for the winter. That our stovepipes needed replacements. That I needed tickets for the exhibition of British watercolors.

Seeing my distress, the figure in my painting spoke again. "Don't worry. Since you're here, you must put everything else aside. Yours is probably a case of sporadic arrhythmia. With medication and some tranquilizers, you'll be out of the hospital within a month."

"You sound so professional." I was impressed.

Her face clouded. "Anybody would be professional if they had to lie in the hospital like I have. Three years and seven months . . ." With that she picked up the stitches of her knitting.

I stared at her in disbelief. This young woman, with no visible signs of illness, had been lying in the hospital for more than three years! I longed to ask about her illness but decided not to probe. So I changed the subject. "How diligent you are! Whom are you knitting this for?"

"This sweater is for our nephew Niuniu, my husband's sister's son. Oh, I've lots of knitting waiting to be done." She opened the door of the bedside cabinet; it was filled with different kinds of yarn, in all the colors of the rainbow. "For the old nanny, my neighbor. For my coworkers. For the son of Dumb Big Brother, in the ward next door. Some of the yarn here belongs to the nurses. Several of them asked me to start a pattern for them. My patterns are never repeated."

"You do it by a book?"

She smiled. "Following a book is so boring. I lie in bed with nothing else to do. I invent my own patterns."

"What a feat!" I was full of admiration.

"What else can I do if I don't knit? At first, the matron forbade it, for fear that I'd tire myself. But I was bored to tears, so she finally gave in. I'm still bored, lying here all day." And she gave a deep sigh.

At a closer look, I could see light wrinkles on her forehead and the beginnings of crow's-feet. Her skin was white and delicate, but her neck and the back of her hands as well as the lobes of her ears all had a waxlike transparency, the result, no doubt, of her long tenure in a hospital bed. She did, after all, look every inch a sick woman. For a moment I was at a loss for words.

Just then, the old woman in the bed by the door began coughing. The sound of her coughing was loud and hoarse. The middle-aged woman who had been sleeping in the bed next to her sat up.

There were four beds in our ward. Bed 21 was the coughing old woman. Bed 22 was a middle-aged country woman. Bed 23 was my neighbor, the young woman. I was Bed 24.

"You meet all kinds in a hospital," my neighbor said. "Such a big hospital. People die here every day, sometimes more than one a day. Death is swift. One minute you're alive and kicking, the next minute you're stretched out and dead." She mentioned death so offhandedly, as she would speak of getting out of bed, eating a meal, or taking a walk. But her eyes betrayed a deep melancholy. She had been in the hospital too too long.

I, too, was seized with a wave of melancholy. For my neighbor and for myself. Were we not in the same plight?

She sensed that her words had unsettled my mood. "My big mouth," she said apologetically. "It never knows when to stop." In a flash she changed the subject. "Elder Sister, is your husband away on business?"

"We are working in different areas. He is in the south. It's hard to get a transfer, and he doesn't want to come to a big city like this."

"Oh, is that so? How long have you been separated?"

"Ten years. Our daughter is nine."

"Well, I suppose every family has its own problems."

"Are you married?"

"My child is five years old. I'm thirty-one myself."

"Oh, who could have told! I'd have guessed you were twenty-six, twenty-seven at the most."

"This younger sister really *is* the picture of youth." The country woman in Bed 22 joined in. "In our village, even unmarried girls are not so tender-skinned as she is. Such a quick mind. And clever fingers, too! Pity her health is not good." She spoke in the thick accent of the Laoting region.

"What's the use of looks?" asked my neighbor. "I'd rather be older by twenty years and have a stronger body."

"What is your complaint?" I finally asked. "You look healthy. Your complexion is beautiful."

"The complexion is illusory. I'm suffering from chronic rheumatic heart disease. The diameter of my bicuspid valve is narrower than zero-point-five millimeters. The transport of blood is obstructed, causing cardiac hypertrophy. . . ." She went on expressionlessly, as if reciting by rote. She lifted a corner of her blanket. "Look! Using steroids year in year out, the metabolism of calcium is obstructed, the bone structure is loosened. Bedridden for so many years, the muscles of my legs have withered. . . ."

Looking at the sticks of her legs, my own heart contracted. But she just calmly arranged the blanket back into place.

The country woman chimed in as she began cracking melon seeds. "It seems that Li Ronggui is not coming." She looked at the young woman. "You might as well wash."

My neighbor snorted. "With or without him, I can get myself a wash." She pressed a bell button at the head of her bed.

The nurse on the night shift appeared, a dainty young girl in white, high-heeled shoes with the collar of a rose-colored sweater showing over her white overalls.

"Xiao Gao, I've been keeping count and I know to-night is your shift. Sorry for the trouble."

Apparently Xiao Gao knew exactly what my neighbor meant. She drew a basin from under the bed. "No trouble at all. I'm happy to serve you, Madame Shao Xueqing!"

"Look out," my neighbor cried as she stretched out a hand playfully. "I'll pinch your saucy tongue." Xiao Gao laughed and averted the hand. She poured hot water from the flask into the basin. After my neighbor had washed, Xiao Gao threw away the water. "Sleep well," she said. "Call when you need me." She then switched off the lights and left.

"This Xiao Gao has a sharp tongue sometimes, but she's good at heart," my neighbor told me. "As for some of the other misses, I never summon them unless I'm really desperate. Of course they empty your pot for you and all that, but you should see their looks. As if you are in their debt for the rest of your life. And if I'd let them, they'd inundate me with their interminable knitting. Behind the matron's back, of course." She regarded me closely for an instant. "Oh, you're tired. You should sleep." And with that, Shao Xueqing lay down with her clothes on.

The room was eerily quiet. I heard the wind in the trees, making a rattling sound. And then a strange cry: *caw, caw, caw.*

"What's that?"

"Cranes. This place used to be a sanatorium. There was a pretty garden, with a pond and many cranes. The year before last, when I was still able to walk, I would get close to them. There are eleven of them. One, a red-crested one, has no partner, and used to moan quite sadly. Did you hear that?"

C—aw, c—aw, c—aw. The cry of the unmatched crane did sound forlorn.

"I have been listening to this for three years and seven months." Xueqing suddenly sat up, the needles clicking in her hands. "Strange, the cawing of the cranes has become part of my day. Something is missing if I don't hear them. The question is, how long will this go on?" Her tone was quite matter-of-fact. So matter-of-fact that it gave me the chills.

The needles kept clicking. She was so adept at it. Even in the dark, the intricate pattern kept evolving under her fingers.

2

I woke up in the middle of the night. Yan Pin was sitting by my bed. The moonlight illumined his haggard face, untidy hair, and unshaved chin.

My heart gave a tug. I clutched his hands and cried silently.

"The telegram gave me such a fright," he whispered as he wiped his glasses. "There were no train tickets. I just bought a platform ticket and jumped on the train. What does the doctor say?"

"Heart seizure. Probably due to nervous exhaustion. My condition is stable now. I'll be back on my feet soon. But now, Yan Pin," I begged him, "please go home to bed. Sleep late. You need the rest. And then—check if our coal briquettes have been delivered. If they have, pile them neatly in the corner of the landing and get some building bricks to wall them in. If they *haven't* been delivered, go to the coal store and put in a request for delivery. Buy one hundred *jin* of our quota of winter cabbages. Store them carefully in the kitchen. Buy two length of stovepipes, one straight, another elbowed. Bring Xiao Yan home from Granny Zhu next door. In the afternoon, go to my school and let them know you've arrived. Return the money that Teacher Li paid for Xiao Yan's new shirt. I think that's all. Please, Yan Pin, go now. Come back at suppertime. To-morrow morning a physician will make his rounds and decide on my treatment."

"All right." Yan Pin got up for his coat.

"And, oh!" I called him back. "Finish the pastries in the container!"

He smiled as he gobbled up two pieces of cake and washed them down with water. He knew I wouldn't leave him in peace until he did as he was told. He tucked in my blankets and prepared to leave. Suddenly he bent down and caressed my forehead. "Poor thing," he said sorrowfully.

"You're exhausted. I am very very sorry." He picked up his bag and left.

"You are such a loving couple." Xueqing said softly in the dark.

"What! You're awake!"

"I wake up at the slightest sound. Elder Sister, it seems your husband is much older than you are."

"By nine years and three months. How could you tell?"

"I caught a glimpse of him by the light of the moon. Left alone to myself all the time, I like to speculate. About people's ages, temperaments, what's on their minds. I usually can tell. For instance, I daresay you and your husband are neither classmates nor from the same locality."

"Goodness! How did you make that out?"

"That's easy. Your different accents. He speaks with a northern accent, although he is now living in the south. As for you, you speak the standard northern dialect, but with a southern twang. And seeing the difference in your ages— well, you couldn't have been classmates."

"How clever. Yes, we met in our travels. Quite interesting, now that I think of it. Eleven years ago, I went to paint in the Rocky Forest in Yunnan and lost my way among the rocks. He heard my shout for help and rescued me. He teaches history. What does your husband do?"

"He works at the glass factory."

"He must be busy." My subtext was: why doesn't he come and see you?

"Busy indeed!"

Evidently my understatement had hit a nerve. Her voice was choked with anger. I realized that I had said the wrong thing, so held my tongue.

"Sorry to disturb your sleep," she said. Her mood shifted just as quickly and she spoke mildly. "Try to get some rest."

The next morning an unusual air of expectancy hung over the ward. The nurses speeded up the cleaning and breakfast was served earlier than usual.

"You're lucky," Xueqing told me as she combed her hair. Her tresses were jet black, but thin. "You're just into your third day here, and already going to be examined by the director of the hospital. If he happens to be away at meetings, you could lie here for weeks on end without seeing him."

"Do you mean to say that everybody must wait for the director himself?"

"Of course not. But he happens to be the head of the cardiology department as well. He is consulted when the senior physicians in the department have some doubts about a diagnosis. They are mostly his former students."

Xueqing plaited her hair into two braids. Then she wetted a corner of her towel in her drinking glass and wiped her face. After these preparations she settled back with her knitting to wait for the inspection rounds to begin.

At the stroke of eight, a group of people in rustling white overalls passed by in the corridor. Apparently, the inspection team had set out.

"There are dozens of people following the director on his rounds. Senior physicians, resident physicians, physicians from other hospitals on study leave, interns, matrons, nurses. They start with Ward two and will be here around nine." Xueqing seemed excited.

At five past nine, her predictions were borne out.

"They're here," Xueqing said. She hastily hid her knitting in her bedside cabinet.

"You're not knitting anymore?" I asked.

"I dare not." She smiled. "Director Jin will scold. He's a jolly old fellow, but strict, too! It's a pity that for the last two years he was mostly in his office. When he was full-time in the department, things were different. Everything so well ordered, even in the sick wards. You should have seen it. Here they come." She was immensely excited.

Suddenly our ward was taken over by at least twenty people. I knew that the little old man in the foreground had to be the director. A host of physicians of all titles and status followed at his heels. The interns and doctors on study leave all had pads and pens in hand.

Stout Dr. Fang started with me and reported on my case. He didn't need to raise his voice. Its natural volume carried it easily across the room.

Director Jin, bending his balding pate over me, listened to my heart. Then he glanced at my file and cardiogram report and inquired after the circumstances leading to the attack. "Check for Keith's node syndrome by catheterization," he said finally, enunciating every syllable quietly and succinctly. He directed Dr. Fang to begin the routine checkups. All the younger doctors were busy at their pads, while Director Jin had already moved to Bed 21.

"Report!" Dr. Fang exclaimed.

But Director Jin waved his hand. The case was familiar to him. He flipped through the file and then examined the old woman's chest, first by tapping with his hands, then with the stethoscope.

A female intern with a pair of glasses perched on her nose pushed to the front and, with her pen, mapped out a square on the area over the old woman's chest. The woman glared at her but held her tongue.

"Now Bed twenty-two. Pericardial flue. Has it been drawn?"

"Not yet," Dr. Fang answered. "She says she's afraid. Wants to wait until her husband arrives."

"What are you afraid of?" Director Jing asked the Laoting country woman.

"A big thick needle poking into my heart. It will kill me."

"There's a flood inside you here. Understand?" The director smiled as he explained. He beckoned an intern to check out the size of her heart area and estimated the amount of fluid. He resumed, smiling effusively. "Now, when you are farming, what do you do when there's a flood?"

"Drain, of course."

"Well, there's quite a flood inside you. The operation is very simple. Dr. Fang is first-rate at draining. It's his forte. Let's say you put yourself in his hands tomorrow? *Good!*" The director then turned to Xueqing. "How are *you*?" he asked.

"Just as usual," Xueqing answered.

"You need more rest. And better nutrition. And also, tell Li Ronggui to massage your legs for twenty minutes every day." He turned to another doctor. "Shall we take Ward seven now? They are your patients, aren't they?"

"Director!" Xueqing called out as the old man turned his back. "I have a request."

All eyes were turned to her.

"Please give me an artificial value." She sat up and fixed

her eyes on the doctor anxiously. Now I understood why she had been so tense the whole morning.

"Impossible under the present circumstances," Director Jin said shortly. "The hospital is not equipped for that kind of operation."

"Then do you want me to lie here and wait to die?"

"How can you say that? We're doing the best we can, but there are problems. We can't experiment on you. You know something about heart disease by this time, don't you? You know it's not a simple operation." He changed the subject. "How's Li Ronggui lately?"

"He has not turned up for the last three days!" Xueqing said accusingly. "He can't be relied on."

"Next time he's here, I'll see him in my office!" So saying, Director Jin turned and led his inspection team to another ward.

My curiosity was aroused. "Your husband—isn't he at work?" I asked Xueqing.

"It would be a miracle if he were to work. He's living off the stipend he receives for nursing me in the hospital. Why mention that good-for-nothing?"

She lapsed into silence and I did not question her further.

The sun was lovely outside. The leaves of the trees in the garden merged into one brilliant mass of gold. After the bustle of the inspection team, the caw of the cranes could be clearly heard.

Xueqing closed her eyes as she lay on the pillow. "What are the cranes feeling?" she asked in a whisper. "Are their caws the sounds of sorrow or of joy?"

After a while she slept. But suddenly after several minutes she spoke out loud: "He'll come. Either today. Or tomorrow."

"Who?"

"My husband, Ronggui."

"He cares for you after all."

"Cares for me?" She smiled grimly. "The flowers need watering. He'll be thinking of his flowers."

There were indeed four pots of flowers on the windowsill, all in bloom.

Now, what exactly is happening between Xueqing and her husband? I pondered to myself. What is this Ronggui like?

3

The old woman in Bed 21 completed formalities for transfer and left. Our ward was now mercifully freed of the sounds of that raucous cough and her abusive language. And the Laoting country wife came to a courageous decision: to proceed with the operation.

In the afternoon an intern took me in hand and sent me hither and thither for all kinds of tests, as preparation for the catheterization. I finished off at the X-ray room and returned to the ward just in time for supper. As I entered our room I saw a man with his back toward me, watering the flowers on the sill. I immediately realized that this was Xueqing's husband, Li Ronggui.

He did not seem the brute that I had visualized. He was slight and sallow and stooped, with pale shifty eyes. His every gesture was slow and deliberate, as if he was too lazy to move.

"This elder sister is a new arrival," Xueqing said, introducing me to her husband. "She teaches art at a university."

Li Ronggui turned and smiled at me. When he smiled, his eyes disappeared, leaving only two dim slits, while his gums showed through his gaping mouth. Just like a gawking schoolboy, I thought. Seeing him in person, my dislike of him vanished.

"It's hard on you," I said, leaving a lot unspoken. "With your wife hospitalized so long and relying on your care."

"That's . . . it," he answered. "I've b-been caring for her th-three years and s-seven months." He stammered onward. "From morning t-till night, work, work, work! M-mother and child . . . to support. No salary, j-just a government stipend. T-twenty-five *yuan*. Hers . . . thirty-four. F-fifty-nine all told. Twenty for Granny to care for child. How . . . live?"

"Come on, come on." Xueqing smiled as she squelched her husband's list of complaints. "Elder Sister is a cultured person. You shouldn't prattle on so." She seemed surprisingly lighthearted. "Ronggui, why didn't you put on your new boots?" Her tone was ingratiating.

He didn't bother to reply, but went on watering his flowers.

"Ronggui, how is Xiao Na's cold?"

Still no answer.

"I'm asking you!"

"Recovered, of course! S-some sick people do recover, you know!"

Xueqing blanched. But she didn't acknowledge her husband's vitriol. "Please bring Xiao Na with you tomorrow!" she said. "I miss her so much!"

"Impossible! J-just recovered!"

"I haven't seen her for six months. Even in my dreams, I think of her."

"Granny won't allow." He waved the watering can at her impatiently.

"Just for a little while?"

"I told you, Granny won't allow her to come to the hospital. Afraid of infection."

She was silent, her eyes red.

"D-don't grumble. Best off with Granny. Just bought her a little fur coat."

"Fur coat? How much?"

"Nineteen *yuan* sixty *fen*."

"Why, that's twenty *yuan*! She's just a little girl. Why would she wear a fur coat? Didn't I knit a woolen sweater for her and pants to match?"

"Granny's paying. N-none of your business." Li Ronggui deposited his watering can next to the radiator.

I took a closer look and found that he had used the recessed area beside the radiator as a storage space. Salt, sugar, washing powder, blanket, clothes—all were jumbled together. Even a box of utensils and a bicycle tire pump.

I laughed. "I see you've set up house here."

"Of course," Li answered as he pulled the only stool in the room over to the window and sat down. He extracted a cigarette from the pocket of his shirt, lighted it, and began smoking. "So l-little to go by, and yet you must live." He turned to his wife. "Why's there a flower missing?"

"Xiao Gao snipped it. I told her they are numbered and you'd miss them. She said she didn't care."

He laughed. "The little minx!"

"What did you bring today?" She tried to sound casual.

He fumbled slowly at a dirty old canvas bag and took out a round lunch box and a paper bag. The lunch box held black beans; there were two fried doughsticks folded in the paper bag. He eyed me surreptitiously.

"Remember I gave you three *yuan* on the morning of the sixth," she said.

"Well, I bought one *jin* of oranges for Xiao Na."

"All right, let's say it's sixty *fen*."

"Sixty-eight! And another *jin* for Niuniu my nephew."

"All right, add another sixty-eight to that. Then add twenty *fen* for the black beans and fourteen *fen* for the doughsticks. That makes just one *yuan* seventy *fen*."

"I n-need cigarettes! Do you object?" He snarled.

Xueqing kept silent. After a while she said, "Ronggui, get some water. I need a wash."

Li Ronggui silently put on his jacket, picked up the thermos flask, and walked away slowly.

Xueqing took the lunch box and nibbled at the black beans. She ate about ten and put the box back. Just then Li returned.

"You don't want them?"

"I do." She ate a few more beans and sighed. "Tell me, does Xiao Na miss me?"

"Who knows? I d-didn't ask."

"Twenty *yuan* for a fur coat!"

"Just m-mind your own b-business! Are you going to wash, or aren't you?"

"I'm washing," said Xueqing as she she drew a piece of worn cloth from under her mattress and spread it across her blanket. She put the washbasin over the cloth and washed her face carefully with soap and water, applying some lotion afterward. "Shall I wash my feet, too?" she asked tentatively.

Li Ronggui pulled over the stool without answering and placed the basin on it. Xueqing opened her blanket and Li plopped her pair of sticklike legs into the water. After soaking her feet a few minutes, Xueqing toweled them dry. Ronggui then took the water away.

"It feels so good to soak my feet. He's on his best behavior today, probably in your honor." Xueqing looked at me gratefully.

"You mean he doesn't do this for you in general?"

"Most days, he's—" Xueqing broke off as Li Ronggui walked back in. He did indeed seem to be in a good mood, humming the tune of a popular song.

"Ronggui"—Xueqing began again timidly—"my chamber pot really stinks. Could you scald it with hot water?"

"All right." And Li bore away the chamber pot.

"He's cheerful today." Xueqing said softly.

"Is he gloomy as a rule?"

"Gloomy? He flares up without reason. Sometimes he just gets up and storms off." She choked back the words as she heard Ronggui approach, still humming away.

"They are serving supper," he told her. "What do you need?"

"Half a bowl of noodle soup. I still have the beans and the fried doughsticks."

Ronggui brought Xueqing some noodle soup. The Laoting woman sent for soup and steamed bread. I also bought some of the hospital food, assuming that Yan Pin was still running errands and wouldn't bring my supper.

However, as I was halfway through, he rushed in, carrying a lunch box, a thermos container, and a string bag.

"Just my luck! My bicycle tire went flat. I had to wheel it all the way here. It's good you haven't finished yet. You can have some chicken broth."

"Why bother to make chicken broth?" I asked.

"Frozen chicken, killed and ready to serve. All I did was throw it into the pot." Yan Pin filled my bowl and then opened the lunch box. "Granny Zhu made this chopped spinach and bean-curd slices. She's also taking good care of Xiao Yan. I've paid Teacher Li for her new shirt. I ran over to the coal store twice. They say they'll deliver the day after tomorrow. I couldn't get any stove-pipes. And there were no cabbages on sale today. Now how did the windowpane get broken? It must be changed. . . . All right, you eat your supper, and I'll take my bicycle for repair."

"B-bicycle repair very far," Ronggui interposed, his mouth stuffed full of fried doughsticks. "Don't b-bother to g-go. Wait a minute. I'll t-take a look."

"Oh, that's too much trouble."

"Leave it to him," Xueqing urged. "Sharing this ward, we're like a family. Don't stand on ceremony."

"Let's have a l-look!" Li Ronggui got his box of uten-sils from its storage place and took out glue, a saw, a pump, and pieces of tire. Yan Pin took a basin of water and the two of them went to tinker with his bicycle.

"Your husband is quite generous." I smiled at Xueq-ing.

"He's not bad when he's in a good mood, but his good moods are so rare."

The Laoting woman came over with a handful of melon

seeds. "This Ronggui is like a donkey that needs to be stroked the right way. Try some of these seeds. They're home-cooked." She extended her palm and offered us the seeds. "Your *own* tongue, Elder Sister, can be sharp, too. How can you expect a man to enjoy serving a woman? And to be scolded in the bargain?"

"What have I done?" Xueqing evidently didn't agree with the other woman. "We just have that fixed sum for every month, and he is always so extravagant. I hate waste. What do you want me to do?"

The country woman continued to expound her views at full volume. "Take my husband. One bottle of liquor every other day. A pack of cigarettes a day. Menfolk, after all, must have their own way."

"Their own way?" Xueqing asked incredulously, and then stopped short. Evidently she didn't want to provoke an argument.

The matron pushed open the door and said to a man who followed her in: "This is her bed. Get her settled and you come back for the forms."

The newcomer was a stout middle-aged man, very neat from top to toe. He nodded to everyone. "Elder sisters one and all," he said, "sorry to disturb you." From the bag he was carrying he extracted a brush. He lifted the blanket and shook it in the corridor. Then, with infinite precision, he brushed the newly changed bedsheet. After putting the bed in order, he arranged the thermos flask on the bedside table and made tea. Then he scurried away.

We were all eager to see what our new ward mate in Bed 21 would be like. A few minutes later, the stout man returned. He and a young girl helped a tightly muffled woman into the room.

"Here, here, everything is in order." The man helped the woman out of her gauze mask, muffler, gloves, outer coat, and padded cotton jacket. The last to go were her padded winter shoes.

The three of us inspected the newcomer closely. She was, after being shorn of her layers of clothing, quite visibly elderly—frail and emaciated.

"Lie down, lie down." The man helped her to bed. His every movement was meticulous, as if he were handling a fragile glass object. "Have a drink." He held the rim of the cup to the old woman's lips. "It's not hot. I've just tried it."

The old woman took a sip, groaned, and lay down.

I exchanged a look with Xueqing. Heavens, she's hard to please. We prayed that she wouldn't be another of those cranky fussbudgets who would disrupt everything in our ward.

"Now you're all set." The man took a towel out of his bag and dusted his trouser cuffs. "What a nice room—white everywhere, and flowers in the window. Right, now I'll go and complete the registration forms. Daughter, look after your mum."

After the man left, Xueqing couldn't help asking the girl, "What's wrong with your mother?"

"Chest pains. We've been waiting for a vacant bed for a long time."

"Who's the man who just left?"

"My dad."

"Your dad!" the country woman butted in. "More like your brother!"

"No, I wouldn't say brother," Xueqing added hastily,

seeing the old woman's black looks. "Perhaps a younger uncle."

I was also surprised. The man looked at most in his mid-forties.

"My parents are the same age, fifty-seven. Ten years ago, my mother even looked younger. It's this illness that has aged her."

"Yes, that's true," said the country woman. "This elder sister has such shining black hair. After you get your health back and gain a few *jin* of meat on your body, you'll be younger by ten years!" She was trying to make amends for her previous remark.

At that moment the three men came back together. Yan Pin praised the two others for the repair of his bicycle, Li Ronggui praised the older man—addressed as Elder Uncle—for resourcefulness, and he in turn said that Yan Pin was very painstaking.

The fact is, as Yan Pin told me, this newly arrived elder uncle saw them tinkering with the bike and gave them a few tips. On their way back, they discovered that they were spouses from the same ward! I also thanked the elder uncle.

"That's nothing," the young girl said. "My dad worked in a bicycle shop for forty years."

"No w-wonder so knowledgeable!" Li Ronggui was genuinely impressed.

"Are you stopping for the night, Ronggui?" the country wife probed.

"Yes, I think I will," Ronggui answered. He seemed cheerful. He washed his wife's clothes and then took up the mop and mopped up the floor, refusing to allow anyone to lend a hand. Then he fetched my hot water. And to crown it all, he volunteered to help Elder Uncle cook poached eggs over the fire in the nurses' office.

After Elder Uncle fed poached eggs to Elder Aunt with a little spoon, we all prepared for sleep. The country wife had already pulled her blanket over her head. Li Ronggui had somehow gotten hold of a board and made a bed for himself by supporting it on one side against his wife's bed and on the other over a stool. He was very snug next to the radiator.

After setting up his own bed, Ronggui went off and came back with four chairs for Elder Uncle. "Got them out of the solarium," he announced grandly. "I know this hospital from t-top to b-bottom." He lay down in his clothes, threw the spare blanket over himself, and wrapped his jacket around his feet.

The rays of the moon shone through the window. The cold white light irradiated one corner of Li Ronggui's blanket. His board creaked from time to time.

Three years and seven months! I thought. One thousand three hundred and sixty-four days. Imagine having to spend every day of the year in the hospital ward, to eat the tasteless food, to sleep in one's clothes over a board. I began to sympathize with Li Ronggui. This tragedy was not easy for him either.

4

"Hurry up, you. I n-need to g-go."

"What's the hurry?" Xueqing asked. "It's barely six."

I closed my eyes. I was embarrassed, forced to overhear a marital spat—especially so early in the morning.

"Why didn't you s-sew it last night? You're wasting my time."

"I'm almost finished."

Li Ronggui's voice was full of anger, but Xueqing sounded conciliatory. Evidently she was sewing buttons on her husband's jacket.

"What's your hurry?"

"Some b-business."

"What business?"

"What b-business is it of yours?"

"Ronggui, what's the matter? Have you swallowed a bucketful of nails?"

"So wh-what if I did?"

Their voices continued to rise. It was impossible to ignore them. I had no choice but to open my eyes. By now everyone in the ward was awake.

Ronggui glared at Xueqing in a vicious fury. Heavens, what if Yan Pin looked at me like that! I'd never stand it.

Xueqing finished off her sewing patiently. As she was biting off the end of the thread, Ronggui snatched the jacket away and threw it over his shoulders, needle and thread still hanging on. What a temper! I had lost all sympathy for him.

"Be careful you don't go too far, Li Ronggui! The leadership is there."

"Leadership!" Ronggui exploded, "Let the heavens come down on me! I'll deal with them!"

I felt helpless. I wished Yan Pin would come.

"I know you, you cursed by the thunder of heaven!" Xueqing exploded. "You just want me to die!"

"Go and die if you want to!"

"Come on, come on," Elder Uncle Ni intervened.

"Husband and wife can always talk. No need to fire off cannons at each other."

In a fury Ronggui picked up his canvas bag and stomped off, the boards of the floor trembling in his wake. With his departure my own tension was also relieved.

"Now what happened? He was quite cheerful last night." Uncle Ni shook his head.

"He's always like that," the country wife said. "Cheerful one moment, quarrelsome the next. But more quarrelsome on the whole." She gave a wipe to her face, and as she started to peel boiled eggs she turned to Xueqing. "Be patient. Don't say a word—and it's over. All men like to act the hero in front of women. Come on, have an egg, freshly laid by our own hens."

"No, thank you." Xueqing turned her face away, but we could hear the tears in her voice.

5

The rhythm of life in the hospital was confusing and monotonous at the same time. It was an unchanging cycle of turning on and turning off the lights, ordering meals, eating meals, ward inspection, medicine time, taking blood pressure, taking body temperature. . . .

It had been over twenty days since I'd entered the hospital. The Laoting country wife in Bed 22 had gone through the first phase of her *drainage* and was waiting for the next stage of operations. My own test was completed and my problem diagnosed as Keith's node syndrome. Elder Aunt Ni was also diagnosed. She had to take steroids and then have an operation. Everything was going well, including Yan Pin's major campaigns to acquire stovepipe replacements, to paste the cracks in the window frames, and to store cabbages and coal for the winter. And what's more, he had decided to move to the city and had already taken the first steps. I felt such relief. I knew that he would have no problem getting transferred. The director of the History Institute had personally inquired after him, hoping to recruit him. I relaxed comfortably, hoping for the best.

Life had improved in almost every way. Only Xueqing and her husband went on in the old way.

6

After several weeks Ronggui seemed in better spirits. He started coming nearly every day, bringing food more tempting than black beans and cold fried doughsticks. Sometimes it was fish, sometimes eggs. The fits of temper became rarer; he even smiled ingratiatingly at his wife. But there was something curious going on. The more amiable he became, the more profound was the suspicion lurking in Xueqing's eyes. This change intrigued me.

I know I did not underestimate Xueqing's powers of detection. During the twenty days in which we were ward mates, I was fully aware of her abilities in this respect. Tied to her bed, she was attuned to everything that went on in the hospital: who was in which ward, who had what disease, the professional background of the doctors, the varying temperaments of the nurses, the stockpile of supplies in the pharmacy, the history of the old woman on duty at the bicycle parking lot, the behind-the-scenes stories concerning investments for a new research center. All the ongoing events were quickly transmitted to her ears. She knew that the hospital chef regularly used the kitchen cloth to blow his nose, that the master cook let his dog lick all the plates, that the hospital staff had written a joint complaint, and that the Party Committee had ordered a thorough overhaul of the kitchen staff. She knew that a certain nurse had never been trained as a nurse, that she gave out the wrong medication, and that when a patient sued, the scandal brought down her supporter from behind the scenes, a certain bureau chief. She knew that Director Jin was going to meet a delegation from abroad. She got her news mostly from the gossip of the nurses and patients from other wards who came over to visit. Xueqing often said of herself, "Me, I am born with sensitive ears and a sharp nose." But what have her ears and nose discovered about her husband?

The atmosphere in the ward was calm. By now the country woman had recovered from the first of her drainage operations. Aunt Ni was also stronger and would take a round or two in the corridor on the arm of her husband. I was reading *Sketchbook from India* and taking a short walk in the garden with Yan Pin every day. One day, we went further than usual and explored the pond behind the patch of wood. We saw the gray cranes, the maiden cranes, and the single red-crested crane. They flapped their wings, stretched their long necks, and gave out their long-drawn-out bellows—cries of discontent, as they sounded to me. The man in charge said that they always flap their wings in autumn in an attempt at flying, but their wings are clipped. I did not want to look at them anymore, those big birds with clipped wings, especially the single red-crested one. It made me think of Xueqing.

The ward was explosively quiet, the sense of an imminent outburst emanating from the growing suspicion lurking in Xueqing's eyes. The quietness of the ward was exactly the calm before a storm.

7

The storm finally broke. Its arrival was heralded by low temperature, a cloudy sky, muffled thunder, and a few streaks of lightning. Human warfare, including that between married couples or family members, followed the same pattern.

I will always remember that sunny afternoon, every window reflecting a square of bright blue sky. The flowers on the windowsill were in full bloom. An occasional fly would buzz in the space between the two layers of glass in the windows.

The Laoting country woman had sneaked out for a visit with some relatives in town. The Nis were whispering together. I was into chapter eleven of *Sketchbook from India*. Ronggui was putting fertilizer on his flowers as he hummed the snatches of a song

"Ronggui, here are two tickets," said Xueqing. "Go and see this film with Uncle Ni."

"Which one?"

"The Little Moon Restaurant."

"Come on, Uncle Ni," Ronggui insisted. "This film is real funny." And with that he dragged Uncle Ni away.

Half an hour later was the official visiting hour. Our ward was rarely honored by visitors at this hour, but on that afternoon, a plump young woman walked into the room. She went up to Xueqing, took out a bag of oranges, and said, "I have always wanted to come and see you, but couldn't. Too busy. Are you better?"

Xueqing never had visitors, so I put down my book and looked the woman up and down.

She was ugly. And made uglier with the wrong kind of makeup. Her meaty face was topped by the fashionable banana coiffure with glazed hair clasps and bits of fake jewelry stuck in her hair. Her Western-style jacket was laced with silver streaks; the turned-up collar of a scarlet sweater showed under her jacket. A pair of tight jeans did nothing to conceal the spindly legs. A strong odor of cheap cologne filled the room.

"I got the message that you wanted to hand something over to me. What is it?" The woman took out a pink handkerchief and wiped her nose.

"What's the hurry? You and I have plenty of time." Xueqing maneuvered herself into a comfortable position on the bed. Her face was pale, but her eyes lighted up strangely.

The newcomer peeled an orange. She placed some orange segments on Xueqing's blanket. "Have some," she said. "They're sweet." Her wide mouth was heavily rouged.

Xueqing took up a piece of orange, looked it over, and swiftly threw it into the spittoon. I was on the alert, fearing something was about to happen. The woman was taken unawares, and the silly smile on her face slowly faded. But she pretended she didn't mind.

"Mi Fengxian," Xueqing began, her eyes burning, "have I ever wronged you?"

"Sister Shao, what are you talking about? I don't understand."

"You don't understand? Ha! You low creep!"

"Sister Shao, we have always been friends, and I am

here to visit. Don't start being abusive. I won't say anything, seeing you are so ill. But if there is nothing else, I'll leave." And she got up.

"Leave!" Xueqing cried fiercely. "Sit down!"

Both Aunt Ni and I were shocked into immobility. Before we could open our mouths, Xueqing started berating the woman. "Mi Fengxian, shall we settle this in court or in private?"

"Sister Shao, I don't know what you are talking about. Is something wrong with you?" The woman wavered.

"You don't understand? Do you want to see the evidence in a court of law? Let me tell you, Mi Fengxian, you think I am helpless in bed, do you? You think I can't sue you? The court is going to sentence you. You just wait and see."

"Shao Xueqing, what rubbish are you saying? I'll let it pass only because you are ill." She bolted toward the door.

"You can't escape! You shameless strumpet, you unmarriageable pumpkin. Go! And we'll meet in court! Let me tell you one thing, though: Li Ronggui has confessed everything."

Aunt Ni and I exchanged a glance. Things having come to such a pass, we didn't know what to say.

Mi Fengxian stopped in her tracks, her face dead white.

"Come over here!" Xueqing commanded.

Dumbly Mi Fengxian staggered back, as if pulled by a wire.

"Mi Fengxian, you have broken up a marriage. Do you realize that it is a crime?" Xueqing spoke in the tones of a judge. "Do you realize that if I die because of this affair, you will answer before the law? If I sue you, you will go to jail. Are you aware?"

Mi Fengxian remained silent, with head bowed.

"Are you deaf?"

Being exposed like that in front of strangers was more than the woman could bear. She burst out crying.

"What is the use of your cat's piss! Tell me, do you want to settle in court or settle privately?"

"It was he, he . . . who followed me. . . ."

"He followed you? Shameless creature. It's all your doing."

"Oh, so you let him off." Mi Fengxian protested. "And who was it who looked me up all the time. For a drink of water. To heat up some food, to borrow the coal shovel."

"You're a pair, the two of you. Please spare me the disgusting details. Just tell me: do you want to settle privately or in court?"

"What do you mean?"

"Either we meet in court at a public trial, or you write me a confession."

"Confession? How?"

"You write: 'I had immoral relations with Li Ronggui. I promise to stop from now on. If I do it again, and thereby endanger the life of Shao Xueqing, I will be responsible for the consequences.' "

Mi Fengxian was silent.

"Are you going to write or not? Either that, or we meet in court!"

Mi Fengxian was like dough in Xueqing's hands. She took up the pen that Xueqing produced and wrote what was required. Then Xueqing made her leave the print of her index finger with gauze dipped in red ink.

Mi Fengxian slunk away. Xueqing folded up the confession into a little square, stuffed it into her purse, and hid the purse under her mattress. She then gave a deep sigh. "Aunt, Elder Sister, people say family scandals must be kept in the family, but what can I do? You've heard everything. Sorry to have disturbed you." She lay down on the bed and stared at the ceiling.

Strange. How had she divined Ronggui's secret?

She lay there unmoving, as if listening to the cry of the cranes. But her staring eyes foretold a bigger storm to come: the confrontation with Ronggui!

8

At five Yan Pin arrived. I saw at a glance that something was bothering him. For the last few days, he was running around, negotiating his transfer. The director of the History Institute was very pleased. So what was the problem? At the moment I was not in the mood to inquire. I was more worried by the coming storm hanging over the ward. I whispered to Yan Pin that in case Ronggui came back and started a fight with Xueqing, he must pull Ronggui away. Yan Pin was mystified, but seeing how tense I was, he promised.

Supper at six. Xueqing forced herself to swallow half a bowl of noodle soup. She was preparing herself for battle. Aunt Ni was also fretting. She wished her husband back, but was also afraid that Ronggui might return with him.

After supper, the Laoting country woman came back from visiting relatives. She was tired and lay down. "Why is everybody so quiet?" Nobody bothered to answer.

At seven Uncle Ni pushed open the door and walked into the room. Yan Pin, who had his eyes on the door, jumped up for action, but there was no Ronggui behind Uncle. We all gave a sigh of relief.

I now asked Yan Pin about his transfer. "I met the director today," he muttered unhappily. "His hands are tied. There are no more quotas for recruiting people from the provinces. And the municipal authorities are not handing out any extra quotas."

My heart sank. Five years ago, there were quotas, but Yan Pin refused to move. Now that he was willing, the quotas are gone.

Yan Pin silently washed the dishes, fetched hot water, and mopped up the floor. After sitting by me for a while, he rose and said, "Sleep well. I'll go now." I kept my face to the wall as his footsteps receded.

"Help me to . . ." Aunt Ni said to Uncle as she gave me a look. They left together. I collected my thoughts. I knew that I, too, had to help avert a confrontation between Xueqing and her husband. It was our duty as ward mates.

The old couple came back ten minutes later. Uncle, usually so jolly, wore a look of anxiety. When he finished his tasks for the day, he walked to and fro in the ward and finally stopped in front of Xueqing's bed.

"My daughter, may your uncle speak his mind?"

"I'm listening, Uncle."

"He has wronged you. It is true. But for your own sake, for the sake of your child, don't make a scene. It doesn't help. I am thinking of you."

"I've done a lot of thinking for the last ten days," Xueqing replied. "I will not let them walk all over me. It's too much. I don't care for loss of face. I don't care for my health. All I want is to get even with him!"

"But you have no proof, my daughter. You must keep cool. You have nothing to show against Ronggui."

"Don't think that I'm helpless in bed. I can see him through and through. Ten days ago—it was a Monday—he came in stinking of cheap perfume. We never use such stuff. I asked him and he muttered something. The next day he showed me a bottle that he had bought. Which of course just showed his guilty conscience. I racked my brains. Finally I hit on Mi Fengxian, that shameless un-marriageable old maid. She always uses those cheap scents—and she had tried to catch Li Ronggui before. She's just man crazy. She offers herself for free. Taking advantage of my illness. The bitch! I smelled that horrible perfume the minute she walked in. She confessed at my first bluff. She's not half a match for me. Didn't she write her confession? Didn't she leave her fingerprint?"

"Ronggui has wronged you, but you mustn't go to extremes. Unless, of course, you've decided to divorce—"

"Divorce! And let him get away with everything! Never! He's made life intolerable for me. I won't let him enjoy life either!"

"But how can you control him? You are tied here, while his legs are his own. What can a piece of paper do?"

"He deserves ten thousand deaths! To torture me, a bedridden woman!" And she began to cry hysterically.

The country wife was awakened by the noise and was completely mystified. "What? What?"

Aunt Ni and I sat on either side of Xueqing and tried to comfort her. Uncle Ni brought hot water. I washed her face. Aunt Ni tidied her hair.

"Daughter, I am thinking only of you when I strongly advise you not to make a scene," Uncle Ni declared. "Just keep quiet. Let me be your diplomat and talk to Ronggui, right?"

Finally Xueqing was persuaded. She promised to let Uncle Ni do the talking for her: Ronggui must acknowledge his wrong, write a confession, and promise to care for her properly.

The ward quieted down. The stars winked at me through the squares of the windowpanes.

Just as we were dropping off to sleep, the door of our ward burst open. To everybody's surprise, Li Ronggui sprang into the room, bringing with him a strong stink of liquor.

All of us women were struck dumb. We all looked to Uncle Ni.

"Ronggui! Ronggui!" Uncle shouted as he jumped off his bed and ran barefoot to catch hold of him. He missed by an arm's length. Ronggui, muttering curses, grabbed his wife's hair and gave her a resounding slap.

Xueqing screamed and hit her own head against the wall. "Hit me! Kill me if you dare! You deserve ten thousand deaths! So the bitch has told you and this is her revenge! Kill me then."

"You—poisonous snake! I'll beat . . ." Ronggui, now held back by Uncle, struggled as he tried to hit his wife again.

Xueqing beat her own breasts as she continued to scream. "I don't want to live. You and she are in league together. I don't want to live." She picked up whatever was close at hand—oranges, drinking mug, toothbrush, medicine bottles, soap dish—and began to hurl them at Ronggui. She screamed like a madwoman.

Uncle Ni tried to push Ronggui out of the room.

Ronggui spluttered: "Poisonous s-snake. Ronggui won't be ruled by a half-dead woman."

The doorway was filled with people, patients from the neighboring wards and their spouses. The lights in the corridor lighted up their faces. Some were dazed, some curious, some angry. Xiao Gao, the nurse on duty, shouted for everyone to return to bed. Then Dr. Fang's voice boomed out: "Everybody disperse. This is a hospital ward."

Dr. Fang and Xiao Gao came into the room.

"What is this, Li Ronggui?" Dr. Fang demanded. "Creating a disturbance in the hospital at midnight?"

"S-sh-he . . . libel." Ronggui began to back down.

"Attacking your sick wife in the middle of the night! This is a case for the Federation of Women to deal with! Let's go!" Xiao Gao headed out, determined to implement her words.

"Dr. Fang! Xiao Gao! My . . . life . . . is . . . too . . . bitter . . . to . . . live!" And with a piteous cry, Xueqing fell back unconscious.

The ward, so noisy a minute before, fell completely silent. Dr. Fang listened to Xueqing's heart. It was as if the whole world were listening. In the silence, the mournful cawing of the cranes could be clearly heard. *Caw caw, caw.*

"Quick! Oxygen tank. Potassium hydroxide. Adrenaline." Dr. Fang issued orders.

Li Ronggui was now completely sober and frightened. "Wh-what?" he stammered.

"What's *what!*" Xiao Gao retorted. "Go and wait in the office. If anything happens, you are the one to answer. This will go to Director Jin's office, no mistake."

Li Ronggui lowered his head and slunk away under the gaze of the people still lingering in the doorway.

Xueqing was soon revived. She was completely exhausted and lay with her eyes closed. The saline solution dripped slowly from the needle point on her wrist. An oxygen tube was fixed to her nostrils.

Poor Xueqing. So pretty, so gifted, a woman who could have ruled easily in her own sphere of life, now perfectly helpless. What would happen to her now? How would she keep up her marriage? I could see no way out.

9

The next night before supper, Ronggui turned up again. It was clear at a glance that he had been severely dealt with, probably disciplined. He came in with a hangdog look and silently took out a lunch box from a basket. He opened the lunch box, ladled some chicken soup into a bowl, and placed it on Xueqing's bedside table. He opened a package of pastry. Then he pulled over the stool and sat down facing the window.

I took the bowl of soup and fed Xueqing with a little spoon.

"Thank you for the trouble," she said to me. Her husband's submission seemed to give her satisfaction. She drank some soup and ate three pieces of pastry.

Ronggui cleared the table, washed the dishes, fetched hot water, and poured out the water for Xueqing to bathe herself. Then he emptied the pot and mopped the floor. After performing these duties, he picked up his basket and left without a word.

The next day, Xueqing was back to normal. The oxygen tank and intravenous solutions were removed and she once again reclined in bed, knitting.

"Now that the leading organizations have intervened, isn't everything solved?" asked Uncle Ni. "Look at Rong-gui. Isn't he better behaved than ever?"

Aunt Ni agreed. "Yes, it's a fact, he's changed."

"All menfolk are like that," the country woman added her bit. "They are not afraid of their wives, but they fear the leaders."

A smile of victory flitted over Xueqing's pale and puffy face. "He's cheap. Needs handling. Thought he could walk all over me just because I'm ill. Taught him a lesson!"

To put down her erring husband, she had paid a price.

Everything had turned out according to plan. She had won. I felt sorry for her.

But things did not go according to plan.

Ronggui came twice every day. The first visit was to bring food. Later he returned for the cleaning-up. He performed his duty every day as if he were a conscript. As far as he was concerned, he could be servicing a corpse. He refused to talk to anybody, probably thinking that we were all on his wife's side. Only Yan Pin, whom he felt was not involved, got an occasional nod. He arrived at ten every morning and left at eleven. In the afternoon, he arrived at five and left at half past six. As precise as clockwork. He was better dressed than ever. He sported a woolen overcoat and stylish leather shoes.

One day, Uncle Ni tried to draw him into conversation. "Not bad, Ronggui. A new outfit from top to toe!"

Ronggui glared back defiantly. "My mother cares for me and bought the overcoat for me! The shoes are a present from my sister!" He was demonstrating that his family was behind him and against his wife.

During the two and a half hours that Ronggui was on duty, the atmosphere in the ward was oppressive. He and his wife avoided looking at one another; if their eyes happened to meet, they glared at each other with fury. They were worse than strangers. They were deadly enemies.

I saw with disquiet how Xueqing was wasting away. She ate very little. In just a week's time, her appearance changed beyond recognition. Her eyes were sunken. The wrinkles on her brow increased. Her crow's-feet had deepened. A wisp of hair over her forehead had actually turned white! Compared with the beautiful young woman I had first seen, she had aged ten years!

We tried to comfort her with words. But all she did was to lie there unmoving, her face a blank. Her bitterness of heart was eating away her very flesh and draining her blood.

I saw with horror that Xueqing couldn't last. From the expression on their faces, my ward mates had drawn the same conclusion.

Outside, the scene was winter. The last lingering leaves had fallen and the rays of the sun were dimmer and fainter. The sky was a pale gray. Everything was depressing.

"I want to leave," I told Yan Pin softly.

He nodded. He was still working on his transfer. "I'll wait and see," he said without much confidence. "The quota problem is temporary, I'm told."

Temporary! I knew what that meant. In the eyes of the personnel department, three to five years is considered temporary!

By now the Laoting country wife had undergone the second stage of her drainage and was ready to go. Uncle Ni had given up his efforts to enliven the place. The old couple would stay in their own corner and whisper. My only pleasure was *Sketchbook from India*. How I missed my own studio!

10

It turned out that I still could not leave. I had to wait for the observation period to expire and for Director Jin's instructions.

I stayed on and looked on helplessly as Xueqing pined away.

One day, as Li Ronggui was preparing to leave after finishing his duties, Xueqing said suddenly: "Bring Xiao Na tomorrow. I want to see her."

"Granny w-won't allow," mumbled Ronggui gruffly.

"You bring her!" Xueqing's voice was low but determined.

Li Ronggui left without a word. The next day on his afternoon shift, Li brought in a little girl of about five years old, Xueqing's beloved daughter Xiao Na.

The little girl looked like her mother, with a pair of striking black eyes. But she was decked out shockingly. She was in a rabbit-fur coat and a furry hat of pink and blue. Her little feet were in a pair of tiny high-heeled shoes. Worse, her hair was permed, her face powdered, her lips rouged, and a pair of earrings tinkled from her little ears. She was a perfect miniature of a vulgar woman. The little thing stood in the middle of the floor, looking around her.

Xueqing sat up, smiling. "Come to me, Na. Come to your mommy."

The child didn't move.

"Mommy missed you so. Come over, darling." Xueqing's tones were so tender. Seeing that the child still wouldn't move, Xueqing took up an apple and two pieces of pastry. "Come, Mommy has kept these for you."

The little girl ambled over and took up her prize.

"Call me mommy, call me."

"You don't look like Mommy," said the child.

"Mommy is changed, sick, old." There were tears in Xueqing's voice. "So you don't know your mommy anymore. Do you like your woolen sweater and skirt and pants?"

"Pretty. Granny Cui in our yard also says they are pretty. I love pretty clothes. See mine has flowers here."

"Mommy knitted them, and then Mommy embroidered the flowers. Call me mommy."

The child seemed to remember and whispered *mommy*.

"Oh, darling, take off your shoes and come in here with me. Can you take off your own shoes?" Then she turned to Ronggui. "Take off her shoes," she commanded. "Carry her to my bed." Ronggui did as he was ordered and then went back to his seat facing the window.

Xueqing held the child to her breast, touching her face, her hair. "How cold are your hands and feet. Come, put your feet here." She put the child's feet into her bosom under the blanket and the little hands under her arms. Suddenly Xueqing exclaimed, "Oh, you haven't greeted your elders yet." She pointed to Uncle Ni. "That is—"

"Granddad!" the child was quick.

"That is—"

"Granny."

"That is—"

"Aunty."

"How smart!" We were all so glad to see a smile light up Xueqing's face. We gave the child chocolate and oranges; the country wife stuffed melon seeds into her little fist.

"Do you miss your mommy?" I asked her.

"Yes, if she buys me a Kwangdong gold watch," she said as she played with the button of her mother's jacket.

"Already talking about gold watches." Xueqing shook her head helplessly. "Come, let Mommy do your hair in plaits. These curls are awful, and this goo all over your face."

"Granny says it is pretty. Granny promised to buy me a ring and a necklace."

"No, that's not good. Let Mommy do your hair in braids and tie them up in red bows."

"All right, but then you must tell me a story."

Xueqing combed the child's hair carefully as she told her the story of the little white rabbit, how old mother rabbit was ill, how little white rabbit went out and looked for fine white turnips for her mommy. The hair was braided and tied. Xueqing wetted her towel, wiped away the rouge and lipstick, and lay down with the child at her breast.

Poor woman, there she lay, all her joy, all her world, all her life concentrated on her daughter. It was a heartbreaking scene. My tears began to flow. I wonder what was turning in Li Ronggui's mind as he sat there smoking, with his face turned to the window.

A nurse rolled in the flatbed cart containing our supper. Silently, Ronggui bought a dish of spinach and took out the fish that he had brought. Xueqing picked off the bones and fed the child some fish. She took a mouthful herself.

After clearing away, Ronggui addressed his daughter sharply. "Let's go!"

"What happened to mother rabbit and little white rabbit?" the child asked. "We haven't finished the story."

"If you don't get home, Niuniu will steal your piggy bank!"

"Oh, I must go, go." The child sprang out of bed onto the floor.

"Xiao Na!" Xueqing tried to hold her back.

"I must go, I must go." The child tried to wriggle herself free.

"Na, you won't forget Mommy?" Xueqing asked as she sought to hold her closer.

"I must check my piggy bank. Granny is going to give me another fifty-*fen* note to put inside. I must go."

Xueqing held the child and kissed her fiercely on the cheeks, the forehead, the eyes. "Mommy's darling, Mommy's life!" she murmured. Her eyes were wild.

The child was frightened. "No, no, let me go!"

Xueqing was exhausted. She released the child's hand and watched Ronggui help with her shoes, coat, hat, and gauze mask.

"Xiao Na—" Xueqing cried hoarsely, but the child was already at the door, waving cheerfully, "Goodbye, Granddad. Goodbye, Granny. Goodbye, Mommy. Goodbye, Aunty." And she was gone.

"Xiao Na—" Xueqing moaned as she drooped her face on the pillow.

"You must try to be cheerful now that you have seen your daughter," Uncle Ni remonstrated with her.

Xueqing gradually stopped crying and lay there motionless, staring out of the window into the darkness.

The lights were turned off. The ward quieted down. As usual, the country wife began to snore. The Ni couple continued to whisper softly in their own corner. Xueqing was still lying motionless, perhaps listening to the cranes.

Their cries were short and tender, as if they were talking in their dreams. Perhaps they were dreaming of the south, its sun, its lakes, its blue skies? That is where they belong.

The south? Yan Pin is also going south. He doesn't want to leave me here, but he must go back to his class. He is quite dejected. No news at all on the transfer.

"Elder Sister!" It was Xueqing's voice in the dark. So she wasn't asleep. "I'm sorry to disturb you. Could you give me some advice."

"What is it?"

"What do you think of my Xiao Na?"

"Very pretty, very smart little girl."

"Supposing she grows up like this?"

"It's hard to say. It seems there is something missing in the way her granny is bringing her up."

"And supposing she is with a stepmother?"

"What nonsense you are talking." I was shocked, "You mustn't give up. Didn't Director Jin and Dr. Fang promise to give you an artificial valve when conditions permit?"

"I'll not last that long. See, Elder Sister, I've got my own solution." She picked up a little bottle. "Eighteen of these would do the trick, and I have fifty-three."

"Xueqing, you're crazy." I was alarmed and tried to take away her bottle.

"Don't worry, I have no use for it now, or I wouldn't show it to you. I wanted to have a last look at Xiao Na, but when I saw her, I changed my mind. Xiao Na is all I care for in this world, and you can see what her granny has made of her. If I die and she gets into Mi Fengxian's hands, she'll be wrecked for life. I must have Xiao Na with me, and if I die, I can give her to my second sister. I have decided to ask for a divorce!"

"You're mad! You mustn't think about such things."

"There was no real love at all in our marriage. It was a mistake from the beginning. Now all we have is hate. He hates me for dragging on and wasting his youth and I hate him for his hard heart. Sometimes I wish him dead, and sometimes I wish myself dead."

"Don't go on like this. Xueqing, divorce is a serious business. If you divorce, who's going to take care of you?"

"My second sister. She is fifty-four and retired. She's been to see me, but I never told her about how Ronggui and his family treat me. She comes rarely because she doesn't want to meet with Ronggui, whom she can't stand."

"Divorce . . . doesn't seem the right solution."

"A man and a woman who hate each other and torture each other every day, and yet stay tied together, is that a solution? Once I thought that since he makes me miserable, I wouldn't let him live in peace either. But now I think differently.

"Tomorrow or the next day I'll get this settled. Elder Sister, thank you for the trouble. Please go to sleep."

11

I waited impatiently for Yan Pin to arrive. I wanted to tell him of my decision. And also about Xueqing's decision. He turned up, producing some wine-filled chocolate candies. They were my favorite candy. He had stood in a long line to purchase them.

"Listen to me, Yan Pin." I grasped the sleeve of his jacket. "Why wait for quotas? We can get our transfer immediately."

He shook his head. "Silly girl, you don't know the full meaning of the word *transfer*."

"No, I know what I'm talking about. I have decided to move south with you."

"Oh, no!"

"Haven't you urged me before?"

"That was the past. Now I can't ask that of you."

"Why?"

"Well, I now realize what a sacrifice it would be for you. The galleries, the art collections . . ."

"Yes, and the cinemas, exhibitions, concert halls. I've thought this through. I lose all those things, but I gain more: a united family, mountains, lakes, trees, wildflowers, healthy air. I'm going to specialize in landscape painting. Don't you remember I once did an autumn painting while sitting by your lake?"

"Let me consider this."

"You'll see that it's the best possible solution. Please— I've made up my mind. And now let me tell you Xueqing's decision. . . ."

Yan Pin had doubts about Xueqing's decision, but he was impressed by her spirit.

Xueqing drafted her application for divorce and Yan Pin helped her with the wording. Her only condition was that she must have the child—and that Li Ronggui was to provide two hundred *yuan* for the child's keep, to be paid within the year in three installments. Everybody around Xueqing—Uncle and Aunt Ni, the Laoting country wife— all had doubts about it. But Dr. Fang was supportive. He said that in her condition, she should not be thwarted.

Yan Pin helped submit her application for divorce to the district court. The court's reply was that in such cases, divorce could be speedily granted as long as the woman insisted. Yan Pin was also sent to take a message to Xueqing's second sister, requesting her presence at the hospital.

The news of Xueqing's application for divorce spread from ward to ward. Luckily there were no busybodies poking in their heads as I had feared.

It began to snow, the first snow of the year. Big flakes wafted down from a purplish-gray sky and melted as they touched the ground.

The country wife, in blue jacket and pants, with her hair carefully combed, sat cross-legged on the bed, surrounded on all sides by half a dozen bags. Her husband had come to take her home. She said goodbye delightedly, inviting Uncle and Aunt Ni to visit and taste chestnuts and walnuts, inviting me to come and paint the native hills. She did not invite Xueqing—that would have been too cruel— but she gave a sign to her husband and he took out a cloth bag, which she held out to Xueqing. "Younger Sister," she said, "here are some dates for you."

"Oh, these are too expensive. I cannot accept!"

"No expense at all. They are from our own tree. I am

not giving them to anybody else. This is specially brought down for you. I'll be offended if you refuse."

The country woman was in tears as she grasped Xueqing's hand. "Younger Sister, I also did some thinking. I guess divorce is right. Rid yourself of all that pain. But take care of yourself."

The snow kept falling. Beyond the window, the earth and the sky were one whirling mass of white.

Before the dinner hour I suggested to Xueqing that she ask Ronggui to go on with his duties for a few extra days.

"No, not at all."

Ronggui came in at his usual time, with his habitual hostile glare. He began to take out the lunch box—dried mini-shrimps in cabbage and steamed unleavened bread. He placed them silently on the bedside cupboard.

"Take them back," Xueqing said slowly and clearly, with her eyes on the ceiling. "And you needn't come anymore. I have submitted an application for divorce."

Ronggui was stunned.

"The court will approve the divorce very soon. You can go. You are free to do whatever you like. Only I must have Xiao Na."

"You? You have—"

"That is my only condition. Xiao Na can't be brought up properly in your family."

"You take c-care of—"

"My family will help. You needn't bother."

"But you—"

"Oh, I'll live very well without you. Better. Please bring my clothes tomorrow, but leave them at the gate. From now on, I'll not trouble you anymore."

Li's face betrayed conflicting emotions: confusion, shame—and relief. He stuffed the lunch box back into the basket and turned to take up the washbasin.

"Leave," Xueqing said coldly. "You are not needed here." She took up her knitting, which she had forsaken for the last few days.

Ronggui put down the washbasin and stood with empty hands.

We looked at him, but nobody said a word. What could we say?

He stood there with lips parted, the muscle in his left cheek twitching, his eyes blinking.

Suddenly I had a hope. Perhaps Ronggui had repented. Perhaps he would be stricken by conscience and his former affection revived. Perhaps he would throw himself before his wife and cry, "No! I won't leave you. I am sorry."

But nothing happened. His parted lips clamped together; his cheek stopped twitching; his eyes went blank. He sighed and stooped to pick up the food basket. "Th-this is your own de-cision." And he walked away slowly.

Xueqing covered her face and cried softly.

"Are you sorry?" I sat on her bed and held her hand.

"No. I just want to cry a little. It is past. Over. I feel better for a cry."

"Yes, have a good cry," Uncle Ni said as he turned to his wife. "Well, old comrade, shall I go and have a peep at our grandson?"

"And why are you standing there stupidly? Don't forget to bring his little cloak!"

It was completely dark and still snowing. The lights were turned on and the curtains drawn. But we could still hear the sound of snowflakes descending.

12

I drew aside the curtains. "Snow! Oh, how beautiful!" I exclaimed.

The world was covered with snow. The sky seemed to have been washed anew, and the bare branches of the trees, bowed down by the snow, sparkled in the sun.

The sun cast its rays over the snow in the garden. Where untouched, it was as smooth as down, while in the shadow of the branches it glowed with a purplish hue.

"I love snow," said Xueqing. "When I was little, I would run into the yard and catch the falling snow with a piece of dark cloth, and the flakes would make a pattern on my cloth, like stars or flowers. When the snow was thick, I would build a snowman, or place a stool upside down on the ground and pretend to go sleighing, or tie a stick of bamboo under the soles of my shoes and play at skating." Xueqing's eyes shone as if reliving a dream. "Skating in the snow was wonderful. The snowflakes whirled in the sky as I whirled on the ice. It made me feel like a bird flying. When was the last time I walked on the snow? It was my first winter here. I could still walk. I wrapped myself up and walked into the garden, over the newly fallen snow. I walked and looked back at my own straggling footsteps in the snow. I was tired and leaned against that cypress tree. The snowflakes up the tree fell over my face, my head, slipping under my neck. It melted— that wonderful wet and cold feeling." She sounded light-hearted, yet there was anguish in her words. I could not bear to look into her eyes. We all kept silent as she talked. "I so wanted to lie down in the snow, to lie down under the cypress tree. The snow seemed so white, so clean, so soft. I could smell its fresh fragrance. The sun shone on me, and the wind blew on me, while the tufts of snow continued to fall from the branches of the cypress over my head. It was wonderful. I wished I could have just lain there, lain there until the stars came out. . . ." Her voice became weaker and weaker as she exhausted herself.

My last day in the hospital. The ward seemed unusually lively.

The nurses with food trolleys walked in with Xueqing's breakfast. One said jokingly, "Madame Shao, pleased to serve you. If you need anything, just say the word and it will be done!"

At around ten, Director Jin came on his rounds. He gave permission for me to leave. Then he turned to Xueqing. "What, no more demands today?"

"I'll not ask for the impossible."

"We will do what we can. Meanwhile you must be cheerful and gain strength." Xueqing caught a hint of something in his words and nodded. "I now understand."

In the afternoon, Xiao Gao came and announced that the matron had called a meeting of all the nurses and they had passed a resolution to take over the care of Xueqing.

"My second sister is coming," Xueqing said. "Either tonight or tomorrow morning."

"She will take care of your daughter and we will take care of you," Xiao Gao announced. "But you must observe discipline. For instance, your knitting must be limited to one hour in the morning and one hour in the afternoon. All the patients in the other wards send you greetings and beg you to take care of yourself."

That same evening, Xueqing had a good appetite. After

supper she sat up and listened to Uncle Ni describe their grandson's day—how he took his milk, how his diapers were changed—down to every detail. In the middle of the recital, Xueqing's second sister arrived.

She was a tall woman past middle age. No accusations, no tears. She just told Xueqing not to despair, that everything would be all right. Second Sister helped her wash before bed and then left.

Xueqing lay down quickly. She fell asleep before the lights were turned off. That was the first time I saw her fall asleep so quickly and sleep so soundly.

Yan Pin sat by me. He had negotiated with my college about using the school car. I could have it either two days later or at five the next afternoon. All right, I decided: let it be five then. I was anxious to get home as early as possible.

13

"Elder Sister, you will not forget me?"

"No. Never."

I walked to the door and took a last look.

Xueqing was reclining in bed with a piece of knitting in her hand. Against the rays of the setting sun, the white sheets, white bedspread, white wall, and the whiteness of the snow outside the window all merged into one harmonious whole. Against this background of varying shades of white, Xueqing seemed beautiful and serene. *The Serenity of Whiteness!* my heart cried out. I will paint you. I will! I will!

Out on the sidewalk, I looked back at the hospital building. The curtains of the windows were drawn, but I could imagine Uncle and Aunt Ni in their corner; I could see Xueqing knitting quietly; I could hear the caw of the cranes in the snow.

The cranes were indeed cawing, a medley of joyous sounds. Or was it my own mood that had lightened? Perhaps the cranes, like Xueqing, were enjoying the snow— celebrating a world that had suddenly turned white.

Goodbye, cranes, I thought as I walked away. I am not coming back. I am going south with my husband.

From The Novelist Quarterly *Xiao Shuo Jia, No. 2, 1985. Translation completed at the Bunting Institute, Radcliffe-Harvard, January 1991.*

FOUR WOMEN OF FORTY

HU XIN

HU XIN, born in 1945, is currently an associate professor of Chinese literature at Jiangxi University and also a member of the Writers' Union.

"Four Women of Forty," her prize-winning first work, published in 1983, is one of the earliest stories in China to depict institutionalized sexual inequality. All four women in the story are victims—of political campaigns, of the double standard for sexual behavior, and of limited opportunities.

Hu Xin's initial success was followed by In the Shadow of the Black Sun, The Bubbling Fountain *(both short story collections), and a novel:* Rose Rain. *All her works combine concern for women's issues with her love for the sights and sounds of her native province of Jiangxi.*

As the saying goes, *three* women are enough to set a table spinning. Not to mention four. Especially four women of forty. These particular women had been classmates for nine years. Life separated them in 1962. But twenty years later, they were brought together as if by a miracle.

The courtyard of the Provincial Women's Hospital was tiny. In the sweltering heat of this southern city, proverbially known as the *stove* of the nation, it was impossible to stay indoors. Fortunately, the hospital was situated on a busy street; the big department store was right next door; and the Workers' Cultural Palace across the street. All the inmates of the hospital who could move about had joined the human wave. So the four women of forty had the stone table and the four stone seats all to themselves. There they could sit under the grapevine in the middle of the court-yard and talk to their hearts' content.

Forty. To women, it is a relentless number. Youth takes leave at its threshold, never to return. Age takes over, never to be shaken off.

Liu Qing—the Liu Qing of yesterday, slender, bright-eyed, haughty, so good at making up nicknames—where was she now? All through six years of primary school, followed by three years of junior high, she was the idol of the other three. She was the center of the group. She was the wonder girl, no doubt about that. She took first at all the exams. Nothing less would satisfy her. How the boys stared in amazement! She had held up her head and said, "I don't see why girls can't beat the boys!"

But after twenty years, all that fire had been spent. A pair of spectacles in yellow celluloid frames put Liu Qing's pinched little face in sharp profile, and her thin and meager frame showed painfully through her old-fashioned cotton white shirt and blue trousers. Age had left its mark on her.

Qian Yehyun, the quartet's cuckoo bird of twenty years earlier, was unchanged—dainty, dashing, dazzling—but only at a distance. She wouldn't bear close inspection. The crow's-feet at the tips of her eyebrows and around her eyes showed through even in the dusk.

Good-natured Cai Shuhua—Big Sister Slow as she used to be called—was her same kindly old self. She was still recognizable with her big smiling face and her comfortable bulk. But her hands! Her hands were strikingly coarse, calling up associations of dishwater, clotheslines, soapsuds, and coal dust. And the petite Wei Lingling was still the clinging vine! Her light yellow short-sleeved shirt was a perfect cut, and so was her dark-brown straight skirt. Her presence exuded elegance and the self-confidence of a mature medical worker. Where was her old bashfulness now?

In spite of the big changes, they knew each other immediately, without a moment's hesitation. Yehyun, in a seductive shirtless nightgown, had emerged languidly from her ward to buy an ice Popsicle. That's when she saw Liu Qing, who was standing five feet away, using a big palm-leaf fan to shade herself from the rays of the setting sun. With one jerk, Yehyun threw the ice cream (and some of her change) into the air and rushed up to Liu Qing. She clutched at her sleeve, screaming, "You wretch! Did you just bubble up from the ground?!"

Liu Qing grabbed Yehyun's shoulders. "Oh, my little evergreen leaf. Are you here in the hospital?" In the joy of reunion, the two women completely forgot where they were.

At the same time, Cai Shuhua, officer of Fuhe District Women's Federation, had just completed some business at the population-control office that was housed in the same courtyard of the hospital. She was crossing the tiny courtyard when she saw two women locked together, a stone's throw away, babbling incoherently. Her professional instincts alerted, she raised a meaty hand in their direction.

"There's nothing that can't be solved by talking," she muttered. "No need for fisticuffs." Suddenly she herself shot forward, hand still raised, and exclaimed, "My little Liu Qing! And, oh, my evergreen leaf!" The three women embraced.

Just then Wei Lingling was crossing the threshold to the courtyard of the hospital ward, a basket bulging with goodies hanging by one hand. At first she was puzzled by the noise of the little group of women by the side of the street, but after taking one glance, she recognized her old friends—and she, too, joined in the general hugs and shouts of delight, oblivious to everything else.

At once they started reminiscing, transporting themselves back twenty years in time, to their carefree young days.

When they were children, their four families had lived in neighboring streets: Tie-Horse Stump, Peach-Blossom Lane, Pine-Tree Lane, and Gan Family Alley. There were no horses in front of Tie-Horse Stump, no scent of flowers in Peach-Blossom Lane, not a twig of pine in Pine-Tree Lane. Only Gan Family Alley lived up to its name and housed members of the Gan family—but that meant nothing to the four little girls. All they cared about was that they must always be together. Walking to school and coming back, they were always together, today wandering through a set of alleys and tomorrow taking a short cut through some old buildings. The flagstone paths held unending charm for them as they walked and chattered on. In this manner, how often they had been late for school— and scolded first by their teachers and then by their parents! But the next day, they would trespass all over again.

Liu Qing would tell stories or devise funny nicknames for their teachers. It was such fun. Or they would crowd into Yehyun's home and write their homework on the rolling board for making sesame cakes. And that was fun. They would go up and down the alleys delivering the clothes that Cai Shuhua's mother had laundered. That, too, was fun. Or they would creep into the Catholic church in Pine-Tree Lane and take a peep at the nuns—wrapped in black from top to toe except for the brim of their veils. They held their breath in terror—and perhaps that was the most fun of all.

The four girls had their share of follies during the Great Leap Forward. They requisitioned the big iron caldron from Yehyun's house and stampeded up to Lingling's apartment to saw off the iron gratings of the windows. Cai Shuhua had burned her feet while carrying buckets of molten iron and Liu Qing had cut quite a figure as a versifier in the new folk-ballad movement. They did not feel particularly bad when the fever was over and all that folly exposed; what really hurt was the parting after finishing junior middle school.

Liu Qing was enrolled in a key senior high school and went to live in a dorm; Yehyun went to a performing arts institute and her family also moved when their little sesame-cake business was merged into a restaurant; Lingling moved into new dorms provided by the hospital where her father worked and she herself went to an obstetrics training school; Cai Shuhua had many little brothers and sisters and she started to work in a textile factory to help support them.

The four women finally calmed down. Lingling's instincts as a doctor were awakened and she questioned the two inmates of the hospital closely. Yehyun had been hospital-ized with an infection of the pelvis. She was cured and ready to leave the next day. Liu Qing had just arrived the day before from the south of Hubei province, where she was a teacher. She was diagnosed with breast cancer and had been sent to this provincial center for further diagnosis and treatment. As an officer for women's work, Cai Shu-hua couldn't help injecting a word now and again deplor-ing the hardships of women.

Twenty years had not passed for nothing. The women had grown into full adulthood. Now that they had calmed down, a little constraint crept into the atmosphere. Cai Shuhua was just off work and had not eaten yet, but at the moment it seemed that any move to depart would be a betrayal of their friendship. So there they stood, savoring the memories of their pure young days as the last rays of the setting sun receded.

The elderly Popsicle vendor took in the scene and strolled over with an offering of four Popsicles. "You must be dry with all that talking!" They all fought to pay, but the vendor waved them off. "That sister"—she pointed to Yehyun—"let her money fly all over the place. I recovered it all."

Lingling suddenly remembered herself and dragged the four of them to the shelter of the grapevine. She poured out the contents of her basket onto the stone table under-neath: four *jin* of apples, two *jin* of pastry, several bottles of fruit juice, and two packs of milk powder. The fact is, the wife of a leading cadre—from the work unit of the aunt of the husband of Lingling's own husband's younger sis-ter—had just been transferred from the county clinic to this hospital. Lingling had been asked to present this bounty to the women for the sake of that far-reaching network of relationships. But the cadre's wife could wait, Lingling decided. She opened the bottles of fruit juice, tore open the plastic containers of pastry, passed the apples around, and asked everybody to dive in.

The four women of forty proceeded to reminisce. Their conversation quickly turned to the subject central to ninety-nine percent of all women: husband and children.

Cai Shuhua had two daughters and one son. Yehyun had two pearls for daughters, as the saying goes; they had already grown into young ladies. Lingling's son—an only child—was considered a child prodigy.

Cai Shuhua's husband was a low-ranking officer at the municipal government. "Just like me, hardworking and well behaved—but not particularly good at anything. Passable, I suppose." Cai's pride in her husband shone through her modesty.

"As for mine," Lingling said, "he's a downright incorrigible bookworm, a hopeless case. All he knows is career, career, he hasn't the faintest idea about how to enjoy life." Lingling's husband was a lecturer in a medical college and a doctor in the affiliated hospital. Her exaggerated complaints revealed all too clearly her deep satisfaction with him.

Yehyun whisked out a cigarette from the pocket of her nightgown and lighted it under the shocked eyes of her companions. "*Lover-wife!* What love is there? Pure sham!" she said through the smoke of her cigarette. "I'm told in ancient times, kings and emperors likened their consorts to their clothes. We've been hearing about women's liberation for the last hundred years, and where have we got? I suppose we've been elevated from men's undershirts to his outer jacket!"

"Oh, come on!" Lingling exclaimed. Yehyun's companions looked at her in consternation and incomprehension.

And what about Liu Qing? "You three have done your duty as women," she confessed, "which is more than I can say for myself. I am not yet married."

The sky suddenly clouded over, as did the look in the eyes of her companions. In China, old maids certainly are not honored; fashions and fads may come and go, but the state of single blessedness has never been one of them. Poor Liu Qing—what should they say to take away the hurt?

Silence. The night air was stifling. The sweet scent of flowers and the refreshing aroma of grape leaves were gone, leaving only the choking smell of Yehyun's cigarette. The street noise forced its way into their retreat while somewhere a cassette player blared forth the strains of Beethoven's Ninth.

"I suppose you have written a lot?" Lingling asked Liu Qing, hoping to break the spell.

"So far, not a word," Liu Qing answered casually as she adjusted her glasses. But her hands were clearly shaking.

Their thoughts returned to that summer night of twenty years ago at their final separation. Liu Qing was enrolled at Teachers' University in Beijing; Lingling was assigned to the X County Hospital; Yehyun was assigned to the County Hubei local opera troupe; while Cai Shuhua was being sent to Shanghai to learn a new and advanced method of spinning. It was during the three years of famine, and the four girls did their best putting together a farewell dinner in Lingling's home. After dinner, they bade one another goodbye in front of the department store.

At the very point of final separation, Yehyun blurted out, "I've got a secret. I can't keep it any longer. I must tell you. Five years from now, I'll be the second Pan Feng-xia, the local opera queen! I'm dead sure." All the girls cheered.

"As for *me*," Cai Shuhua countered, "in five years' time, I am going to be the second He Jiangxiu, model spin-ner." Nobody had expected this from the slow and plod-ding Cai Shuhua. They cheered for her, too.

Lingling looked at the others shyly, but she was not going to be left behind. "As for me," she said, "I'll never marry. I'm going to be a second Dr. Lin—you know, the famous obstetrician Lin Qiaozhi . . ."

As for Liu Qing: her companions decided that she would be a writer. Even her name was the same as the famous novelist who wrote *Walls of Iron* and *The Start of a Great Cause*. "Yes, of course I wish to be a writer, but I am in a teachers' university, training to be a teacher. So probably I'll have to settle for another role: the Russian village schoolteacher Varvara." Liu Qing had swung back her long braids as she proclaimed her prophecy.

Apart from the dumpy Cai Shuhua, all those girls growing up during the three years of famine were thin and undernourished, looking like straggling bean sprouts; but the fire of idealism burned fiercely in their breasts.

Five years? What is five years? Even twenty years passed by in a flash! At the beginning, they corresponded. But then during the turmoil of the Cultural Revolution, what with the ups and downs of personal fates, people kept

166

to themselves and they actually stopped writing! In the intervening years had they realized their ideals?

"Come on, why so glum?" said Liu Qing, "This is such a precious meeting. Twenty years! Who knows when we'll meet again! Come, let's say something about the last twenty years. Anything, an incident, a thought. Come on, spin the button, east-west-south-north-middle. Cai Shuhua, you begin, then Yehyun, then Lingling, and last is me." Liu Qing suddenly became very animated, and the mention of their old game—spin the button—made them all laugh.

"Let's talk about the happy side," said Cai Shuhua.

"No!" Yehyun insisted. "Let fate decide." She then tore off a button that had been dangling from her nightgown. It was a celluloid button, the right side a blaze of colors, the reverse a dull gray. Yehyun tossed it up with a flick of her palm and caught it again. "If the right side comes up, talk about your happy experiences. If the wrong side comes up, tell the sorrows and the bitterness. I don't care about your theories of idealism or materialism, I must have this my way." She passed the button to Cai Shuhua.

Cai Shuhua laughed good-naturedly, tossed up the button, and watched it fall—on the wrong side.

"Now I'd call that preposterous," Yehyun said. "Just look at you, with father-in-law and mother-in-law above you, sons and daughters under your feet, and a husband to lead you on in marital harmony, you've got the three-generation family intact. What do you know about sorrows and bitterness? You, rolling in perfect contentment!" She went on: "I suggest everybody's confession must begin with a proverb or quotation; after all, we are all educated women."

There's no arguing with Yehyun, so Cai Shuhua began her story.

"Well, you could say about me that 'the slow coach has its share of good fortune.' My life has been completely plain and uneventful. In 1965, after a stint at the socialist education campaign in the country, I was reassigned to the district Women's Federation." She wiped a bead of sweat from her nose.

"That's not a proper proverb," Lingling interrupted, dissatisfied. "It's just a common saying."

Cai Shuhua thought hard for a moment. "Here's one: 'Even the hen loves its young. But to be a good mother, that's another thing entirely.' How do you like that? I think it's Gorky."

Liu Qing came to her rescue. "Yes, that will pass. Go on with your story."

"As you know, our generation has this saying: 'Everything is ended at middle age; our hopes are with the next generation.' So we yearn for our sons to turn into dragons and our daughters into phoenixes. The only way open to them is through the university, or at least through technical college. All my spare time is taken up by housework. My mother-in-law has bad eyes. My husband Lao Yang is not in good health and he's loaded with work at the office. So my day is a round of shopping, washing, cooking, even hauling coal. I won't allow the children to take out the garbage on Sundays. So long as their studies are good, I'm satisfied to do as much as I can. Well, last week, their reports came back, and guess what!"

"The gods have rewarded your maternal devotion." Lingling proposed.

"Hardly! Our daughter Xuejun, in her second year in junior high, failed in three subjects! Xuewen, in fourth grade, failed his math! Even little Xuedong, who is in his first year at school, only passed with a measly sixty. I was so angry! I gave them all a good scolding!"

"Laying the foundations is most important," Liu Qing said. "You must look for the root of the problem. Why are the three youngsters not interested in their studies? You know, interest is half the secret of success."

"Oh, you'd never guess. They have their side of the story. Xuejun was full of tears. 'All you can do is scold,' she cried. 'Just look at Wenwen's parents. They bought her a cassette player to study English, and she can listen to songs, too, whenever she wants! And look at Xiaoyen! She has a tutor—every Sunday she has special coaching. Her mommy says how can you win if you don't get an extra start? And Guanping's mommy, even for just ordinary tests, her mommy goes on sick leave and helps with her revisions.' Our second daughter Xuewen also joined in: 'Last week the sixth graders sat for middle-school exams, and all the daddies and mommies were waiting outside, with fruit juice, bananas, and cream cake. Now, when I take that exam, will any of you bother to take me there and wait outside?' Even our little son complained: 'It's true, it's true, Xiaoming and Xiaopan, they have milk and cake for breakfast, and what do we have? Leftover rice! Leftover rice all the time!' Heavens, how they fired away, one volley after another. Not that I approve of all these parents, but still their words hurt."

Yehyun laughed. "Always remember, our sons and daughters will be blessed with their own good luck in their own good time. No need for us to serve them hand and foot. The rod makes the filial son. Chopsticks feed the un-filial wretch.''

"Why don't you be serious!" Lingling gave her a look of mock disapproval.

"Yes, I've also been thinking," Liu Qing said with deep concern. "The parents in the city have become slaves of their children. Youngsters just lie back and rely on parents for everything, like hothouse plants, or clinging vines. This won't do!"

"But guess what my husband said when we were in bed!" Cai Shuhua exclaimed. "He insisted that the children's words should make us think, that I should take it easy at work. He informed me that my so-called women work was at the bottom of the list. Party, government, army, workers, youth, and women—that's the order they come in. As for my district women work, he said, it's still lower down the scale. For petty quarrels, there's the neighborhood committee; for bloody violence there's the security branch; for divorce there's the court; there's even a special office for birth control. So where do you fit in? he asks me. And he reminded me that I am a mother who has overstepped the one-child-quota limit—all the more reason I should spend more time on the children, he argued. Can you imagine how I felt? To tell you the truth, at first I was sorry to leave my loom, but later I began to love my new job. You can say it's all dealing with trifles, but it suits my temperament. I've been doing it for sixteen years and I can't bear for people to look down on it. I just don't be-lieve that you must shirk your duties as a women-work officer to qualify as a good mother. That night, I had a regular fight with Lao Yang, our first real fight. Well, that's all, I'm afraid I've been rambling." Cai Shuhua stopped suddenly as her two big coarse hands rubbed against each other uneasily.

Lingling sighed. "Oh, this is like a warning bell to me."

"Like a whip, striking at my broken heart, me a mother but in name," Yehyun said in self-mockery. She snuffed out her cigarette on the stone table and said, "It's my turn." She picked up the button. "Yehyun, Yehyun, like a drifting leaf, like a floating cloud." She tossed the button carelessly and it landed, wrong side up.

"Now for the proverb: 'Frailty, thy name is woman.' " Yehyun's ten fingers locked and unlocked nervously. "And here's some more: 'Men's words are like darts,' 'Contempt can kill, especially women.' Now, aren't these proper proverbs?"

Lingling wanted to stop her, but Yehyun went on without heeding. "One does not tell lies to genuine friends. I have been married once and remarried twice. In other words, I am thrice married and twice divorced. This is more than can be accommodated by *one incident*, but since my various incidents all concern marriage, I have not strayed from the subject, have I?"

Lingling reached out and placed her fingers on Yehyun's wrist. Her pulse was too fast. Lingling frowned, but Yehyun softly pushed her hand away.

"In the eyes of the world, I am a fallen woman," Yehyun told them. "Who'd guess that I had fallen so low precisely because I had pursued my dream of being a real woman?" She raised her eyes to the skies. The stars twinkled in the firmament, so high, so faraway, so inscrutable. Twenty years ago, when Yehyun had first spread out her wings to take flight, she was so naive. Her courage was boundless.

"During the first few years, my singing career zoomed along. I was actually second to the leading lady of the company. I was drunk with success. And love also came in the shape of Sun, a schoolmate who had graduated two years earlier. A writer and actor rolled into one. I didn't want to marry so early. In school we were taught that an artist's youth should not be wasted in pregnancy and confinement. Sun said we could marry and not have children—or wait at least ten years. But barely a year into our marriage, Sun's mother started her attack. First it was the force of tradition—continuing the line; then it turned to abuse—'What's the good of a hen who doesn't lay eggs?' It was preposterous, the way she talked, as if I was being kept by them—me a working women with my own income. But I gave in. The year after our marriage, Rangrang, a girl, was born. I thought I'd done my duty."

"Now there was peace. Right?" asked Cai Shuhua, as if she was the pacifier in the family quarrel.

"Don't forget the two thousand years of Chinese history," Yehyun said contemptuously. " 'Beget a son; daughters do not fill that requirement.' " By then, Sun had already been reassigned to the propaganda department of the county Party Committee and had forgotten his vows. He kept nagging me all the time: 'Mother is saying it for our own good. Since we are bringing up one, we might as well bring up two for the same amount of trouble.' And so our second child was born. Tingting—another daughter. It seemed that their family was blighted. I didn't want to be embroiled in any more protracted arguments with mother and son. At the beginning of the Cultural Revolution, I came back home, got a certificate, and had an operation. Back at the opera troupe, the leading lady was dethroned and made to clean the latrines with a placard round her neck advertising her crime. I was also labeled a revisionist little weed. But I was from a good family background—small dealer was part of the city proletariat. And anyway they needed people to play the heroines in the model operas—Li Tiemei, Sister-in-Law Ah Qing, Xiao Chang Pao—so I appeared on stage again. It seems that the walls indeed have ears. Anyway, the news of my operation got about and of course all hell broke loose in the family. I just ignored them and kept on my set course. But soon, rumors appeared—that I was loose, depraved, that I made passes at so and so on stage, down to the last detail. The only thing that had sustained my relationship with Sun—mutual trust—collapsed, and we went to court." Yehyun's hands fumbled in the pocket of her nightdress for cigarettes. Lingling held her wrist, and Liu Qing handed her a bottle of orange juice. Yehyun took it and downed it in one gulp. Cai Shuhua handed her a handkerchief and she slowly wiped the corners of her mouth.

"Perhaps it is my fault. Now Rangrang has no mother, and Tingting no father. But my temperament has always been like that, obstinate, how can they expect me to coax and wheedle?"

"The Women's Federation could have reconciled you two," Cai Shuhua said with regret.

Yehyun smiled wryly as she shook her head. "Sun married almost immediately. His mother went about bragging, 'At thirty, a man blossoms out; at thirty, a woman is a hag. My son has married a virgin girl! Now who'd look at that stinking bitch? How many years longer can she carry on?' Out of spite, I decided on the spur of the moment to marry Big Brother Chemical Fertilizer—the head of the work team that was sent to supervise the opera company. Many people advised me against it, saying he was not a real worker at the chemical fertilizer plant, that his former wife left him because of the beatings he gave her. But I ignored all those warnings. He promised me a proper wedding celebration, and that was enough for me. As for our life after the wedding, I can't bear to think back on it. My irresponsibility has exacted a heavy penalty. Within a year, I left the house after a severe beating, with just the clothes on my back, dragging Tingting with me. My poor daughter was half-dead with fright. I wanted nothing, except divorce. Even that was not easy. After a year of wangling, I finally got my divorce. But he was not over with me yet. A few days later, he brought his gang to the theatre to taunt me. I shrieked and called the bullies names. They knew they were in the wrong and sneaked away. But I was the defeated after all. I had lost what is most precious to a woman—her good name. How can you expect people to penetrate the surface and understand all the intricacies of my case? And I was, after all, an actress, still young, with the remnants of good looks. From then on, I had to bear the contemptuous looks of all virtuous women. Highly placed women looked down their noses at me; trouble-making women made up stories about me; good women pitied me for falling so low. What's more, all virtuous men avoided me like the plague to protect their own reputations, while others made lewd innuendos."

"You are going from one extreme to another," Liu Qing broke in. "Life was not as easy as you had first imagined, but it cannot be total despair and isolation." Her voice was soft, but her tone firm as she cut short Yehyun's dismal recital.

"Oh, I don't need words of comfort, not even sincere ones. They're cheap." Yehyun closed her eyes and shook her head obstinately. "Let me finish. The year before last, I married for the third time. He is definitely elderly, a leading old cadre of the prefectural Federation of Arts and Literature. I had known him as early as twenty years ago when I first reported to work. We have been in touch all this time, in a work relationship; he was my superior. He is well read and open-minded; he respects me and admires me; his wife has been dead these ten years, and all his children are independent. Upon our marriage I was entitled to reassignment at prefectural level, and my daughter Tingting, still under fourteen, was entitled to move with me. I decided to be the virtuous wife and start out again at the prefectural center. On our wedding night, we got a card sent collectively by his children. It has only these words: *A bitch replacing a beaver*. Isn't that funny! Definitely my idea of humor!" Yehyun laughed hysterically, catching the attention of several passersby. A few white-capped little nurses poked their heads out of top-story windows of the ward.

The three friends had nothing to say. What could they say, after all?

Yehyun stopped laughing. "What went wrong?" she murmured. "Is it my fate?" Then she seemed to wipe everything away as she lighted another cigarette and gave it a vigorous pull. "And so what, after all. The earth has not stopped moving. It's your turn now, Miss Wei." She was her old cynical self again.

Wei Lingling, the picture of dejection, tossed the button carelessly in the air. It fell to the ground, right side up, a blaze of colors. Lingling fanned herself with her handkerchief in silent disgust.

"Life is made up of all the colors of the rainbow. Tell us your story," Liu Qing prodded her. Night had fallen. It was getting late.

"All right. My proverb: 'Is being virtuous wife and dutiful mother a woman's born lot?' Will that do?"

"Good." Yehyun stuck out her thumb in commendation.

"Sacrificing oneself for husband and children is commendable, but not enough. One is imprisoned in the home."

"Come on, don't talk in riddles," Cai Shuhua remonstrated.

"I don't deny it. I have an enviable home. I married at thirty-two. By then, my husband, Lao Muo, had already made a name for himself in his research on virus, and lately he's been moving upward steadily. His parents are in Hong Kong. They have sent us presents—color TV, stereo, washing machine, cameras, all the requirements of a modern home. We live much better than most of our peers— that is the truth. For the sake of husband and son, I have given up my profession and taken up administration; glancing at the papers, knitting sweaters, and strolling around makes up the female administrator's working day. All my energies are used to take care of my husband's well-being and to tutor my son in his studies. My skin, coarsened by years as the village doctor, has now turned soft and white; everybody says I am younger than my years. Shouldn't I be satisfied? But when alone, in the stillness of the night, something gnaws at my heart, a sense of loss, a sense of futility. What does it mean? Perhaps I don't realize how lucky I am?"

"You've lost your soul," said Liu Qing, not at all joking.

"You're right. I have indeed lost my soul. I gradually figured out that I had felt the same way before, fourteen years ago, when I was disqualified as an obstetrician and made to work in the fields. They said I sided with my reactionary father and had mistreated patients with good class background. Something akin to political sabotage. And there was no way to defend myself. For a full six months, from winter to summer, I went about like a lost soul. You see, I had already worked six years as an obstetrician. I was used to the groans of women in labor; the first cry of the newly born infant was music to my ears; it was my joy to see the tired but blissful looks of the mothers; I was even used to the smell of antiseptics. But suddenly I was condemned to farm work—head bowed to the yellow earth, back toward the sky, as it is called. I was devastated.

"I will never forget that summer evening. It was during the wheat cutting. I crawled back to my lonely hole after a day of backbreaking work in the fields. My whole frame felt like it was falling apart. But I still had to do my own cooking. I sat in front of the stove dispiritedly, starting the fire, too tired to wash myself. From the window, I caught a glimpse of the summer sky. Suddenly I was seized with such a longing for you three. I had an illusion that you were there with me. I cried and laughed by turns. I shouted with joy. I was not alone anymore. But suddenly the sound of piercing screams recalled me to reality. My professional instincts led me to the source; it was Aunty Cheng's next door. Her daughter-in-law was in labor and she was convulsing—eyes rolling, teeth clenched. Aunty Cheng was kneeling in the middle room praying to Buddha; the young woman's own mother was crying hysterically; two old busybodies were hanging up cleavers and scissors over all the doors while babbling some mumbo jumbo—they were exorcising evil spirits! I rushed into the room, took the woman's pulse, and gave orders: 'Quick! Chopsticks! Towels! And get the midwife!' Perhaps my authoritative tone worked. Anyway, Aunty Cheng stopped praying and helped me wrap the towel around a chopstick and eased it between the young woman's upper and lower teeth, to prevent her from biting off her own tongue in her convulsions. Just then the midwife trudged in with the first-aid case on her back—the slatternly wife of the head of the Production Brigade. As soon as she saw the woman on the bed she froze in her tracks: 'Heavens! I can't deal with this! You better take her to the commune!' I silenced her with a look. The commune was over a dozen kilometers away over rough mountain roads. How could the woman make it in her condition? Supposing something happened on the way? I took a deep breath and asked her, 'Do you have the suction cup with you?' I knew that she had recently taken part in a crash course for midwifery set up by the county center for educated youth—though she was neither young nor educated. 'I suppose so,' she said uncertainly as she fumbled in her case. Luckily, she fished it out. 'Good. Now you work with me! And—Aunty Cheng,' I ordered, 'you prepare boiling water, soap, and two lanterns.' I turned to Genshen, the husband: 'You put the suction cup and the rubber gloves into a clean cooking pot and boil it for half an hour. When you're done, bring me the pot. Don't touch anything with your hands!' My head was clear, just what doctors need in moments of danger. I had regained my soul! I felt like a commander directing an army, or a soldier ready for combat. No melancholy now, no depression. I stayed with the woman and treated her with acupuncture, assisted by the midwife. When the things were boiled, I washed my hands carefully three times, put on the rubber gloves, and did an examination of the woman. Her womb was open. In the brief interval between her pains, I took the suction cup and fixed it firmly over the infant's head. Between the midwife and I, we managed to suck out the air inside the suction cup, thus creating a vacuum. Then we sucked softly, once, twice, and the pull of the suction helped the infant out. It was purple all over! Asphyxiation! Without a moment's hesitation, I inserted the tube of the suction cup into the mouth of the infant and sucked with all my force at the other end of the glass contraption. A nauseating smell assaulted me and before I knew it, a mouthful of the amiotic fluid was down my throat. I went on sucking and finally cleared the water from the infant's respiratory system. After that, I gave it the kiss of life and lo, the infant gave its first cry. I felt the earth spinning and then lost consciousness. When I woke up, the sun was shining through the window. Aunty Cheng brought me a big bowl of noodle soup with a poached egg on top. The tears were streaming down her face. 'You are Hua Tuo, the doctor saint, come back to life!' she cried. 'Come, eat. May Buddha watch over you and get you a good husband!' From that time on, all the villagers insisted on calling me Dr. Wei. They had reinstated me, long before my *official* rehabilitation." Wei

Lingling paused in her account and helped herself to some orange juice. She sipped slowly and deliberately, as if re-living those happy memories.

Her companions looked at her with admiration, sharing her happiness.

"But now . . ." Lingling gave a deep sigh.

"Well, there's no need to be so hard on yourself. You are now playing the green-leaf role—supporting the blooming flower." Cai Shuhua, Old Slow, actually resorted to a literary flourish.

"But I'd rather be a wildflower myself," said Lingling vehemently, tears shining in her eyes, or perhaps it was the fire of her passionate longing. The human heart is such a mystery. An old complaint goes this way: "There is no end to a man's longings." But should people forsake their longings?

Liu Qing raised her wrist to the light of the moon as she tried to make out the time from her weather-beaten mechanical watch. "It's nearly eleven. Could I give it a miss?"

"The last couple of days, the main gate has been under repair, so they don't lock up—" Yehyun realized that she had broached a painful subject and stopped short.

An embarrassed silence.

Wei Lingling spoke up suddenly. "Liu Qing, when I go back, I'll ask my husband to use his influence and see if he can get you transferred to a better hospital in Shanghai."

Yehyun threw away her cigarette and stood up. "I know what I'll do. I'll send a telegraph to my old man this minute. I'll ask him to wire me three hundred *yuan* and also extend my sick leave by another month. I'll take you on a pleasure trip to Shanghai, Wuxi, and Suzhou."

Cai Shuhua's big hand wiped away the sweat of her nose. "Right!" she said. "And my husband was a classmate of the personnel department chief at the Bureau of Education. I'll talk to him tonight. He must look the fellow up and get you transferred to the provincial center. It's the least I can do."

Liu Qing's glasses were blurred with tears as she struggled for speech. Suddenly she grabbed the button and tossed it up. The button bumped off the surface of the stone table, rolled over into the grass, and settled there. The three women bent down in the dark to retrieve it. But it was Yehyun's matches that solved the problem. She lighted up one match after another as they crouched and scoured the patch of grass under their feet. Finally they spotted the button, right side up, twinkling in the darkness. "Hurrah!" shouted Yehyun and Lingling as Cai Shuhua also jumped to her feet.

The four women looked at each other excitedly. Their silence spoke more than words. Perhaps they should stop here?

Liu Qing took off her glasses and wiped it with a corner of her shirt. "Yes, the button is right. I am happy, truly happy." How time had wrought changes. Liu Qing moved her hands exactly as a peasant woman would.

But now Liu Qing wanted to have her say. She resumed her seat. "Sit down," she said, "and let me tell you my story."

Her three friends sat down dubiously. What was she going to say? What could she contribute?

"How I wish you would understand me and trust me like in the old days!" Liu Qing knitted her brows as she looked into the night, as if looking for something.

"Wang Xizhi in his preface to *Orchid Pavilion* said: 'What has been joy turns to ashes in the flash of a moment; nevertheless it leaves its mark. Even so our lives, whether long or short, constantly changing, will end. As the ancients say, life and death are of paramount concern. What a sad reflection.' " Liu Qing's recital was so fluent, like the bubbling of a fountain, but her words struck cold into the hearts of her listeners.

"We today should face the fact. Once we close our eyes and our ashes are scattered over lakes and rivers, what does honor or disgrace matter? Commemorative funerals are a show for the living. Oh, what I want to tell you is—I have already tasted the joys of a sincere commemoration."

"Stop it, what nonsense you are talking!" And Cai Shuhua put her big hand over Liu Qing's mouth, as if to avert bad luck.

Lingling continued to fan herself with her handkerchief. Tomorrow, she decided, she must make Liu Qing have a general examination. Perhaps she had been emotionally hurt?

Yehyun savagely wrenched off another button of her nightdress.

"Now you are all so gloomy, as if you are saying a last goodbye to my corpse," Liu Qing said, smiling as she pushed Cai Shuhua's hand aside. "Of course I'm human. If death comes so early, of course I'm afraid. And sad. Especially as I am single, and sensitive, and literary, and a woman. For example, the day before yesterday, at four in the morning, there were few stars in the sky and the wind was chilly. I made my way all alone to the bus station, a tattered bag in my hand. I had completed the formalities for transfer at the county hospital the day before and had

refused when the head of my school offered to send someone to help me on the way. It was the harvest, every hand
was needed, and most village schoolteachers have just this
time to take in their own crops. And anyway, apart from
some loss of weight and strength, there is nothing wrong
with me. I can take care of myself. I made the head of the
school promise not to tell anyone of my departure. I made
him go back to the village. I thought I had the strength of
will to handle it alone. But halfway in my solitary walk, I
regretted my decision. I was overpowered by loneliness. I
thought back to the last few days at the county hospital.
The looks on the doctors' faces, the half utterances of the
nurses, the oversolicitousness of my school principal—all
made me think that I must be seriously ill. To be cut off
at forty, that was so cruel. I had been a rural schoolteacher
for fifteen years. For nine years in village primary schools.
For the last six years in the middle school of the commune.
The villagers look up to me, the school relies on me, but
if I must describe my life, I can only say that it is silent
and unknown. Well, as I was saying, I dragged myself to
the bus station. The place was bustling with life. Vendors
were hawking meat-stuffed buns and sugared pancakes.
Cooking stoves were set up in a cleared-up space, some
vendors fried doughsticks, others boiled pig's-blood soup.
Melons and other fruit were displayed for sale. The market
had completely destroyed the serene beauty of early dawn,
but on the other hand, it was so full of vitality. My heart
trembled in my breast. Life, after all, was worth living."

The night was still and silent. The last batch of patients
returning to the ward looked at them curiously.

"I knew that the big bus to the prefecture always
parked at the northeastern corner of the parking lot. Like

the local villagers, I did not go in by the regular entrance, but made a shortcut through a crumbling wall. I was surprised to see such a crowd. Were they all going to the prefecture? Were they still carrying on their little businesses during harvest time? I was confused. I stopped to have a good hard look through the morning mists, and I was petrified.

"Heavens, whom do I see! Right there in front of me were my students. Some were former students, by now manly young fellows and well-behaved village girls. And among the youngsters, not only my students, but their little brothers and sisters. They surrounded me on all sides. But the school principal, Wang, had just headed back the night before! It meant that these children—young or old, all my students are my children—must have started off the minute they got wind of my going and had walked over twenty kilometers all through the night to arrive on time. The first rays of dawn lighted up their sweaty faces.

"I heard my faithful, loving students as they shouted to me, 'Teacher Liu! Get well quickly and come back! We'll come and meet you. . . .'

"I rushed up to the children and my tears just flowed. I bent down and held a scruffy little one to my breast. It was Xiangmei's baby brother. I allowed girl students to bring their little brothers and sisters to class. Otherwise, so many little girls would have to leave school. I kissed the baby's dirty little cheeks. I wanted to have a good cry, to cry it out once and for all!

"They were tears of happiness. I had lost my father as a child, and then my mother shortly after my graduation. I had no parents, no siblings, no husband, no children. I was just a plain village schoolteacher; I had not yet seen one of my own students go to college. But I had gained such a treasure, such a pure and devoted love. Truly."

By now, Liu Qing was unable to speak for crying. Again she used the end of her shirt to wipe her glasses, and then wiped her tears with the back of her hand, just as the villagers do. Her three companions seemed to understand and looked at her lovingly.

"Truly," said Yehyun. "What she said was true."

"I can't control myself," Liu Qing put on her glasses and sighed. "Anyway, the crowd grew and grew. Passersby stopped out of curiosity. The buses hooted their horns, accompanied with the shouts of the drivers. Goodness, I was going to miss the bus! A ticket collector came over and dragged me through the crowd. 'You are the schoolteacher. You are going to the prefecture. Get on the bus quick!' I tried to explain, but she just dragged me on. 'I know, I know,' she said. 'Your principal had asked us to help you.'

"Finally I made it up the bus. I was ready for the scolding of the driver and the complaints of the other passengers. But, surprise, surprise, everybody on the bus greeted me and offered me their seats. Actually, the best seat, the front seat, was reserved for me. In the rush, I had lost my bag. But several of my students were hoisting a bulging bag onto the bus. Was that mine? Before I had taken in the situation, other students were clambering on the bus. There were shouts: 'My eggs!' 'And mine are left behind!' 'And mine!' Heavens! Eggs are most precious in the summer, the best nutrition available. I tried to remove their gifts from my bag, but Xiangmei held my hands while others were adding more. It was utter confusion. Suddenly the driver stood up from his seat and handed over an empty water pail. 'Put your eggs in here,' he growled. "They'll be safe. They won't break. Hurry!'

"The bus moved slowly. Suddenly I felt such a strong urge to live on. As the bus turned to take the high road a little old man ran up to its side and shouted at me: 'I told ... not to ... won't listen ... get well ... back ... wait for you ...' It was the school principal, Wang. I bit my lips so as not to cry out loud."

Lingling held her handkerchief to her mouth to muffle her crying. Yehyun and Shuhua handed Liu Qing some juice and fruit. Liu sipped the juice and the tension relaxed somewhat. Liu Qing turned to Yehyun. "Yehyun, I have forgotten the rule. Here's my proverb: 'When I die, I leave with you, O silent world, my last words—I have loved.'"

"Tagore!" In unison Lingling and Yehyun identified it.

Liu Qing went on with her story, not heeding their interruption. "For a long time, I had thought that it was for love that I was so attached to that barren corner of the earth. The object of my ardor was a graduate from medical school. He was assigned to this commune the same time as I was. Forsaken at the faraway corner of the earth, we shared the same fate. But just as our love was about to blossom he lost his life. Answering a patient's call during a rainstorm one summer night, he lost his foothold and slipped down a crag. Did he love me? I don't know—and do not need to know. I know that I love him. With all the force of my life."

Her three friends were stunned. So this is love, which they thought they knew about.

"It was his love for the villagers that gave me inspiration, his unswerving attachment to his work that gave me strength. As I love him, I must love my work. Those poor, irregular village schools, those simple country children. My ideal rests with them."

Liu Qing stood up and made a gesture of dismissal. "I now declare the reunion heart-to-heart talk closed. We must hold hands to greet a better tomorrow."

"You are still our center," Lingling said.

Four pairs of hands held tightly together as four women of forty said goodbye under the moonlit night.

Career, ideals, struggle, love, marriage, family. It is so hard for women. Questions at every turn. But where are the answers?

First published in Hundred Flowers *magazine, 1983. Translated at the Bunting Institute, Radcliffe-Harvard, December 1990.*

THE SUN IS NOT OUT
TODAY

LU XIN'ER

LU XIN'ER is one of China's most hopeful female writers specializing in women's issues. Lu graduated from the Central Institute of Drama in the early 1980s and is now settled in Shanghai as a professional writer. Her earlier works are fired by idealism and filled with images of women who overcome obstacles. Her recent works have taken a more ironic note.

In "The One and the Other," two women are contrasted. One, a widow, lives only through her husband—dead or alive. The other, a professional success—a liberated woman—stays single and carries on a lifelong affair with a married man.

In "The Sun Is Not Out Today," a group of women share a moment of solidarity as they wait for abortions.

In this moderate-sized city, the first signs of life every morning occur at the vegetable stores and the hospital. The vegetable vendors are ready with their weights and scales at half past five, according to established practice. But now with the appearance of free markets, there is no need for customers to get up early to form a line. At the hospital, also according to established practice, registration begins at half past seven. But nowadays it is getting harder and harder to register.

Dan Ye arrived at the Maternity and Gynecological Hospital at six. A crowd had already gathered outside the forbidding iron gates. Mostly men.

The day was cloudy. A grayish mist obscured the rising sun. There was no discernible moment of dawn between the night and the day.

It's just as well it's cloudy, Dan Ye thought to herself. She leaned against the cement lamppost by the side of the iron gates, her face a grayish blur. The lamp over her head was still lighted, lighted but not giving any light. It was just a yellow blur, like a half-ripe grapefruit. She lifted her head sideways and looked at the yellow lamp, the gray sky.

> When the sun is not out,
> Color yellow is sunlight.

The lines flashed through her mind.

Wipe that out! She kicked herself mentally. Why think of poetry? *His* poetry . . .

"Stand in line! Stand in line!" A dumpy little nurse appeared outside the iron gates to hand out registration slips.

A waiting line began to form. After some pushing and shoving, some kind of order emerged. The people stood close to each other, as if fearful that any little crack in the line might let in an intruder. The long line zigzagged along the pavement. Predictably, the men smoked and read newspapers. Some just gawked.

Another two men joined the line.

Dan Ye eyed the bus station in the distance. He did say he would come, but she had forbidden that. Forbidden him, but still expecting. . . The bus station was just another gray blur.

"Registration is getting harder and harder," said an old woman standing next to Dan Ye. "I was here yesterday."

"For whom?"

"My youngest daughter. It's a sin, it is. Her baby just one year old and now again . . ." The old woman's flabby mouth puckered up in worry. "And you, are you also brooding?"

Dan Ye was embarrassed. She was not accustomed to this kind of familiarity. But the term was vivid and to the point. All women, high and low, must brood like any old hen.

"You can tell at a glance by the complexion," said a middle-aged woman next to them. "The little chits at our factory, I can tell by their looks the minute they are in trouble." The woman's hair was cut short and combed back smoothly. Her jacket of dark gray nylon was without a crease in its folds. Everything in her tone and demeanor denoted serious commitment. Just like a judge.

"And you are . . . ?" the old woman asked.

"I am the birth-control officer for the union in my factory; every Monday and Wednesday I come and line up to arrange their abortions."

"All that work!" The old woman was impressed.

"The birth-control program at our factory gets honorable mentions from year to year." The woman scrutinized Dan Ye's college ID badge. "You are a collge student? You must be thirty."

"I teach in college," Dan Ye could not avoid answering.

"How old is your eldest?" the officer asked, slipping into her professional role.

Dan Ye shook her head. Vague, noncommittal.

"Nowadays, all that people care for are clothes," the old woman said. "They don't want more children. Not like in my time. We just produced them one after another."

The birth-control officer gave Dan Ye a significant glance. "Not all are so conscientious, though. Today, for instance, I am here for this girl, not yet registered in marriage, and already pregnant. The silly thing doesn't want an abortion. Afraid the fellow will jilt her."

Dan Ye didn't care to hear about other people's affairs. Nor did she want others to know hers. She turned around and removed her college badge.

The dumpy nurse made her way to them. The men in the line gazed at the stack of registration slips in her pudgy hand. Their eyes followed her, mesmerized.

The woman officer looked about her anxiously. "Why, they have not turned up . . ."

"Oh, how responsible you are!" The old woman was sincere in her praise.

At that moment, a young couple appeared at the iron gates. They seemed in some sort of argument; the man was voicing words of reassurance, too low to be heard, and the woman shouting, "Don't you dare cheat me! If you do . . ." Her words boomed as if they came through an amplifier.

The woman officer was relieved and waved to them. "They're here at last."

The young woman saw the birth-control officer and averted her eyes. The young man, however, dashed over, pulling the girl behind him. "Sorry to trouble you."

But the woman officer did not take it personally. "Hurry upstairs and wait in line," she commanded the woman.

The young woman shook off the man's hand and strode forward. She was well made—tall, slim, with delicate skin and shoulder-length hair.

"What is your problem?" The nurse stood in front of Dan Ye.

"The doctor gave me an appointment for today."

"Artificial abortion!" The nurse's voice was as loud as her waist was thick. "Take your registration slip, go up to the second floor, and wait outside the operating room!"

"So you have also come to scrape it off!" The old woman's deep-sunk eyes were full of pity. "How bitter it is to be a woman!"

Dan Ye was shocked into immobility. She felt all eyes directed toward her.

"Nobody here with you?" The old woman was concerned.

Dan Ye managed to smile unconcernedly. In spite of herself, hope flared inside her breast. She looked across at the bus station. A bus drew into the station, but drove off immediately. The station was deserted.

The sun was still not out.

At the turning in the stairway leading to the second floor, a wooden plaque carried the warning: MALE COMRADES NO ADMITTANCE. So, from here on, women only. What a privilege! On the second floor, a row of doors on the right proclaimed by painted signs that they were the gynecological consulting rooms. Next to them was a birth-control consulting room. The open space in the middle was the waiting area, with rows of benches evenly spaced out. A corridor led to the operating room. One word in two large characters glared from the frosted glass of the entrance: SILENCE. The corridor was flanked by two benches, one against each wall, for the comfort of those awaiting operations.

The benches were already occupied. The silence was impenetrable, like the tightly shut frosted glass doors of the operating room. People continued to arrive, walking up listlessly. With so many people packed together, there was bound to be conversation. The silence was soon broken.

"Does it hurt?"

"It's bearable. Anyway, better than labor pains."

"I am so tense, I didn't sleep a wink last night."

"The trick is to relax your muscles. And don't cry out. Doctor's can't stand the hollering."

"There's no limit to the pains of women."

"Silence!" This stern admonition came from a tiny room on one side of the main entrance to the operating room. It was dignified with the title of CHECKPOINT.

Checking what? The card to your medical file, your employment card, your marriage certificate, your residence registration booklet, the letter of recommendation from your work unit? The checkpoint was just a narrow strip, with a table and a chair. At this moment on the chair behind the table sat an old nurse. Her eyes were fixed on the wall clock, as she waited for the two arms of the clock to point precisely to eight.

"Hand in your medical file card. Go and relieve yourselves." The old nurse emerged from her place behind the little door. She had high cheekbones and two protruding teeth, which interfered somewhat with the dignified air she was trying to assume.

The two benches emptied. An old woman selling toilet paper at the entrance to the toilet was in a flurry of business. At the sink, someone was in the throes of morning sickness—one hand clutched to her chest, the other hand holding on to the tap. The woman did not regurgitate anything, though the convulsions went on. The women beside her stopped in concern. In turn, some of them were infected by her vomiting spasms and they dashed away.

"You go in first," Dan Ye told the woman at the sink. "When you feel better." There was also a lineup for toilets.

The woman turned her head to answer. "Thank you." A beautiful woman, Dan Ye thought. Her paleness enhanced her beauty.

Dan Ye was intrigued. "Please take my arm." Is she newly married? An actress?

"It doesn't matter, I can cope. Actually, I will be onstage tonight."

"Tonight? Can you manage?"

"Yes."

"Do you play a leading role?"

"An established actress has the lead. I am her understudy. She allows me to take over for seven performances. And so far I have only done two."

Doesn't your husband care for you? Dan Ye wondered. Then her thoughts lighted on her own condition. But does *he* care for *me*? Didn't he say that he would come along? Of course, she herself had forbidden . . .

"I didn't tell my husband," the actress said, as if answering Dan Ye's unspoken question. "He loves children. But this is my first appearance in a major role. If I succeed in these seven performances, I will be given the opportunity to appear fourteen times in the next play." The actress was quite frank. "And you? You don't look as if you've had children."

"I have classes this term," Dan Ye murmured.

After relieving themselves, they all filed back to the bench. By then, even more people had arrived. But nobody complained. They squeezed against each other, shoulder to shoulder, finding place for everyone.

"Which of you is Fan Hong?" The old nurse at the checkpoint took up her place, standing between the two benches. She was going through the stack of medical file cards, checking thoroughly for all the required documents. "Where is your letter of recommendation from your work unit?"

The good-looking girl with shoulder-length hair rose shamefacedly, as if she were a negligent schoolgirl. "Director Feng of the Worker's Union in our factory . . ."

"Oho! So this is how you union people get their honorable mentions—by fixing up abortions for the likes of you without official approval from the factory authorities! So that these unplanned pregnancies go unrecorded and unreckoned! This is not the first time this trick has been pulled!"

The old nurse struck up a familiar diatribe: "According to regulations, our hospital doesn't deal with cases like yours. Nowadays there are special clinics for the likes of you. Outside the city. Everything self-paid. Your pay gets docked if you take sick leave after the operation. Even so, consider yourself lucky. You are longer penalized."

The girl named Fan Hong stood with head bowed, as if arraigned before a law court. The tears rolled down her chest.

"What's the use of crying over spilled milk? A woman should know which end is up." Apparently, the nurse relished lecturing.

Holding their breath, the occupants of the two benches also attended the lecture.

Fan Hong wiped her eyes with a little handkerchief; the harder she tried to stifle her sobs, the more the tears rolled down.

As soon as the old nurse turned her back, the two benches broke out in solidarity. The women nearby rallied to comfort her. "Don't cry. Crying will spoil your eyes. This is just like a birth."

"Be careful next time."

"Might as well get married right away and keep the baby. You must give birth to one child anyway, so why go through this extra pain?"

"In these cases, the woman is always the loser."

Only Dan Ye was silent. *Loser?* She searched her heart and did not know how to reckon the gain and the loss. There was no set of scales upon which to reckon up human love. He said he loved her. When she first heard that, she had cried. She could hardly believe it. And then she had believed in his love, had thoroughly believed in him. Every day, for five years, she had taken the roundabout way to wait for him under the stone bridge, just to see him briefly, talk about her teaching, his poetry, or nothing at all. . . .

"He . . . he did it on purpose," Fan Hong said. "He was afraid I'd throw him over. He calculated the days of my period. I didn't know. He is seven years older than I am." The girl's voice broke. "When I discovered I was pregnant, I thought I might as well get married. But now his parents do not agree to the marriage, say I am too young, too flighty. . . . They have asked the Workers' Union to talk me into this abortion." Faced with these women, strangers yet completely understanding, Fan Hong, for the first time, let down all her barriers. She confessed all the secrets that she could never have borne to reveal and had had no one to tell.

The two benches broke out in indignation.

"Don't let him get away with it so easily. Make him take you back in a taxi after the operation. Make him buy you good things to eat. Recover your health before anything else."

"Might as well break with him once and for all. You've learned a lesson."

"Go to the Workers' Union and accuse him! Get him a reprimand!"

The girl's eyes were red and swollen. "He was frightened of a scandal. He gave me some herbs, but it didn't work."

"You must never take medicine on your own. It's dangerous."

"Being a woman is a misfortune." The actress sighed. "I don't want to give birth to a girl. Never."

"Some people are all in favor of girls," the woman sitting next to the actress said. She was a hunchbacked, wizened creature, one skinny shoulder blade higher than the other. She looked like some kind of stunted plant. "My husband always complains that I can only produce boys."

"Let me see your palms." A primary-school teacher, shed of her classroom reserve, clutched the hands of the little woman. "You'll have a string of girls. That is, if you are *allowed* to have them."

"How true!" the hunchback exclaimed. "The last one I aborted was a girl!" The fortune-telling had come true, and a flush of excitement brought a dash of color to the little woman's wan cheeks.

"And so, it is you!" The old nurse emerged from behind the glass doors of the operating room and fixed the hunchback with her eye. "No wonder the voice is so familiar! So you are here again? And you have the cheek to boast about your last? How many times have you been here? As I see it, you're playing a game with your own life." She spoke slowly and deliberately, every word a barb.

"I—" The little woman tried to avoid her eye.

"Why did you not take precautions?"

"The uterine device didn't work. I can't help it. After my last abortion, only three days after, he forced me." The little woman squeezed her two palms between her knees, while one shoulder blade went up and the other down.

"Three abortions in six months! How can anyone stand it? If everybody behaves like you, we won't be able to cope with all the work, even if our feet were turned into extra hands!" The old nurse spread out her arms to include everybody. "Even as it is, we have two dozen of you every morning, every single morning of the week!"

The two benches grew silent, their occupants lost in contrition for their sins.

Dan Ye felt suffocated. In moments like this, everything beautiful was desecrated, as the sun is by the thick slab of gray cloud. Did she do wrong? Yes. She knew she was doing wrong, made hundreds of resolutions to stop, but as soon as they met under the stone bridge she plunged again into the abyss. . . .

"With so many abortions, I don't know whether you can be operated on anymore." The old nurse was in a dilemma.

The little hunchback paled with anxiety. "Oh!"

"You go in first and let Dr. Tang have a look."

Submissively the little woman crept through the forbidding glass doors painted SILENCE.

The two benches again burst into indignation.

"This kind of husband should be dragged to court!"

The primary-school teacher bit her fingernails in vexation. "It is no crime. This is also *my* third abortion. What an abominable nuisance! When I take the kids for morning exercise, I skip rope like mad, hoping to abort the thing. Whenever my period is late, I am sick with worry. When I discover I am pregnant, I get so desperate, I act like crazy, shouting at him all the time."

"Men have no consideration. For us, it's off to work at the crack of dawn. And after work, it's cooking and washing. At night, you're so tired you just want to sleep, but they won't leave you alone!"

"What can we do? It's our duty!"

Dan Ye was shocked. These women were so frank, so naked—no hedging about. Their candor made her want to speak out, too. What should she say? That he was married, had a son, that he told her he loved his son. She understood—he did not cheat her.

"So!" The old nurse's face was as chilly as the frosted glass panes. "You are all nicely worked up and excited! Very well. But let me tell you, if you don't conserve your energies now, you'll collapse the minute you get to the operating table." She studied the faces before her. "Who is Qiu Ying?"

"I." The actress stood up.

"You are not from this city?"

"That's right. I am touring in a show."

"Letter of recommendation from your work unit?"

"I don't want the theatre company to know."

"Then bring your marriage certificate."

"I don't carry it with me."

"No certificate, no abortion." The old nurse was adamant. "Rules are made to be kept."

"But I truly am married," Qiu Ying protested eagerly, though she didn't know how to verify her statement.

"True or not, who can tell?" the old nurse retorted knowingly. Evidently experience had taught her not to be too credulous. "I've made it clear. This hospital does not treat cases of pregnancy before marriage."

"But I really and truly am married. I must have an operation now. I must be on stage tonight." The actress was now begging.

"I work by rules. Without a certificate, the doctor will not do the operation—even if you break in and lie down on the table."

"Could you make a special case for her?" the primary-school teacher pleaded. "She's been here since early morning."

"And she's vomiting so badly," Dan Ye added.

"Who would come to this place if they weren't really in trouble?" Fan Hong, the girl with long hair, muttered.

"When I say no, it's no."

"Give me back my medical file card!" The actress snatched it away and walked out, her high heels attacking the cement floor.

Two rows of eyes from the two benches followed her.

"I've seen the likes of her, with their *really and truly's*." The old nurse was full of scorn.

Dan Ye stood up and rushed after the actress. She now realized that all women were equal before this frosty glass pane, beautiful actresses or wizened hags, women with college badges or those without.

She caught up with the actress. "Please keep your child," she said. "I'm sure it will be beautiful just like you. The hardship will be over sooner or later."

The actress smiled at her in gratitude. "And I am sure your child, too, will be like you, elegant and refined."

Dan Ye's heart trembled like a lone leaf swept up by the wind.

The actress turned and walked down the stairs.

The two benches were silent again.

The old nurse disappeared into the checkpoint for good. Evidently her duty was done. In her stead, a young nurse took over. Regular features, soft voice, a model of a nurse.

"When you finish with the thermometers, go in and change. Please be quick."

Another flurry of activity. The frosted glass doors swung to and fro as everyone scrambled to enter. The young nurse decided she might as well keep the doors open. Thus the interior of the entrance gaped at the women like the scoop of a bulldozer.

Dan Ye hesitated at the threshold. She took one look out of the sealed windows. The sky was still overcast. The yellow street lamp was probably extinguished by now. So. No sun. And no yellow either. Where then was the radiance? Just a passing speculation. She realized this was the first time she could think of his poetry and remain detached.

The rest area next to the operating room was quite

large. About a dozen beds were ranged against the walls. Small white tables were sandwiched between the beds.

The little hunchback was the first to emerge. She lay down on the first bed with her face to the wall. She clenched her fists, hitting the unresponsive cement walls weakly. "It's killing me, it's killing me!" she cried.

"It's the uterus contracting," the nurse said as she put down two mugs of Ovaltine by the bedside stand. "Drink this, drink it all," she urged.

Fan Hong lay on her bed as if in a swoon, her long hair spread appealingly across the white pillow.

The primary-school teacher lay facedown on the edge of the bed, a helpless sight. She had started vomiting as soon as she got on the operating table.

After a while, the rest area was completely quiet. The women all lay peacefully. The room was like a dorm during the noon break.

It was over. Over and gone, as if it had never happened. There was no more conversation. They were strangers after all. The confidences on the waiting benches seemed lost in memory, like wisps of floating cloud.

"Which of you has ordered a car?" The nurse's voice startled them all. "Please leave as early as you can. Another batch of operations is over. Others are arriving in a minute."

Fan Hong was the first to sit up. "He hired a car to take me here and has ordered it to wait." Her eyes were recovered from their swollenness, and the sense of injury was also gone.

"Taxi waiting?" The nurse was amazed. "Nowadays, some people do have style, I'd say."

The nurse handed Fan Hong a certificate of sick leave. "Stay in bed for a couple of days," she advised.

"Yes, he has promised to ask leave and stay with me for a few days," the girl said confidently as she shook back her long hair. "And why not? By now everybody knows about us—the Workers' Union, my own workshop." She seemed to accept the situation calmly now.

"I also have a car." The little hunchback wriggled up painfully. Now her body looked more than ever like an empty sack, with the limbs hanging about her limply. Only her hunch gave her a third dimension. "He drives a truck. He's coming to get me at ten." She looked at her wristwatch on its faded chain and began to hurry, looking for her clothes, her shoes.

"Take your time. Weren't you in pain?" the nurse reminded her. "So what if you make him wait a little?"

"Oh, no, he still has a job for the morning. He's never late for work. His team has kept a record of excellence for years and years." Her eyes shone softly, with quiet satisfaction.

"Eat well. You must make up for your lost nutrition."

"Oh, he never stints his strength at work, and he never stints his food either." The little woman's voice positively tinkled with complacency.

"Come for an examination after your first period," the nurse said as she flipped through the woman's medical file. "From now on you really must be careful."

The little woman blushed and bowed her head submissively.

Suddenly an unfamiliar voice was heard at the door. "Is Sung Lizhen in there? Your husband is very anxious." A message was slipped through a crack in the door.

"Yes, yes, I am all right." The primary-schoolteacher seemed to derive much comfort from the message. She smiled in embarrassment and barely concealed pride. "I can also leave now. He will take me back on his bicycle."

Two beds were vacant. Two women, doubled over in pain, were led in by nurses. The patients lay down on the newly vacated beds. Dan Ye walked in by herself.

"How can you . . ." Everybody gasped.

"I . . ."

"She is more than three months gone," the nurse explained. "She must be hospitalized for induced birth. There's no point in delaying," she added.

"Induced birth is just as bad as a regular birth."

"Plain torture."

Dan Ye heard the whispers, but did not pay attention. She was not afraid of pain. She did not think it torture. Although he admitted contritely that he had injured her. Although her heart had contracted in pain. At those times, the stone bridge itself seemed to be swaying above her. Yet still, after the acute pain, she had experienced an inexpressible happiness. She had loved, after all.

The nurse handed her a slip of paper. "Hurry downstairs and complete your procedures for hospitalization."

Dan Ye took the paper, gave it a look, and crushed it in her hand. She walked out with great composure.

The SILENCE painted on the frosted glass had finally prevailed. The rest area next to the operating room was as quiet and peaceful as a maternity ward after a safe delivery. The two benches outside the entrance were deserted. No more unrestrained confidences. No more relief in complaints.

Dan Ye sat down on the bench. Hospitalization. In-duced birth. Three months gone. Only through this as-yet-uncompleted cycle could she ever know what it is to be a woman. No, she did not want to start all over again. In a flash, she came to a decision. *He*, or *she*, must be *elegant and refined*, just as she had envisioned over and over again in her mind's eye. Like her. And like him. She threw the slip of paper under the chair.

Going down the stairs, Dan Ye saw again the MALE COMRADES NO ADMITTANCE sign. He had said that he would always remember this day. She wanted to forget it.

The male comrades were all waiting docilely in the hall on the ground floor. The hall was huge, but the crowd nearly filled it. That stocky fellow, looking as if he was hewn out of rock, must be the little hunchback's husband, Dan Ye thought. Some of the men looked elegant and re-fined, others hardboiled and streetwise. But all their eyes were fixed on the stairs. Every figure, every sound, every movement coming from the stairs would cause a wave of expectancy in the hall.

Dan Ye walked through swiftly with her head down.

"Have you finished?" The actress was standing at the entrance to the hall.

"You haven't left?" Dan Ye asked in surprise.

"I am so sick. How can I go on stage tonight?"

"Are you sure you don't want the child? What a pity."

"The father is a director. He's going to be promoted deputy head of the company. I can't rush into pregnancy and child raising at this moment. I'll lose myself and he will lose interest in me. I need time. I must keep my good looks. I must succeed on stage. So that he can't do without me. I'm keeping this from him. He mustn't know. . . ." Qiu Ying's handsome face could hardly disguise her anxiety. She took out two slips of pink paper, theatre tickets. "I'll go and talk to the doctor. I will invite him to the play. He will believe me."

"Give it a try," Dan Ye murmured. "Give it a try." She was bracing herself. Give it a try. See if a tiny life illegally conceived has a right to survive. Dan Ye treasured her love. More, she treasured the life so naturally born of that love. For that, she was prepared to pay the price. She was prepared to sacrifice even more.

The little hunchback walked slowly down the stairs. The stocky man immediately went up to her. She held his arm and together they walked through the hall. Her two eyes looked placidly out of her pinched little face. As she met the actress and Dan Ye she smiled at them gently.

The actress was a bit uneasy. "I'm going upstairs," she said.

"And I am leaving." Dan Ye was perfectly calm. She left the hall, walked down the steps. She took out the college badge and pinned it on her breast.

The road was packed with vehicles of all kinds: taxicabs, minibuses, trucks, and a sea of bicycles. Further on, there was the bus stop. And a handful of people waiting for the bus.

He must have come and gone, Dan Ye thought. She leaned against the cement lamppost and looked up at the sky. The sun had broken through the masses of clouds and gave out a weak light. A yellow globe. Like a ripe grapefruit. The sun was out. No more stone bridges. No more taking the roundabout way. No more. A lingering echo of her heart seemed to merge with the faint yellow sunlight pouring from the sky:

> When the sun is not out,
> Color yellow is sunlight.

From Selected Short Stories in Reprint, *Xiao Shuo Xuan Kan, 1987. Translated at the Rockefeller Study Center, Villa Serbelloni, Bellagio, June, 1990.*

THE ONE AND
THE OTHER

LU XIN'ER

"Come on, Elder Sister Song. You should order a taxi for such a trip! At your age!"

These young chaps at the office really travel in style!

Over twenty *yuan* for a single trip, she had mentally calculated. Up to fifty for double! Song Huishan could not bear to part with so much money. She could take the bus. Only fifty to sixty cents a trip. As she had told her colleagues last night: if she caught the first bus, she would get a seat. Almost like a private car, and so economical. Gaining two benefits at one stroke, as the saying goes.

Now it was close to five A.M.. There were a few lingering stars in the sky as she made ready to leave. Song Huishan put on a plain suit of nondescript whitish gray, tailor-made for this occasion. The evening before she had packed fruit—peach, tangerine, apple, banana—in a quadruple set of stiff paper containers, four boxes stacked neatly one on top of the other. (These fruits were available throughout the year.) He's basically vegetarian, she said to herself. In the other world, he must never be short of fresh fruit. She had thought of everything.

Song Huishan had been a widow for three years. Today was the anniversary of her husband's death. Again she had been kept awake through the night, going over their

208

whole life together. She had scoured the shops the day before for white roses, his favorite flower. True, the bunch she got had lost its scent, but it was still in full bloom. Even during their hardest years, she would skimp and save to buy him roses, displaying them in the big vase on the windowsill.

It was still so dark. Song prepared breakfast and laid it on the table to cool. Two little bowls of millet, yellow and thick, with a few dried red dates and white beans swimming on the surface. The blue china bowls, placed across from each other on the table, were flanked by a pair of chopsticks with a dragon-and-phoenix design. Four side dishes formed a pattern in the middle of the table: peppery dried carrots, sweet-sour cucumbers, dried tofu soaked in soy sauce, and dried bean curd, tightly wrapped and soaked in oil and vinegar. It was said that these four dishes had been a favorite item in Confucius's own diet; *he* had researched it. Everything on the table was ordered according to *his* taste, as was everything else in their lives. Probably it was because they had no children. Anyway, Song Huishan was content that it should be so. She knew all his ways and enjoyed ministering to them, down to the most minuscule detail. But he was gone. Gone so swiftly, without leaving a word.

The room was dark, with only an eight-watt fluorescent light, its glass cylinder murky with age. He could never stand being flooded with light. And, of course, darkness was more economical. He had always been frugal. She had caught his habits and never wasted a cent. On her yearly visits to the cemetery, she would first get on the inner-city bus and then change to a suburban line, four hours coming and going. It's a day's work. She couldn't make it without asking leave for the day. Luckily, her colleagues were understanding. They reckoned it as a business trip so that nothing would be deducted from her monthly bonus.

Everything was in form. Song was on the point of leaving when someone knocked at the door. The sound was light, like a kitten scratching its little paw against the door.

"Who is that?" Song was surprised that anyone should be knocking at this hour.

"It is I." The voice was as soft as the knock.

"You!" Song was surprised that Hua, of all people, should be standing in the doorway.

Hua Qing, Song's neighbor, lived in Apartment 301, across the landing. The two women had been colleagues as well, both working at the Bureau of Textiles. Song was in the administrative department, a model worker, while Hua—not too long before—had been a designer, at the top of her profession. The administrative offices and the designers' studio were both on the second floor, facing each other across the corridor.

Right from the beginning, the two women couldn't get along. Hua was petite and beautiful, always dressed elegantly, walking softly like a cat. Her whole manner was subdued, even bashful, but you could see at a glance that she exuded a sense of superiority.

Giving herself airs! Song had thought.

Song had no patience with that narcissistic type. She herself was easygoing. She got along with everybody. Except this precious miss. Before the Cultural Revolution, there had once been a scene at the designers' studio. The wife of Chief Designer Yin had stormed into the room and overthrown Miss Hua's desk, shouting insults and obscenities all the while. The entire bureau was thrilled with this display. Since that day, stories of the liaison between Mr. Yin and Miss Hua circulated freely among the gossips, with many graphic details. After that incident, Hua was temporarily reassigned to another department and later permanently removed from the staff of the bureau itself. At the same time, Mr. Yin acquired the habit of seeing his wife off to work every morning, walking right up to the bus stop, waving until the bus was out of sight, acting the loving husband. A model couple, they were dubbed at the bureau. But Hua never married.

"The utter futility of it all!" Song had said to herself at the time. How could she step between husband and wife! Served her right! If a third party had turned up between him and herself—but no, that was impossible, beyond imagination. They were truly one and indissoluble.

Before Hua left the bureau for good, she managed to receive a housing allotment, the little apartment that made her Song's neighbor. People said it was very tastefully furnished, with the first phone in the whole building installed at self-expense, and the first refrigerator.

"Elder Sister Song, why don't you pop in and have a look?" Hua asked shortly after she was installed in Apartment 301. "Phone, fridge, full-scale modernization." The young fellows at the bureau were full of envy.

Song was not interested. All she cared for was that she loved her husband and was loved in return, that they were happy, and their lives rational and satisfying. But three years ago, he departed, leaving her single and solitary— just like Hua. "But I am different," she kept telling everyone who mentioned herself and Hua in the same breath. "Entirely different," she kept repeating to herself. But the people at the bureau persisted in referring to them as the pair of women who lived singly in Building 5, one in Apartment 301, the other in Apartment 303—two women who did not speak to each other.

That day, to Song's complete surprise, Hua had come to tell her that she had ordered a car to the cemetery. "You needn't leave so early to catch the bus. I've ordered a car, just for myself. You can accompany me." Hua was in a silver-gray woolen suit, stylishly cut.

Song refused outright. "I'd rather take the bus." *His* anniversary. She wanted to be alone with him. She didn't want to share him with anybody, least of all a woman like *her*.

"This is the day of the marathon. The buses on the suburban lines stop running after seven in the morning."

"Oh . . ."

Yes, Hua was more knowledgeable. She herself was completely unaware of the marathon. In the past, he read the papers and listened to the news broadcast regularly, and if there was anything interesting, he would always repeat it to her. After his death, she stopped the subscriptions to his newspapers.

"We leave at six."

"Whom are you commemorating?"

"A relative who died last year. It's still early. Why don't you come and sit in my room?"

"No, no."

Song had set a rule for herself. During the whole week commemorating his death, she observed the three abstentions: refrain from visiting, refrain from participating in social events, and refrain from receiving visitors. It was for his sake. It had become a rule with her. Even now she placed him before other considerations.

But on that occasion, Song had no choice but to accept Hua Qing's offer of a ride. In the car, they had chatted a little. It was the first breaking of the taboo.

Shortly after that, Little Wang from the designers' studio came over to Song's office.

"Elder Sister Song, do me a favor. Please take a message to Hua Qing. Ask her to make some designs for wall hangings. Some Latin American companies are coming next week to place orders. You live so close. You'll spare me an errand."

"So! The designers' studio can't do without Hua Qing after all!"

"Well, before she was removed, she had been in charge of designs for export products—and her designs were always popular."

"Ask your chief designer, Mr. Yin, to talk to her!" Song said knowingly.

"Come on, Elder Sister. Surely you know what a shrew Mrs. Yin is! If she finds out, the whole designers' studio will be in trouble. Please just this once. I've never asked you for a favor before."

Little Wang went on begging with sugared words until Song finally agreed. That same evening, after cooking dinner, she called on Hua. She planned to step in, deliver her message, and leave.

Hua was just sitting down to dinner. In the middle of the carpet was a small low table. Around the table were a few rush chairs. The chairs were high-backed but set low against the carpet, Japanese style. On the table was a bowl containing a potato salad mixed with peas and sausage—a pretty pattern of white, red, and green. On another plate were pork chops and an omelet. Orange juice sparkled in a decanter.

"Oh, this is Western-style food!" Song had seen it only in movies. Her husband stuck resolutely to Chinese food, so she had never set foot in a Western-style restaurant all her life.

"Please join me. There's lots of food." Hua opened the refrigerator and began extracting more food.

"No, no, I've already done my cooking." Song glanced at the open refrigerator. It was chockful of goodies, like a magician's box. She herself only had a kitchen cabinet. Leftovers were placed in a bamboo basket strung to the rafters of the kitchen.

"Please stay. For company's sake." Hua laid another place at the table.

"All right then. I won't stand on ceremony."

Song sat down cross-legged on the low chair. Though it was an uncomfortable position, the novelty was exciting. It was a plain meal, but she savored everything slowly and carefully, enjoying every mouthful. A good part of her own life was already over, and yet all that she had ever known thus far were *his* preferences. She had never enjoyed anything for herself. And for the last few years, she had usually eaten alone, with his place laid on as usual.

They ate and chatted and Song began to relax. After sipping Hua's exquisite dragon-well tea, Song became downright talkative.

"Hua Qing, why don't you marry?"

"Aren't you living singly yourself?" Hua retorted with

a smile. There was not a trace of regret in her expression. Though nearing fifty, she was still neat and trim.

"My case is different. All my life, there was only one man for me and he is gone."

Song had spoken truly. For a year after her husband died, she couldn't bear to mention his name, even less their love. It would put her into a melancholy mood for days. Now the ice was broken.

Song and Hua chatted away. Of course, the conversation revolved around what they knew in common—the goings-on inside the bureau, all the office gossip, all the news of life within the bureau. Song had never felt so good. At work, she had gone about in the old way for several decades, congenial—but only to a certain extent, always prudently refraining from saying more than she should.

Without the two women being aware of it, the hour crept to midnight.

"My goodness! It is so late!" Song exclaimed.

Song felt deeply satisfied. But she was also surprised at herself. How had she stayed to dinner? And how had she drifted into talking so much? Back in her own apartment, as she lay on her bed, her excitement had still not died down. She continued to savor this new and pleasurable feeling. She slept soundly through the night, without being haunted by uneasy dreams, without being haunted by him either.

From a sense of duty, Song Huishan invited Hua Qing to dinner that same weekend.

Song went to market during the noon recess and bought a chicken, a fish, half a *jin* of shrimp, and a box of quail eggs. Back home after work, she busied herself for a good while, stewing, deep-frying, and stir-frying, finishing up with a platter of sticky rice with eight embellishments for dessert.

Hua Qing brought wine and they thoroughly enjoyed the meal.

"Did you really enjoy it?"

"Indeed I loved it!"

Song was pleasurably flattered. It was as good as hearing praise from her husband. "He used to say that compared to my cooking, no restaurant, however fancy, could tempt him."

"I can't cook myself," Hua said. "I eat Western style to save time and trouble. Sometimes I buy cooked meats, I just don't have the time."

Hua Qing had been reassigned to the Institute of Art and Handicraft and was again one of the top professionals. Her designs combined folk art with modern painting and had a style of its own.

"You are busy and you get results. As for me, I am also bustling about all day long at the office, but when the day is over, there is nothing to show."

"Everybody has strong points and weak points. So long as we do our best, we have done our duty."

"It is good of you to say so." It was the first time Song had expressed her sense of inferiority.

Song felt that Hua was a very considerate person, not at all the arrogant and unapproachable creature of her first impressions. As to her affair with Chief Designer Mr. Yin, that was all past and forgotten. Nobody mentioned it now.

This meal again lasted deep into the night. It was only later when Song was clearing the table that she realized she had omitted to lay *his* place. How had she forgotten? Or had she felt it unsuitable? It was the first omission in the three years since he had gone.

Thus backward and forward, the visits between 301 and 303 continued. Whenever Song cooked something special, she would have Hua over. "For company's sake," she would say. She enjoyed being needed, as she had been needed by him. The only problem was that Hua was always so busy. She would often eat at her workplace and come back late at night. Also, she was often away on business—meetings here, exhibitions there, once even a trip to Canada, carrying her own designs with her. Whenever she was away, she would leave the key with Song.

"Please keep an eye on things," she requested.

"Leave it to me."

Hua Qing's trust gave Song Huishan a sense of responsibility, filling an emotional gap. Every day she would check the gas, the electricity, and the faucets in Hua's apartment. Sometimes she would sit on the low chair and go over the sensations of her first visit. Hua was a caring person. If she was away for long, she would write Song a letter. When Song received the first letter from Hua, she was so moved her hands shook. She read it over and over again for the warmth it brought her heart. *He* was lazy with the pen. When away from home, he would never write, except for an emergency. She was so grateful for Hua's letters, storing them beneath her pillow, reading and rereading them.

Soon the busybodies at the Bureau of Textiles had another story: the two women living singly in Apartments 301 and 303 had hit it off and were like two sisters.

Two years passed. Song Huishan was fifty-five, and Hua four years younger. Everything went on as before.

The only difference was that Song's apartment was now adorned with twin sofas in woolen coverings, while a Japanese-style rug covered one side of Hua's wall from top to bottom.

The day she brought back the rug, Song was stunned. "Two thousand *yuan*! Two thousand!"

Song's own pair of sofas had cost her five hundred *yuan*. Hua had virtually made her buy them. Even after they were transported to her apartment and planted in her bedroom, Song still smarted from the drain on her finances. She kept tossing about in bed, unable to sleep. When *he* was alive, except for the purchase of old porcelain, they never had many expenses. The most expensive piece of furniture they owned was the three-compartment clothes cabinet, and that barely cost two hundred.

She got out of bed in the middle of the night and sat on one of the sofas. It was indeed very comfortable. But that only added to her sense of guilt. *He* had never enjoyed such a high-class sofa.

Hua tried to talk her out of her anxiety. "What's the use of saving all that money? The point is to enjoy life. The cost is not much, when you come to think of it."

Song was in possession of several deposit checks, adding up to five or six thousand *yuan*. Such a sum seemed considerable, but actually wouldn't go very far. Song rarely dipped into her savings. She had to think ahead to her retirement, when there wouldn't be any more bonuses, just a bare pension. If she grew infirm, she would have to use hired help. She well knew she had to put by something against a lonely old age.

When her husband was alive, she had not felt the absence of children. She still remembered the year she went from doctor to doctor, asking for help. After a group consultation, they decided she was unable to conceive. How she had cried in secret! "We might as well divorce and you can marry again," she told her husband sincerely. He refused. His sister offered them one of her own children, which he also refused. "There are thousands of childless couples," he had said. She was so grateful. She didn't know how to repay him. In fact, though, she expressed her gratitude all the time, in every detail of their daily lives. He made life full and meaningful for her. Life was like a basket immersed in water, full to the brim. But when he departed, it was as if the basket was suddenly lifted from out of the water, lying exposed in its emptiness. After he was gone, friends advised her to remarry. It was unthinkable.

Hua Qing never gave her such advice.

Sometimes they broached the subject of marriage. "Hua Qing, are you sure you'll never marry?" Song asked her friend.

"Quite."

"What about the future?"

"I'll go on as I am."

"Won't you miss something?"

"Those who marry, with home and family, are not necessarily happy. The meaning of life is not in these external forms."

"Of course, now that you're busy, you don't miss anything. But later when you retire . . ."

Hua was optimistic. "When I retire, I can still go on designing. I'll work less. You and I can go traveling together."

Song didn't believe in traveling. She had never learned to enjoy herself even in her youth, and the older she grew, the less interest she had in gadding about.

The two women never saw eye to eye on any topic. Actually, their differences grew. One day, they came close to quarreling, all because of a telegram that was delivered to Song.

"Oh, Hua Qing, what shall I do?" Song slapped down a telegram sheet on the table in exasperation. It was a telegram from her husband's sister, giving notice that her son, Song's nephew, was coming to spend a month of his summer vacation with her.

"What's the problem?" Hua inquired. "Let him come. He can keep you company."

"I don't need company! I'm perfectly happy living alone!" Song shouted angrily.

"What's come over you?" Hua could not understand her friend's attitude. This was her nephew, after all, from her husband's side, and he was only staying for the holidays.

"I'll wire back for him not to come."

"Oh, no, you shouldn't do that." Hua Qing blocked the door.

"It's my own business." Song was obstinate.

"Are you not on good terms with his sister?"

"She's doing this to spite me, sending her son over, knowing I cannot bear the sight of . . ."

Song was on the point of tears. Such a nuisance. Staying for a whole month. Where could she put up an extra bed? There was only the sitting room/study, with all her husband's antiques and porcelain standing untouched. His writing materials, his brush pen, his inkstand, his paperweight were all there on his desk in their familiar places. Even the wastepaper basket, long out of use, had not been replaced. Where could she house another person? Put him in her own bedroom? No, she was accustomed to sleeping alone. Even the presence of the pair of sofas had cost her many sleepless nights! The telegram itself had put her in such a flutter. It was unthinkable what the arrival of a big, hulking country boy would do.

"Give it a try, Elder Sister. If it doesn't work out, your nephew can come and stay with me."

"No, I won't drag you into this. It's not just a matter of a day or two."

"Oh, I don't mind. We won't be in each other's way at all. And we can have some fun together. I like young people. The young people at our school are always asking me to join them—swimming, movies, dancing, concerts." Hua insisted that Song shouldn't turn down her nephew.

"All right," Song agreed. The next day, however, she invented an excuse and sent a telegram turning down the self-invited guest.

Hua Qing didn't bring the matter up again. For several days in a row she returned to her apartment very late. Song knocked at her door in vain. On Saturday, Song made her way to Hua's institute and sat in the porter's lodge, waiting for her. Hua finally emerged after everybody else had left. Their conversation was strained.

"Haven't seen you for so long," Song began. "What's keeping you out so late?"

"I'm organizing a meeting. Putting together some material."

"I've got chicken today. I'll prepare it the way you like."

"I've still more work to do. I'm going out for a bite, and then I must come back."

Listlessly, Song Huishan turned and walked home. The chicken had been left to simmer over a low fire, but by the time she returned, it was overcooked, nevertheless. She fluttered about restlessly. She had no appetite for food. Nor was she in the mood for TV. Whenever she heard a sound on the stairs, her heart would pound. Later, lying in bed, she strained her ears for the least indication of her friend's return. But there was absolute quiet. Only at dawn, when people on morning shifts were leaving for work, did Song manage to fall asleep. Even then she was disturbed by dreams. She dreamed that a smiling Hua Qing came back with a kitten in her arms.

Song couldn't figure it out. "Why a kitten?" she asked herself.

Even less could she explain why she was so restless and why she had dreamed a dream in the first place.

The anniversary of her husband's death came around again with the arrival of autumn.

"Are you going to the cemetery tomorrow for your relative?" Song Huishan asked Hua Qing. "I have ordered a car. I've also packed lunch." This time Song had taken the initiative. She had changed. The month before, through the maneuvers of a friend, she had even acquired a refrigerator.

"Of course I'm coming," Hua Qing replied.

"What relative are you commemorating anyway?" Song was dimly aware that deep down Hua had a secret.

Hua answered vaguely—and Song dropped the subject.

222

The two of them agreed to leave early the next morning.

The cemetery, hidden behind a patch of leafy willows, was wrapped in a hallowed silence. Here and there, a few wisps of incense drifted hazily.

Song stood in front of her husband's gravestone in silent commemoration and then sat down for a while to keep him company. In front of his gravestone she placed four platters of fresh fruit, gleaming in their red-and-yellow skins. She had gone to some trouble getting them straight from the orchard and had given some to Hua.

The sun overhead, now at its zenith, sent out a pleasant warmth. It was noon, time for a snack. Song Huishan walked around the tomb, then placed her hands on the gravestone, saying softly, "I will come back in the afternoon."

She followed a footpath through a patch of wood. Suddenly she saw a familiar figure in front of her emerging from another patch of woodland. Chief Designer Yin. She couldn't be mistaken. Why was he here?

Hua Qing was waiting for her at the gate of the Commemoration Hall building. "I was hungry," she said. "But I didn't want to disturb you."

"Yes, I've stayed a bit longer. Oh, just now . . ." But Song didn't finish her sentence.

The two of them sat down before a stone table under the shade of a tree. Four stools cut out of granite felt smooth and cool to the touch. Song took out the lunch she had packed—tofu and other vegetarian food.

"Hua, is this to your taste?"

"Mmm, it's good."

"When are you leaving this afternoon?"

"I need to leave early. There's some business at the institute."

"Business." Song pondered over the word.

"Just now I saw Chief Designer Yin," she ventured, speaking slowly and looking closely at Hua.

No reaction at all, as if she had not heard.

"Hua Qing, did you see him?" Song asked point-blank.

"I saw him before you did." Hua smiled.

"Was he embarrassed?"

"What on earth for?"

"What do you mean?"

"Elder Sister Huishan, let me tell you. The relative whose death I am commemorating is no other than Mr. Yin's mother."

"His mother?" Song didn't know whether to believe it or not. And then Hua changed the subject.

But Song wanted to solve this puzzle. His mother? Then that means . . .

The two women left the cemetery at three in the afternoon, silent all the way. The driver dropped off Hua Qing at the Exhibition Center. Song poked her head out of the car window and said, "Have supper with me."

"Don't wait. I can't be back for supper."

"Business? At night?"

Song Huishan was depressed. Hua Qing's flurry of activities always made her feel, in contrast, like an unmotivated drifter. Back in her apartment, she didn't feel like cooking. Eating alone always robbed one's appetite. She sat back on the sofa, exhausted. His enlarged photograph, in black-and-white, looked down on her from the wall across. The metal frame gave out a cold light. His eyes, too, seemed to look icily on her. She decided to go out for a stroll.

Outside, dusk had descended. The crowds in the street were thinning and the street lamps were being turned on one by one. Lights illuminated the big glass panes of the shop fronts lining the street.

Song walked on slowly, as if pushed gently by a moving tide. She passed the flower-and-bird shop, the department store, the clothes store. She reached a big dry-cleaning establishment with a renovated front. The huge plate-glass windows glittered in the dusk.

She had been here the week before to leave a woolen coat, worn last year but never cleaned. She decided to see if it was ready.

Song was on the point of walking into the store when through the window she caught sight of two figures within. The outlines were blurred, but she recognized them at a glance: Hua Qing and Chief Designer Yin.

"So that's it. . . ." Song crossed the street and walked away hurriedly as if she had done something shameful and was running away from it.

She walked faster and faster. Her thoughts were in a turmoil. Past events cropped up in a whirl, obliterating the present. During those days gone by, what a beautiful creature Hua Qing had been, so handsome, so slim, gliding about silently.

Song didn't know how to explain what she suspected. She stumbled to the No. 11 bus stand and got on the bus. The bus was on a circular route, stopping at all stops, with no beginning and no end.

"So that's how it is. . . ." Song Huishan sat on a window seat of the bus, looking out of the window distractedly. A thought flashed across her mind. Should she move? Move to another apartment where she and Hua Qing need not face each other across the landing?.

The bus went on and on. Song Huishan lost track of how long she had been riding. She just sat there unmoving, with no inclination to get off.

First published in Cultural Encounters, *Wen Hui Yue Kan,* *1987. Translated at the University of Kent at Canterbury, July 1989.*

LOST IN THE WIND
AND THE SNOW

NIU ZHENGHUAN

*NIU ZHENGHUAN, born in 1950, was a Ping Pong cham-
pion in her native Gansu province in northwest China before her
athletic career was interrupted by the Cultural Revolution. After
various jobs in cultural affairs, she graduated from a writers' training course in Wuhan University and is now a teacher of expository
writing in the Lanzhou Trade Institute, while she keeps writing
and publishing steadily in her spare time.*

*The much-anthologized short story "Lost in the Wind and the
Snow," her first work, describes the sale of women during the famine
of the Sixties. The recurrence of this phenomenon in the Eighties—
for reasons other than famine—brings the theme up to date. Note how
women are never addressed directly but only in relation to the males
(husband, son, brother) and how this affects the telling of the story.*

Jin Niu's wife sat on the adobe platform bed, sewing on
the sole of a shoe for her husband. Jin Niu himself squatted
on the floor, whittling at the handle of a hoe. His wife
remarked that she would like to go to her native village
during this slack period to visit her family. "I will come
back in time for the New Year," she promised.

Jin Niu demurred. "Yes," he said, "the work in the
fields is over, but there is so much to be done in the house—

wheat to grind for the New Year, vegetables to store up for the winter.

"Can't you do some grinding when I'm gone?" his wife asked. "As to vegetables, I've stocked up a lot. The dried peas and eggplants are at the top of the chest, the salted peppers and celery at the bottom of the jar, the pickled cabbages in the big clay container, and there are two strings of red pepper hanging under the eaves. Besides, there are several dozen heads of fresh cabbage. You and Pillar and your father will have plenty to eat. There's enough to last the three of you through the winter."

"What do you mean, the *three* of us?" Jin Niu shouted. "Aren't you coming back?"

His wife's heart gave a thump. "Who said anything about not coming back? I'll be back for New Year, and the first crop of vegetables will be up by then."

Jin Niu devised a fresh objection. "All the children hereabouts receive new clothes for New Year. If you leave, our Pillar will be in his old clothes."

The wife reached over to the little cupboard on the platform bed. She took out a bundle wrapped in a piece of cloth, opened it, and showed it to her husband. "They are all here. Padded jacket, padded pants, overalls, new shoes, the hat which you bought last time you were at market. Pillar's shoes wear out so quickly, I'm going to sew him another pair when I finish this."

Jin Niu had nothing more to say. "All right, then, when are you leaving?"

"Tomorrow, I think." And thus the matter was settled.

Having secured her husband's permission, the wife immediately set about to get ready. She spent the whole day putting the house in order. Then she went to Second Aunt next door and asked her to keep an eye on her household while she was away. Then she came back to cook supper. By the time supper was ready, the lamp had to be lit.

Her father-in-law took out a bundle of tobacco leaves, his own produce. "Take them with you, a present for my in-laws, though we have not yet met. Tell them to come for a visit when times are better so that we can get acquainted with each other, and Pillar will see his maternal grandfather."

Pillar howled. He wanted to go with his mother.

Jin Niu said not a word throughout supper, but kept his eyes on his bowl. Now he picked up his son and said, "You grow up quick and then we will *all* go together to visit your mother's family." But Pillar was not taken in and still cried for his mother. To quiet him down, Jin Niu promised to take him to the railway station the next morning.

Jin Niu was reluctant to let his wife go. Her absence, he felt, would create hardships. She had come to this part of the country four years ago and settled with him. Since then, his whole life had changed. Every morning before he set out to work, a bowl of hot soup and two steamed buns would be at the top of the trunk over the platform bed within easy reach. When he came home from work in winter, she would hand him a bowl of steaming noodles. In summer a big basin of mung-bean soup would be cooling on the kitchen table. She was a filial daughter-in-law. The old man's teeth were bad, and for him she would make special pancakes, soft and thin. She would buy pieces of rock sugar and boil it with pears to relieve his cough in winter, a treat that not even Pillar was allowed to share.

To Jin Niu, who had lost his mother when young and

only managed to get married at the ripe age of thirty, this wife was so important. He couldn't do without her for a single moment. Their son was three years old already, and throughout these three years she had cared single-handedly for him. To think of all the times Pillar wet himself and soiled himself and his endless needs by day and night. When he was in the mood, Jin Niu would buy Pillar a handful of candy or plait him a grasshopper cage. But now that his wife was going, could he handle everything?

His wife came from the upper reaches of the Wei River, from neighboring Gansu province. She had arrived on a day in spring, during the famine of 1960. Jin Niu had come back from the fields to find a crowd under the willow tree at the end of the village. He went up and saw a young woman sitting on the stone under the tree. She was in her early twenties, poorly dressed but clean. Her eyes were dull and her face had that grayish undernourished look. A little bundle wrapped in a checkered cotton scarf held some old clothes, which showed through the edges of the scarf.

Behind her, a slightly older man leaned against the tree. "We are from upriver," the man explained. "We have been starving for a year. We dug wild herbs. Now they're all gone. We peeled the barks of trees, and that's all gone, too. Everybody who can move has run away. Now that we're out, we don't have the strength to walk back. This is my sister. She is too worn to move another step. Is there a good-hearted person here who would take her in? That would be storing up a good deed in this life toward the next."

Two big tears ran down the woman's face and dropped on her shoes. The people around her sighed for pity. "Poor girl, so young," said one of the villagers.

Second Aunt signaled Jin Niu with her eyes. Away from the crowd, she whispered, "Keep her. She's good-looking. And coming from another province, she won't cost you much in bridal money."

"But Aunty," Jin Niu reasoned, "that would be taking advantage." He turned to go, but Aunty held him back.

"Now who has ever seen the likes of you," she asked, "thirty already and talking such nonsense? Don't you hear her brother saying that this is doing a good deed?"

Just then, the man's voice was heard again. "If we go back, we starve and die. Please, someone keep her. At least she will live. She is very capable."

Jin Niu considered a moment and made up his mind. "All right, Aunty. You go and talk to them."

Through the good offices of Second Aunt, Jin Niu took in the young woman as his wife. That same day, the brother and sister were accommodated in a side room of their house while Jin Niu stayed with his old father in the main room. According to local custom, bridal money was mandatory, even for a girl who was running away from starvation. Jin Niu's father fumbled at the bottom of his trunk and counted out two hundred *yuan*. He handed the money to Second Aunt and asked her to present it to the girl's brother as bridal money, all formal and proper—and asked her to select an auspicious day on which to hold a wedding feast and entertain family and friends. Second Aunt was gone but a moment before she returned, followed by the man.

Nothing would induce him to take the money. They were running away from famine, he said. All he wanted was to see his sister safely settled. There was nothing to buy anyway. If they insisted on a bridal gift, he would accept some grain. He could use it to save lives. Father and son could not prevail against him and finally made him a present of a sackful of grain.

Jin Niu invited him to stay for the wedding feast and give away his sister in marriage. But he insisted on leaving immediately. To save the rest of his family from starvation, he said.

Jin Niu and the young woman saw him off. At the edge of the village where stood the big willow tree, the man shouldered the bag of grain that Jin Niu had been carrying and bade them go back. The young woman cried piteously.

The man seemed debilitated from hunger and bowed down under the weight of the grain. He said to the young woman, avoiding looking at her directly, "Sister, you stay here. I'll come and see you when I can. He is a good man." He pointed to Jin Niu and dabbed at his own face to wipe away the sweat—or perhaps tears. And then he walked away. His sister leaned against the tree and cried in despair.

Jin Niu looked on helplessly. He had never been in close contact with a woman before, much less a woman awash in tears. Finally he spoke to her. "If you really want, you can collect your belongings and follow him." But she just stood there and continued weeping. It was Second Aunt who caught up with them and saved the situation. At last, with a little persuasion and a little prodding, she got the young woman back to Jin Niu's house.

One year later, a fat baby boy was born to Jin Niu. For two generations running, the family line had been handed down through single male issue. Thus the boy was named Pillar, to hold up the line. Only then did people stop calling the woman Younger Sister. She became known as Pillar's mother.

Pillar was three years old and his mother had never

returned to her native village for a visit. She never expressed the wish to her husband. Her brother, now known as Pillar's uncle, had visited several times. Every time he came, Jin Niu would give him forty or fifty *yuan*—derived from selling grain—and also a hundred *jin* or so of wheat to carry back. Every time she had to part with her brother, Jin Niu's wife was immensely sad. Her brother always tried to ease her heart by assuring her that everything was all right back home—and that she was always welcome for a visit.

Jin Niu should have taken his wife to visit his in-laws according to custom. But the expense of the marriage and then the birth of their son, coupled with the dip into their savings from the brother's frequent visits, made for difficulties. The family was living from hand to mouth. A train ride for the two of them to neighboring Gansu province would cost Jin Niu at least fifty *yuan* both ways, not to mention gifts that were indispensable for such a visit.

Jin Niu lay on the heated platform bed but couldn't sleep. He looked at his wife sewing new shoes for their son. "Pillar's mom," he called to her.

"Um, you sleep. I want to finish sewing on these two pairs of shoes for Pillar. The soles are already done."

"Are you really leaving tomorrow?"

"Um."

"Don't go. After the wheat harvest next summer, let's take Pillar and make a family visit together."

She stopped the work in her hands. "Didn't you give your permission this morning?"

"Well . . ." Jin Niu started, but he had nothing to say. He suddenly sat up in bed and began putting on his clothes.

"What are you doing?" his wife asked him.

233

"Go if your mind is made up. I'll borrow some cash from Second Aunt for you to take on your journey. Also, there's still some wheat from our private plot. I'll pack it for you to carry."

She forbade him to borrow money, saying her family had used up enough of his money over the years. All she wanted was to return to her native village and have a look. "Where are our eggs?" he asked.

"There." She pointed to a corner of the wall. "Are you hungry?"

"Um."

"Let me make you some poached eggs."

"No, no, you go on with the sewing. I've got nothing to do anyway."

Jin Niu took a handful of eggs and started a fire. His wife went on with her sewing. The room was quiet except for the crackling of the wheat stalks in the fire. Jin Niu divided his attention between the eggs boiling in the pot and the needle and thread in his wife's fingers, looking from one to the other. His wife's brow contracted as she concentrated on her work. She finished one shoe and measured it against the foot of her son sleeping on the bed. She hastily dashed away the tears filling her eyes.

The couple was always spare of words. Actually, today, they had talked much more than usual. But Jin Niu cared dearly for his mate. Those eggs in the pot were for her to take on the road. Jin Niu had no complaint against her at all, except that she spoke so little and rarely laughed. At first, Jin Niu thought that she missed her native home. Later he accepted it as part of her temperament, which was quite similar to his own, he felt. Now seeing her distressed, he feared that one of his earlier remarks had hurt her. So he said clumsily, "Don't tire yourself out. Remember you are traveling tomorrow. You can always finish it when you come back."

She sighed. "I'm going. Take good care of our baby. Protect him. Don't let the other boys bully him."

"Sure."

"He is still so small. Don't hit him if he does anything wrong."

"What are you talking about? How can I bear to hit him?"

Silence. Jin Niu finished boiling the eggs. Seeing that she was still at work, he gently took away her sewing. "Come to bed. You are worn out." He put out the light and took her to bed.

The next morning, Jin Niu accompanied his wife to the train station, carrying Pillar on his back. The woman took with her a little bundle wrapped in a checkered cotton scarf, the same scarf she had carried with her four years before. It held her old clothes and her father-in-law's present of tobacco leaves.

Babbling all the way, Pillar alternately perched on his father's back and nestled in his mother's arms. It took them a good three hours to reach the railway station. As soon as they arrived Jin Niu left his wife and son and went to the ticket office.

The train had just pulled in. Pillar was in his mother's arms. She backed away as she saw the train make ready to depart after a brief stop.

"Mom, your train is leaving," Pillar said.

"If your father doesn't make it back in time, then I won't go."

Just then, Jin Niu rushed over and pressed the ticket

into her hands. He helped her up onto the train, which had started moving.

She held on to the handle of the door and turned back. "Pillar," she shouted, "be a good son to your father!"

Jin Niu, who was holding the child, cried, "Quick, Pillar. Tell Mommy to come back soon!"

She just managed to catch Pillar's infant voice before the train gathered speed. The tears ran down her face and she pressed against the window for a last look. Pillar was in his father's arms waving his little hands.

She walked through several compartments without finding a seat, so she found a space by the door and sat on her own bundle. After a few stops, the train reached the provincial center of Xian, where nearly everybody got off. She found a seat in the nearly empty train before it filled again with passengers. The train started moving again and she turned her face to the window, not wishing to be recognized by any chance.

The trees along the side of the rail tracks had shed their leaves and stood stark and bare. The train moved so fast, the trees fell away one by one in quick succession, while more and more rose to view. They were like the question that kept turning up in her mind and would not go away: *I am going—but have I treated him fairly?* She could not find an answer. She took her eyes away from the trees and looked beyond toward the great expanse of wheat fields.

Planted in the fall, the wheat was now two or three inches high. Looking at the tender sprouts of wheat that would soon have to go through the rigor of winter, she thought of Pillar: *I am sowing evil everywhere. Pillar is also a little sprout. How can he survive without his mother?*

She seemed to hear Pillar crying, "Mommy, Mommy."
No, it is not Pillar. It's another boy's cry, also calling,
"Mommy, Mommy." It is Lock's voice of four years ago.
It is Lock, whimpering and wiping his wasted little face
with his dirty hands. She felt as if she were holding him in
her arms again, sitting under the sunlight of early spring,
weak with hunger. "Hungry, Mommy. . . . "

The child's cry tore at her heart as he tugged at her
flabby nipples. Crying, the child fell asleep. Her husband
came back, carrying pieces of bark and some firewood in
the basket on his back. He took down the basket and gazed
at Lock. "Has he eaten anything?" he asked her.

"No," she said in a weak whisper.

He walked into the room and came out with a coarse
clay pot: "Let me see if they are dispensing gruel today."

"What's the use of going. There's not a single drop of
grain around, not for months. Who can expect any gruel?
Except the leaders, of course. And the bookkeeper. And
the cook."

With the Great Leap Forward movement to make iron
on a national scale, all private cooking utensils were forci-
bly taken away and melted down. The whole village was
made to eat in the commune kitchen. Since the previous
winter, the kitchen was only able to provide thin gruel,
and now not even gruel.

"Then what shall we do? I've only found this bit of
bark. How can baby eat this?" They looked at each other
under the sunlight of the early spring.

After a long silence, she finally spoke with an effort. "I
will go to Shaanxi. It is the only way to keep alive."

He was not sure he heard her. "*What* did you say?"

This time she sounded more determined. "I will go to Shaanxi."

He squatted down limply and stared at the empty pot in his hands. She wetted a finger and gingerly wiped away the tears from the face of the child sleeping at her breast. "Everybody is going to Shaanxi," she continued. "How can we stay here to starve? Lock is barely two years old."

His eyes moved to the child, who was crying fitfully in his sleep. He seemed to make up his mind. "Yes, I suppose there is no choice. I'll see you on the way."

Hearing him acquiesce, she, however, began to waver. "*If* I go, it will mean finding someone else. Can you manage . . ."

He sat there like a stone. After a while, she said tearfully, "I'd die willingly, if I can save this family. After I go, just think of me as dead. When things get better, get somebody else, so long as she treats Lock right."

He only sighed and said, "If it is decided, you should leave as early as possible. The important thing is to stay alive. You'd better leave tomorrow. When we get to Shaanxi, let's say that we are brother and sister."

They now entered Gansu territory, and the train went in and out of tunnels drilled through the mountains. Between intervals, she could see the rural landscape with beautiful clear skies, unending stretches of yellow earth, and the sluggish waters of the Wei River. Waves of inexpressible longing swept over her as she looked on the familiar scenes of her native land.

Gradually she dozed off and was pursued by dreams. In her reverie she saw her home downriver. Jin Niu was trying to snatch the bundle in her hand. "How can you cheat me?" he demanded. "How can you leave Pillar and me?" And she cried as she tried to snatch back her bundle. Sometimes her dreams carried her upriver to her old home. She stretched out her hand to take Lock, but Lock resisted her embrace and backed away from her in fright. She pursued him saying, "Lock, Lock, I am your mother. . . . "

She woke up with a fright. She looked out of the window and saw the familiar scenes of her home county. The craggy mountains in the distance, the turbulent waters of the Wei River dividing the plains into north and south. Her home was on the south bank. The wooden building was the mill, the landmark of her village. Her eyes were suffused with tears.

The twenty-third of the last month of the old year, known as the mini–New Year, had passed. Still there was no sign of his wife. All the neighboring families were busy killing pigs, making steamed buns, frying pancakes. It was two months since she had gone, and Pillar clamored for his mother all the time. Jin Niu put together a hasty meal just as he used to do in the old days when there was just him and his father.

On the eve of New Year, Second Aunt came over and made them some stuffed dumplings. Jin Niu offered the first bowl to his father. Pillar threw a tantrum and refused to get out of bed, so Jin Niu took a bowl of dumplings to him and the boy gobbled it down in one breath just to spite the adults. Jin Niu had no appetite.

He mused to himself: *She promised to return in a few days. It is two months and no sign of her. No letter. What has happened? Has she fallen ill? Did the train overturn? An accident on the way?*

The minute these thoughts occurred to him, Jin Niu

was on pins and needles. He deeply regretted not going with her. *It's all my fault, thinking only of money. What shall I do if something happened to her?* On the third day of the New Year, after he had visited his mother's grave, he told his father that he was going to fetch his wife.

Lock's mother was in the kitchen preparing food. This was the first New Year after their reunion, and friends and relatives were coming over to eat, drink, and celebrate. She was cutting cooked meat and carrots. Her husband came in and tapped her on the back. "Arrived!" he whispered. "So what if they've arrived," she said without raising her head. "No need to be so tense. I'll be ready in a minute."

"No, it's *him*!" her husband exclaimed.

She sensed something unusual in his tone. "Who?"

"*Him*. Pillar's father!"

In the shock of hearing the news, she cut her finger and the blood gushed profusely. Her husband was alarmed and squeezed her wounded finger to stop the bleeding, but she had no time for the cut. "What . . . what shall we do?"

"Take care of your hand first."

Lock's mother wrapped her finger as she asked, "Have you seen him?"

"Yes, he ran straight into me, in there." He signaled toward the north room. "I told him you were busy in the kitchen and that I'd let you know."

"But what shall we do?"

"Give him some food first. Then we'll make him feel at home."

She followed him out of the kitchen and entered the north room.

The first thing that Jin Niu noticed about his wife was

that she had put on weight. The curves of her figure stood out nicely. Her complexion was also improved; there was a look in her eyes and an air about her that made her a different person. Though for some reason, she looked at him without expression. She avoided looking him directly in the eye. She just stood there rubbing her hands together. "Didn't expect you," she said in a low tone.

"I was worried, so I came," Jin Niu said affectionately.

She merely lowered her head. "I thought perhaps I might as well stay over the New Year and go back later. . . ." She was guilty about the lie and could not go on.

Jin Niu imagined that her constraint arose from fear of his displeasure, so he reassured her. "Come to think of it, you have not spent New Year with your own family for several years now. You were right to stay a while longer. It's just that I was worried, not having heard from you. So here I am."

Lock's mother didn't know what to say. Her husband came and saved the situation. "Well, it's good to have you here with us. Such a rare occasion." Then turning to his wife, he added, "Why don't you light the charcoal burner for *gu fu* to warm up?" *Gu fu* was a familiar form of address for the husband of one's sister while impersonating one's own child. "We can then offer him some tea."

Before long, the friends and relatives began to arrive. Lock's father served up the food and urged everybody to eat. The first glass of wine was offered to the visitor from afar and Jin Niu could not refuse. Then the other guests followed one upon another, offering to drink with him, and he could not refuse them either. Seeing his wife—as he thought—safe and well, his tension was relieved and he found himself ravenously hungry. He ate and drank without restraint and was soon overcome. Lock's father led him to a spare room and left him to sleep it off.

Jin Niu wanted to ask when his wife would join him, then thought the better of it. She must still be in the kitchen, he figured. He fell asleep the minute his head hit the pillow.

After a fitful sleep, he woke feeling ill and fumbled for a lamp. He felt a wave of nausea and threw up all the food and drink. He then did as all country people do; he lifted one edge of the bed matting to look for a piece of paper to wipe away the mess. As he was fumbling he came across a photograph of his son's mother and the man she called her brother. They were sitting side by side; on the picture were printed these words: IN MEMORY OF OUR WEDDING. He thought he had made a mistake, so he took a closer look. No mistake. It was the two of them, only looking much younger. He was stunned, overwhelmed with a feeling of being cheated. "I must get this cleared up," he said to himself.

He threw his clothes over himself without bothering to button them up. Then he opened the door. As a cold gust of wind hit him he shivered and was completely awake. It was the dead of night. The north wind clattered through the bare branches of the trees; it had begun to snow. He closed the door and went back to the platform bed. The charcoal in the burner gave a steady blue glow. He sat down and was lost in thought.

All through the night he racked his brains as perverse ideas cropped up in his head and clashed with each other. The charcoal in the burner had long been reduced to ashes. In the distance a cock crowed.

Jin Niu stood up and stamped his feet, which were

numb with cold. He buttoned his jacket and went out into the courtyard.

Jin Niu knocked hard at the west door.

"Who is it? What do you want?" the woman's voice asked from within as she cracked open the door. Jin Niu pushed her aside angrily and stepped into the middle of the room. While the woman was opening the door Lock's father had descended from the platform bed and lighted the lamp. He clasped Jin Niu's hand, still calling him *gu fu*, as if addressing his sister's husband. Jin Niu shook off his hold roughly. "Cheat! You have the face to call me *that*!"

Lock's father and mother clung to him, each holding on to one of his arms. They made him sit on the bed. "Please do not be angry," Lock's father continued, but did not know how to go on. Then he regained his presence of mind, first of all changing the form of address. "Elder Brother, please listen. At the time, there was really no way out for us. We acted in that way just to keep alive." He began to weep soundlessly.

Lock's mother broke down. "It's all my fault! If I could just die, everything would be solved. Why don't the heavens strike me down with sudden death?"

Her cries woke Lock, who was sleeping on the platform bed. The child woke up frightened. He sprang out of his ragged bedroll. "Mama, mama!" he wailed.

Jin Niu, sitting on the edge of the bed, put out a hand and helped the boy back into his bedroll. His hand hit a cold damp adobe surface. There were no bedding underneath. A wave of pity overtook him. All the words of recrimination that he had prepared through the night forsook him. For a moment he was dumbfounded.

Lock's mother continued to weep in gasps while her

husband looked at Jin Niu pleadingly. "Please forgive us, Elder Brother. We are not thieves and cheats. We were desperate. At the time, all other ways to keep alive were cut off. Is there a man who would willingly exchange his wife for a sack of grain?"

Jin Niu had never imagined the situation would turn out like this. He had been prepared for words and blows. But this couple stood before him like a pair of lambs, asking him for pity, for mercy, for forgiveness. He lost all his former resolve and did not know how to act. Suddenly he gave a hoarse laugh. "Ha! What am I doing here? Ha! Ha! Ha!" Two rows of tears stole down the corners of his eyes.

The couple continued to plead for forgiveness. "We will forever be in your debt," said Lock's father, "and our child after us."

Jin Niu gave a deep sigh and stood up. "It is time for me to go."

"Go?" exclaimed Lock's mother. "Now?"

"What do I have to stay for?" he answered quietly.

Seeing that his mind was made up, Lock's father told his wife to prepare some food for Jin Niu to take with him on his way back. He took the padded jacket off his own back and put it over Jin Niu's shoulders, but Jin Niu shook it off. Lock's mother took out the cotton bag that Jin Niu had used to hold the eggs he cooked for her on her last trip. She filled it with steamed buns of white flour. Jin Niu slung the bag over his shoulder and left without a word.

Jin Niu made his way slowly to the railway station. His head was numb and empty. What had happened, after all? He had fits of dizziness and nausea as he tried to review the events of the previous night.

The train station was deserted. There was no one in

sight, neither on the platform nor in the waiting room. Snow covered the tracks and the fields beyond. He was alone in a cold white world. He shivered and went into the waiting room and crouched over a seat, his teeth chattering, his back chilly—as if he had been doused with a bucket of water. His heart contracted painfully with the cold.

"Anybody going east?" a voice behind the window of the ticket office asked. Before Jin Niu had time to get up, the window was slammed down.

A train rumbled from afar and approached slowly. The sounds seemed to rumble in his own head.

Jin Niu remained where he was, feeling sometimes clearheaded, sometimes in a daze. Four more trains heading east came and went, but he did not get on any of them.

He did not want to leave just like that. On the other hand, he didn't know exactly *what* he wanted.

The day came to an end and night descended. Jin Niu could see by the light of the snow. He wanted a full explanation. Somehow or other, he found himself again at Lock's house. He raised his hand to the door.

He needed her. Pillar needed his mother.

His hand was poised, but at the last moment Jin Niu did not knock at the door. He turned and walked away. *He* needed her, yes, but Lock needed her, too.

The snow had now become heavy, descending in cascades, and the wind was piercingly cold. Jin Niu dragged his feet wearily in the wind and the snow with nothing particular in mind.

First published in Gansu Literature and Art, *No. 2, 1980. Translation completed at the Bunting Institute, Radcliffe-Harvard, January 1991.*

SILENT

COMMEMORATION

WEN BIN

WEN BIN joined the Communist Revolution in 1949, when she was barely seventeen and worked for the newspaper of the People's Liberation Army. Later she transferred to the Xinhua News Agency and then went on to study literature at the Northwest University in Xian. She began writing and publishing after the Cultural Revolution and is now engaged in a major work based on the anti-Japanese war.

"Silent Commemoration" has been variously interpreted. The center of the story is not the daughters' regret and silent commemoration of their mother, as is generally assumed, but the fact that even as the children mourn her they can only think in terms of clichés.

It is a reversed generation gap: the illiterate old woman's innate yearning for beauty and love are beyond the mental capacity of her daughters, in spite of—or because of—their ostensibly superior upbringing.

Moon festival. The first moon festival after ten years of turmoil. I gaze on the moon, listening to the rustle of the wind. Thoughts of the loved one, lost to me forever, send icy shivers through my heart.

For the last few years, whenever I find a quiet moment

to myself, the image of my mother, who died on a moon festival, rises up before me. Her slight form, her wan looks, her desolate life haunt my thoughts. Quietly she came into the world, quietly she left. . . .

There is an old saying: "It takes mothering to understand a mother." Perhaps that is why, now that age has crept up on me and I have raised a couple of children myself and seen something of the world, only now do I begin to understand what I should have known all along. The thought of this is an inexpressible torment. Why is it that one must spend a lifetime and pay the price in tears and blood, just to earn a slice of common sense?

Mother has been departed from this life for over ten years. I keep intending for us, her children, to go as a group to honor her grave. But we were all scattered. (And then there were the ten years of turmoil!) So this heartfelt wish has never been materialized. Not one among her daughters has gone to add a handful of new earth to her grave. It has lain deserted through the years, probably overrun with weeds. If she has any feelings where she is lying under the earth, how she must long for her daughters! And we, her daughters, how can we ever be forgiven?

At the time when I left home, Mother was still in her thirties. Of medium height, she was always dressed in dark blue or black; her gowns, though old and worn, were always scrupulously clean. Her black hair was combed back and tucked in a big bun at the back of her head. She always tried to look middle-aged, or even older. But vintage clothes and the bun at the back of her head could not hide her beauty and vitality. Of course, poverty and misfortunes had robbed her of the freshness of youth. But her features were delicate as ivory. On top of that her long eyelashes and her clear, limpid eyes, sensitive and mournful in expression, made her a real beauty. Her beauty was introverted; it was like a little brook in the depth of the woods. It only revealed itself slowly, trickling through her everyday words and deeds.

When I was a child, I loved to help Mother wash her hair. Her hair would fill the basin. It was long, soft, and gleaming. I would flutter around her, seize her thick hair, and try to submerge it in the basin of water, which could hardly hold it all. Mother would complain of this head of hair. It was such a burden, a misfortune even. Though not in my opinion. After it was washed, her hair would lie on her shoulders in a shining mass, the ends curling up softly. How beautiful it was—just like a picture!

But Mother, so young and beautiful, was already by then in her eighth year of widowhood.

Another old saying: "A woman's beauty carries with it her tragic fate." That was what people would say about my mother. My father's family was not very well off. He had married young, but his wife had never given birth to sons. My grandmother was concerned that the line of the Wang family would be broken, so they decided to secure a concubine for his son. In the old society, nothing was easy—nothing, that is, except acquiring a woman. That was cheap and easy. Mother was a country girl bought by the Wang family to procure sons. At the time she was just fifteen.

The vagaries of life are strange indeed. The more you long for something, the more it will elude you. Mother gave birth to eight girls in quick succession, though only five survived. Three of her babies were either dumped into a pail of water to drown or held by their legs and flung out into the wilderness. A concubine was among the lowest of the low. Add to that the fact that she had only produced girls. Mother literally staggered under her burden of guilt and disgrace.

It was the custom in our locality for women in childbirth to sit round the clock. According to local belief, the blood emitted in childbirth was contaminated. Even ghosts would be affected if they were splashed with it, so women had to be drained of this blood during childbirth. Before the birth, all the bedclothes on the *kang* would be removed; the *kang* would then be spread with a thick layer of ashes, and a bundle of straw would be thrown over the ashes. And that was where the birth took place. After the child was born, the mother was not allowed to lie down, but made to sit round the clock starting from the moment of giving birth. If one round did not drain her, she would have to sit through another twenty-four hours. In some cases, the mother hemorrhaged to death.

I still remember the birth of my little sister. Members of the family spread some ashes on the *kang* and then cast down some moldy hay. Crickets and other insects were skipping in and out of it. Mother dreaded these pests; now she had no choice but to sit over them. I remember how her blood had soaked the ashes and the hay. Her face was ghastly pale while beads of sweat stood on her brow. She sat against the wall; sometimes she would slip down but would immediately be jerked back into a sitting position. She was in such pain, but because she had again given birth to a girl, the whole family turned against her, some cursing, some gnashing their teeth. The room where she had given birth seemed to be under a curse. Men would go out of their way to avoid it. Some poured water over the threshold to exorcise the evil spirits. The women, too, would not go near her, afraid of catching the curse. Mother would go pale and relive that horror whenever childbirth was mentioned. She once said that all of her daughters were paid for by her blood.

A woman who could only give birth to girls had no place in the scheme of existence. She worked day and night and was the most downtrodden of women. Having no son, she suffered acutely in the company of women who boasted sons. She was a bundle of quivering pain and guilt.

To this day, I cannot understand my father. He was a technician. He should have been somewhat enlightened. Surprisingly, he took the job of carrying on the family line very seriously. To all the daughters he brought into the world, he never paid the slightest attention. To us he was a stranger. He died suddenly when he was barely forty. My grandmother died one year before my father. With her dying breath, she bemoaned the fate that deprived her of a grandson.

Mother was wild with grief at Father's death. She wanted to lie down and die. But all those children tugged at her heart, so she had to go on living. It was hard.

When we were all in the throes of grief, a distant cousin on my father's side, turned up. He had been well-to-do, but had squandered everything on opium. Now this degenerate scarecrow of an elder decided to camp on our doorstep. Mother rebuffed him, saying, "Living or dead, we are nothing to you!" The opium fiend left in a huff, saying as a parting shot: "Well, chastity is a widow's duty. See that you remember that!"

At the end of her resources, Mother sold off one room of our house and bought an old mule. With that and a gristmill, she began grinding wheat to keep us fed and clothed. The deadly monotonous grind of the mill and the weary tap of the mule as it made its rounds—these were the sounds that greeted us children as we got up in the morning and sent us to sleep as we lay in bed at night. From dawn to nightfall, mother sat in the dark little grinding room, her bound feet stepping on the springs of the flour sifter. Her body always seemed to be enveloped in a cloud of flour dust. My baby sister lay on the cold floor of the grinding room, seriously ill, but Mother could not even find time to hold her.

Then in the silence of the night, under the dim light of an oil lamp, Mother would do sewing for hire. Wedding clothes, burial clothes—she did everything. On the fifteenth of the lunar New Year, she would make fancy lamps. And for the Dragon Boat Festival on the fifth day of the fifth moon, she would sew and embroider all kinds of fancy purses on order. Never was she idle, not even for a night. She coughed more and more, and then began to spit blood. People said Mother was consumptive. But in my eyes, it seemed her energies were inexhaustible. Her movements were so deft, her hands so nimble.

Year in, year out, she would sit in the same place under the dim light, head bowed, working away. I would gaze at Mother's shadow against the wall and lose all sense of time. She was so beautiful, so moving. Whether doing embroidery or making paper lamps, she was always so intent, losing herself in the work. In embroidery, she drew the thread with such loving care, and whenever she finished a flower or a bird, she would hold it up for a last close inspection, and then I could see her long, fluttering eyelashes. At those moments, it seemed that she was enthralled by her own art. Whatever Mother did, she threw her entire being into it; everything she created with her hands vibrated with life. I was often lost in wonder at Mother's embroidered flowers, which seemed to drip with dew, and her butterflies, which seemed to dance in her hands, and the gracious and elegant long-stemmed blades of grass and bamboo shoots. One and all, they always fired my imagination with a sense of the goodness of life.

When the yearly festivals came around, Mother would always contrive to make new shoes for us, no matter how poor we were. The embroidered designs on our shoes were never repeated from one year to the next. During the festival days, when we walked along the streets in our new shoes and accepted the surprised delight of onlookers, we were so happy and proud.

Mother's life was indeed full of sorrow and hardship, but with her own two hands she created joy and beauty for her children and for the people around her. That might have been some compensation for her—and given her heart some comfort.

The lunar New Year festival came around, a festival full of rejoicing for the rich but such a grievous trial for the poor.

On New Year's Eve, Mother grabbed us to wash our hair as usual. She also got hold of two big turnips, which she sliced and boiled, making us share. She beamed as she said, "Boiled turnips are so delicious, and good for you, too." But her smile could not conceal her sorrow—or our situation. We knew that we were completely destitute.

In her despair, Mother suddenly remembered that a

trader in the city had once borrowed from Father a small sum that was never returned. She thought if she could retrieve the money, it could keep us going for a while. Mother took me with her to call on the fat wife of the trader. The woman ignored the question of the debt but looked Mother up and down saying how young she was, how attractive, how *beautiful*. Screwing up her eyes to inspect Mother, she said that her husband was looking for a second concubine. "One's fate is predestined," she said. "Why don't you give away the younger children and bring along your two eldest and be the second concubine? You'll never want for food and drink. Isn't that better than struggling for yourself?" The end of the affair was that Mother fled in tears without collecting a cent of the debt. On her return home she collapsed and had to spend several days in bed.

On the third day of the New Year, my little sister was brought down by hunger and disease. She lay on the *kang* dying while we watched helplessly. Just then, a neighbor child brought in a man who was apparently looking for Mother.

A peasant stood in the doorway, tall and broad-shouldered. He was dressed in coarse homespun cloth, a blue turban, cotton stockings, and hemp shoes. A pair of shining eyes twinkled in his bronze face. You could tell at a glance that he was kind and trustworthy. He carried a bamboo basket on his back and a cloth container over his arm.

"Elder sister," he said, addressing Mother, "do you remember me? I am the fifth son of the Sun family."

Tears cascaded down Mother's cheeks as she heard his voice. She couldn't speak a word, forgot even to ask him to step inside. A full minute passed before she recovered herself. Then, sending us off to boil water, she bustled about arranging stools. In the presence of an old acquaintance from her home village, who turned up just when she was absolutely at the dead end, Mother could not find words to express herself. She just kept wiping the tears from her eyes.

Mother told us our guest was from her home village—a distant relative of her own family. They had grown up together, she said, and we should call him uncle.

Uncle brought us local products from Mother's village: oat flour, gingko fruit, apricot kernels. He also presented her toys plaited out of grass: deer, horses, lambs, and floral bouquets.

Mother let the tears fall as she handled the familiar objects. "You still remember," she murmured, "after so many years."

"How can I forget!" Uncle said. "These were your favorite toys when you were a child!"

My little sister grabbed at the toys, but Mother said they were plaited by Uncle's own hands and mustn't be spoiled. She carefully pinned them on the wall.

Uncle's arrival brought joy and color into our life. Mother seemed to grow younger. She used the flour Uncle brought to make steamed bread. She made the loaves in a variety of shapes and designs: squirrels, roosting birds, phoenixes opening their wings. As she looked at the domestic treasures from her village Mother's thoughts must have reverted to her innocent and carefree childhood, to her own family and the scenes of her native village.

The fifteenth of the lunar New Year was at hand. This holiday was also the Lamp Festival. Every year during the

Lamp Festival, Mother would be hired to make dozens of lamps. Among the sea of lamps on display, many—crane lamps, lion lamps, lotus lamps—were her handiwork. In our little town Mother made quite a name for herself in lamp making.

This time we did not need to beg and wheedle. Mother collected some of the material left over from the lamps she had made and constructed several lamps for us children. She made them very fancy, especially the rabbit lamp.

As she bent over her work, she sang: " 'Long are the rivers, high are the hills. My home is in the valley of ten thousand flowers. In the valley of flowers, birds abound, old and young sing mountain songs. Sing in the morning and laugh with the sun, sing in the evening and dance with the stars. Sing at morn and sing at eve. The mountains and the rivers will rejoice . . . .' "

That was the first time I remember hearing Mother sing. Her voice was low and melancholy, filled with longing for her childhood home and friends. I sat in the shade and watched her singing as she worked. Her hands moved mechanically. Her eyes gazed absently into the distance and she seemed lost in the song. Under the light of the lamp, her eyes shone intensely. And at that moment my heart surged with love for Mother.

Later, when I recalled these details of early life, I was struck by the pity of it. Mother, although illiterate, was abundantly skilled and talented—and yet all she could do was to slave away at the gristmill from morning to night, all her youth and vigor worn away and wasted.

Mother finished making the rabbit lamp, a unique design of her own. The rabbit was white and furry and cuddly, its ears white on the outside and red inside. The loveliest part of the animal was its eyes, flashing like red crystals. The eyes were actually just a few pieces of white and red paper, but Mother's hands worked like magic, clipping here, pasting there—and a lovely little rabbit was created. The little creature seemed to be peering around with eyes innocent and bright and timid, looking at this strange world into which it had just arrived.

The festival was observed for three consecutive days. The first day was for showing the lamps. On that night, people, all bearing lamps, surged into the streets. The second day was for watching the lamps; all the population would turn out, women who rarely showed themselves or old people too feeble to walk. The third day was for destroying the lamps. Nobody knew the origin of this practice, but in the middle of the carnival atmosphere, people obliterated all the lamps in an act of celebration. Also, throughout the festival, it was the custom to snatch away lamps. To have one's lamp snatched away was a tribute to its superior craftsmanship. Thus lampsnatching was a form of compliment.

That year, on the first night of festivities, the streets were filled with lamps of every color and description. Our little town looked like a fairy world. Formerly, on these occasions, Mother was always afraid of losing us and would only stand with us at the street corner. But now everything had changed. There was Uncle. So we promenaded and thoroughly enjoyed ourselves. Uncle put my little sister on his shoulder. I followed with my elder sisters and we joined in the throng.

My little sister held high the rabbit lamp. Its white color and special design made it conspicuous, it outshone all the gaudy lamps in the procession. Before the evening was over, the lamp was snatched away. Uncle then took us to watch the dragon lamps and the local acrobats. We were delirious with happiness.

Uncle quartered himself in the house of a family nearby. He was a hard worker, never idle. In the mornings he would come over to our house. He would sweep the court-yard, tidy up the gristmill room, tend to the sick mule, mend our leaking roof, and carry sacks of wheat for grind-ing.

One day, mother was sifting flour and Uncle was sit-ting nearby with my little sister on his lap. He sang a tune to make her sleep: " 'Long are the rivers, high are the hills. My home is in the valley of ten thousand flowers. In the valley of flowers, birds abound, old and young sing moun-tain songs. . . .' " His voice was deep and strong, full of expression.

I clasped him on the back and asked, "What song is that? My mommy can sing it, too."

"We country people are used to singing mountain songs," Uncle answered shyly. "Herding sheep on the mountains, we sing alone. And peeling the leaves of the master's corn on the threshing floor, we sing together. Yes, Lan, your mother often sang this song when she was a child . . ."

I turned to look at my mother, but she was staring ahead, her eyes wet, as if reliving the times when she used to sing mountain songs.

Uncle took pity on our helpless state and decided to stay on for a while to help us over the spring famine period. After a few days, he managed to find work in wool cleaning in the suburbs. The workshop was mainly several large pools dug in the ground where the dirty wool was soaked. You could smell it miles away. The workmen had to strip and jump into the pool and tread on the wool to wash it. This went on day and night, summer and winter. The work was killing. But Uncle threw himself into it, just for the sake of the pitiful payment of several *jiao* for each day's work. He said he didn't mind any hardship under the sun, as long as he could help us.

Uncle was working at wool cleansing for about a month when it happened—the opium fiend turned up suddenly at our door, blustering with rage. "You have disgraced our ancestors. How dare you! A widow should behave like a widow, no showing her face outside the main gate, no stepping through the inner portals. And you, you have brought home a strange man."

Mother screamed in protest, and the opium fiend roared. Soon the noise brought all the neighbors. Mother turned a ghastly white and her teeth chattered, but the bully kept on scolding.

Uncle came back from work, and the opium fiend caught him by the collar. "Don't think that the Wang family has died out! Living, she is a member of the Wang clan, and dead she is a ghost of the Wangs'. Don't you dare take advantage of a widow. Take care or you'll get scorched."

Uncle could have lifted the scarecrow and thrown him over the wall. But mother was trembling by the side, so he loosened his hold. "What filthy nonsense are you talking?" he retorted. "Everyone knows that I am a relative."

The opium fiend hooted. "Relative! As if all the world doesn't know that you are sleeping together! Leave this minute! Don't say you haven't been warned!" With that, he stalked away, toying with the bird cage in his hands.

To our consternaion, that same night, Uncle was thrown out by the family with whom he lodged. And then some unknown enemy threw a stone at him in the dark. Mother was afraid for Uncle's safety, so with tears in her eyes, she sent him away. When she came back from seeing him off, she collapsed and coughed up blood by the mouthful. She was laid up and could not leave her bed until the next summer.

In remote little towns like ours, rumor could thrive on a mere nothing. So one can imagine what a disaster that row with the opium fiend was for our family. We were pariahs. Wherever we went, people would point to Mother and exclaim: "That is the shameless widow." We could feel their disdain, their hateful looks following us everywhere. We never ventured out after dark, but even so, some scamps would throw stones over our walls under cover of night.

Sensing a renewed opportunity, the fat wife of that trader in town turned up again. There she sat in the middle of our cold and empty room, one leg wedged on top of the other, as she lectured mother in that ghoulish voice of hers. "Elder Sister, you know the old saying 'Slander follows the widow's footsteps.' But, of course, you are yourself to blame, too. How could you take up with that wretch of a field hand? As I told you, my husband has no son. He would like to take another concubine. It's perfect for you. I will treat you like a sister." Finishing her speech, the woman waddled off haughtily, as if she was doing us a favor.

Mother was pale and quivering with shock. My little

sister called out in hunger, but Mother seemed to hear nothing.

The moon festival came around again—the festival for family reunions. Considering her own fate, Mother always approached this as a day of sorrow. I remember her face, pale and wan, as she went about by day. At night, when the moon was up and it was time for families to watch the moon and feast on sweet moon cake, Mother broke down and cried out to the heavens in heartrending tones. She bewailed the misfortunes of the poor widow and her children and their desperate plight. I felt that the world was tumbling down around me and the room itself filled with terror. I could not bear the sight of my weeping mother anymore and bolted from the room. I ran to the big elm tree at the entrance to our alley and squatted at its foot. The alley was empty and in complete silence, and the moon peeped at me through the foliage of the tree. My elder sister found me later when the night was far gone. She had to shake me violently before she could wake me up.

Mother witnessed the decease of the old era through sorrow and tears, that harsh era that had devoured the most precious years of her life.

At the time of the Liberation of the mainland, I was a soldier in the PLA and had been out of touch with Mother for a full ten years. Our country was then launched into a program of economic construction, and I was discharged and sent to study engineering.

In 1953, I learned that Mother was alive and well. How ecstatic I was! That same night, when all my classmates were asleep, I wandered alone on the college grounds, thinking of Mother. It was early autumn, the skies were clear and high; I lifted my eyes to the stars and all the images of Mother from long ago came crowding back into my memory: her flowing hair; the gentle smile; the lovely eyes, revealing her innate intelligence and a wistful melancholy; the hands that had often caressed me; her stubborn struggle to hold on to life. Yes, Mother had survived. She had caught up with the new era, of which each day would burgeon with joy and beauty. True, we, her daughters, were scattered—some in the capital, some in the provinces—but even our third sister who had stayed on in our native village was now placed by the local government in a teaching job in primary school. As I looked back on those miraculous changes, my heart was seized with gratitude.

I got into touch with my sisters, and we decided to reunite for the moon festival at my eldest sister's home in Beijing.

In company with our third sister, Mother traveled all the way from the northwest of the country to Beijing. She was dressed in a black jacket and a pair of trousers of coarse homespun cotton. The edges of her trousers were tied together at the ankles. She and my third sister each carried a bamboo basket on their backs. We hardly knew them. The change was shocking. Mother's hair was still twisted into a bun at the back of her head, but it had lost all its gloss; the skin on her face was a yellowish gray and the crow's-feet stood out so clearly as if they had been carved onto the sides of her temple. She was barely over forty, but she looked worn and shriveled. Her face was covered with tears. She looked at her five daughters one after another as we stood in front of her.

What a happy moon festival it was! Mother and her daughters rejoiced. Comrades from the units where we were working or studying all came over to congratulate us on our reunion after having lost each other for so many years.

At night, after the guests dispersed, we sisters went to bed, but Mother was too excited to sleep. She sat at the bed of one daughter, then moved to another. Deep into the night, in my dreams, I felt the caress of Mother's soft eyes. I opened my eyes, and sure enough, there she was, looking at me tenderly. Yes, her daughters, lost to her for so many years, were back at her side, all grown and doing well. What a tumult of emotions must have surged up in her breast as she contemplated these miraculous changes!

Our newly reunited family was full of vigor and hope. My brother-in-law, husband of my eldest sister, had been through the war and was doing research in theory at the party school. My eldest sister, though barely twenty-five, was the editor of a supplementary page for a daily newspaper. My second sister and her husband had become playwrights; throughout the days of our reunion, they burned the midnight candle to catch up with their writing. My youngest sister was a student in a school of the performing arts; she wanted to be an actress. As for myself, I also had secret ambitions: I wanted to become an engineer to serve the needs of economic construction. Even my third sister, teaching primary school, was inspired by our aspirations and decided to take the national examinations for teachers' college. I felt that our family was a microcosm of our country. My sisters and I were fired by a sense of responsibility; whenever we got together, we would always get into discussions and sometimes even heated arguments about national affairs and the future of China.

Mother rarely let herself relax. Evidently she still felt the strangeness of her new environment. For instance, she would not sit down at the dinner table with my eldest brother-in-law. "You go ahead and eat," she would say. "You are busy. Never mind me, I can eat anytime." She would always wait till everybody had finished and then peck at the leftovers, sitting alone in the kitchen. If my eldest brother-in-law came over to speak to her, she would stand up respectfully and invite him to sit, as if he were an honored guest.

We had become more or less strangers after so many years of separation. That is understandable. But Mother's every word and gesture denoted such timidity, such humility, it made my heart ache.

Our eldest sister saw through Mother's heart. She was straightforward. "Mother," she said, "I know what is bothering you. You are uneasy at living in your son-in-law's home. But what's the difference between daughters and sons? You must treat this as your own home."

Her husband reassured her. "Mother, I am just like your own son, just the same."

Mother blushed. "Yes, yes, just the same," she agreed uneasily.

My youngest sister was in the first flush of youth and could not bear the slightest hint about the inferiority of girls. She struck in, ready to pick a quarrel. "Now, who says girls are not as good as boys? Mom is still carrying a feudal head on her shoulders!"

My second sister was always sharp-tongued, and she chimed in. "Mother, our eldest sister expects you to set up home here with her, but Little Sister says you still want to go back. You can't bear to part with Third Sister's baby boy, your precious grandson. All your life, that's all you've ever wanted—a boy."

Little Sister put her arms around Mother's shoulders. With her face next to Mother's, she asked slyly, "Now, Mother, will not this bevy of daughters make up for one little grandson?" Mother lowered her head and smiled, but would not say a word.

Mother was indeed reluctant to stay on in Beijing. We were right in our conjectures: she could not bear to part from her little grandson, the only male in the next generation. But we all insisted, and Mother stayed on against her own wishes.

To keep her from being lonely, I took her to Tiananmen Square, the Palace Museum, the Temple of Heavenly Peace, the Summer Palace, and other sites and attractions. Little Sister was in love with theatre and would drag Mother along to all the performances in town.

Mother gradually got accustomed to life with this big family. She took part in the meetings and the study sessions held by the Neighborhood Committee, and she also took up all the housework, shopping, and cooking. On Saturdays, when I came home from college, I would always see Mother standing in the doorway waiting for me. And the minute I set foot in the house, I would encounter the sweet aromas of cooking. Mother cared for us as if we were children. In cold weather, she would put food to warm over the fire, waiting for us. When it was hot, she would let the food cool before we were ready to eat. And when we slept at home, she always got up several times at night to cover us.

Our eldest sister protested, "Mother, you're spoiling everyone."

"What am I good for," Mother answered, "if not to serve you?" Mother always thought nothing of herself. She brought warmth and love and comfort to the family. She gave us strength and support, but she regarded it as a matter of course.

But Mother changed as life went on. She became younger, her face filled out and acquired some color, her health improved. Most important, she regained the vigor and confidence of former days. She was interested in everything. At the time, my head was full of my own studies; when I came back for weekends, I would wax enthusiastic about affairs at college. Mother always followed my stories attentively.

Our little sister was a movie fan. She would come home from a film and describe the plot or imitate the acting. And Mother was always there to listen and encourage her.

Most wonderful of all, Mother fell in love with the radio. She knew the daily schedule by heart. The six-thirty morning news was the start of her day, never to be missed. She listened to it as she prepared breakfast. Then she would relay the headlines to us as we ate. As she spoke it seemed that all the bubbling new life of our country was brought before our eyes. Mother had a remarkable memory and was very receptive to the new things coming into her life.

We were all busy, each of us pursuing our own careers and ideals. Our elder brother-in-law was engrossed in philosophy. He even ate his meals with a book in his hands. Our elder sister's time was taken up in editing her page for her paper. My youngest sister and I, as students, spent most of our time in college. Our second sister in a province in the south and third sister out in the country were, needless to say, also busy. Our entire nation could be described in one word: *busy*.

Every Sunday when we saw Mother, we noticed a change for the better. Her health improved steadily; her spirits were more cheerful; even her movements exuded confidence—and she was learning fast. Her assignment of new words to learn for the day was written down on a little blackboard hanging in the kitchen. Sometimes she would ask us questions about issues related to this new society.

Our little sister decided that Mother had no reason to make herself look like an old woman. She insisted on cutting Mother's long hair. The change was astounding. With her short hair flapping about her ears, Mother seemed even younger. At the beginning, she was ashamed of her new looks; she even feared going out shopping—and she would hide when there were callers at the house. By and by, she got used to the new hairstyle.

One day, I was in town to attend an exhibition of foreign technology, and I stopped at home on the way. As I passed under the window I heard the sound of singing: " 'Long are the rivers, high are the hills. My home is in the valley of ten thousand flowers. In the valley of flowers, birds abound, old and young sing mountain songs. . . .' " The sound was soft and low, but deeply moving. The words and the tune were familiar, but I could not remember when and where I had heard it. I stopped in my tracks to listen. The song gathered to a crescendo, then gradually died down. It was like no song on earth. It plucked at the heartstrings.

Who was the singer? Could it be my tomboyish little sister? Was she capable of such sensitivity? I pushed open the door to catch her unawares. And what a shock I had! There was no trace of my little sister at all. Mother alone was sitting in front of the window, bending over some sewing, singing as she worked. I suddenly recognized the tune: it was the one that Mother had sung when she was making lamps for the fifteenth of the lunar New Year festival. Then, however, her voice was melancholy; now her voice was full of joy and hope and fervor. I was afraid to interrupt her thoughts and her singing, so I stood quite still where I was.

She happened to look up. When she saw me, her song stopped immediately and she blushed crimson.

"Mother," I said, "I've heard that song before."

"Don't be silly, Lan. How could you have heard it before? I was cheerful and just made it up."

Later that day I told my little sister that Mother could sing beautiful mountain songs. Little Sister then begged Mother to sing for us. But Mother denied everything. She even insisted that a neighbor had been singing and that I had made a mistake.

One Sunday, I was home as usual and helping Mother make stuffed dumplings. My little sister rushed into the room shouting in excitement.

Elder Sister was in the inner room correcting an article.

"Now what are you up to, Rash Warrior?" she demanded, poking her head into the kitchen. "We can hear you miles away." Elder Sister often called our little sister Rash Warrior or Havoc-raising Boar, from legendary figures, because she was so tomboyish. Mother and I could not help laughing at the epithets.

As was her custom, my little sister ignored Elder Sister. "Mother, I saw a classmate to the railway station today, and guess whom I met at the station?"

Elder Sister snickered. "I suppose you met a movie star and got an autograph!"

"Nothing of the sort!" Little Sister replied. "Mother, I was talking to my classmate in the street next to the railway station. Then this tall peasant came toward us and asked directions to the station. I took one look at him—and who do you think it was? Our uncle!"

"Uncle? Then why didn't he call on us?" I asked.

"Beijing is so big," Little Sister said. "How do you expect him to find us? He came to visit his nephew, who is serving in the PLA. His nephew put him on a trolley on the circular line to give him a look at Beijing. He said he squatted in a corner of the trolley, and after riding around and around he got out and found himself in the same place where he boarded. He didn't see a thing, but thought it was great fun nevertheless."

Elder sister and I laughed at this drollery.

Little Sister continued with the story. "His nephew was afraid he'd lose himself as he wandered about, so he wrote down his address on pieces of paper and put one in each of his pockets."

"One should never forget friends in need," I murmured. "If I'd been you, I would have dragged him back with me."

"Uncle wanted very much to have a good look at us all, Sister Lan, but the train was leaving. There was no time at all."

Mother was silent throughout this conversation. She continued to work mechanically, occasionally dropping her chopsticks and letting her pastry slip onto the cutting board.

"Mother, have you heard what I was saying?" Little Sister asked.

Mother looked away toward the window. "I am listening, listening," she said with feeling.

"What a scatterbrain you are!" Elder Sister scolded. "Why didn't you ask after his family and circumstances?"

"We talked so much, he nearly missed his train! Yes, I remember he said he is still living alone."

"Yes, that's how it is in the countryside," Elder Sister said, standing in the doorway. "If you are too poor to marry when young, you never have a chance afterward. But you should have asked for his address. We should be in touch. We're relatives, after all."

"Uncle said Mother has his address. He said to tell Mother to take good care of herself. And also to send him a word now and then so he won't worry."

I recollected the events of long ago and sighed. "Right from the old society down to the new, Uncle was always concerned for us. People are good, after all."

Mother never said a word. From the expression on her face, I sensed that she was gripped by a strong emotion. She went out to fetch water and did not return. The pot over the fire was left unattended. Probably it was the first time Mother had let something like that happen. I went to look for her in the next room. She was standing against the window, gazing at the distant clouds in the sky, and the tears were sparkling in her eyes.

That summer, my elder sister was away on a business trip and my little sister was head over heels in love. I myself was deep in my studies. Every hour of the day was accounted for. I only returned home to sleep. I began to notice that Mother sometimes sat alone in the dark in the little courtyard. She would gaze at the stars, lost in thought. I would drop off to sleep the minute I got home. I never noticed what time Mother went to bed.

One Saturday night both Little Sister and I came home very late. The little imp dropped on her bed the minute she arrived and started snoring. She was completely exhausted.

Just as I was going to bed myself Mother pushed open the door gently. I asked her if she wanted anything. She didn't answer. I reached out for the light, but she stopped me. She sat on the edge of my bed and caressed my hand. "Lan, Mom has something to say to you. May I?"

I got a shock. I felt gripped by a sense of guilt. We were just buried in our own affairs and nobody bothered to talk to Mother. Mother noticed my sense of guilt. "I understand that you are all busy," she said. "You have something to work for. It is good." Then she sighed deeply and resumed. "Lan, all her life, Mom has had nobody to care for her, nobody to love her. She is all, all alone, like a solitary ghost. . . ." She sounded so mournful. Yes, it was true, I thought: Mother was indeed deprived. If she had our chance to work and study, she would not be so lonely. Perhaps we should send her to a spare-time school.

To my surprise, Mother raised a totally different issue. "Lan, Mom will be a burden to you sooner or later. I figure, I cannot go on like this forever, all alone." I was at a loss for words.

Little Sister, who was sleeping beside us, woke up at this moment, just to hear the last words. She jumped up and turned on the light, giving Mother and me a fright. "What! Mom! You are going to get yourself a husband? You don't want us anymore? What a joke!" Then she burst out laughing. Mother, blushing deeply, also laughed constrainedly.

The next day, as we were all seated at dinner, my scatterbrained sister blurted out: "Elder Sister, do you know, Mom wants to find an old partner."

"Don't talk such nonsense," Elder Sister replied. "You are slandering Mother." Everybody thought it a good joke and laughed very hard.

Mother blushed to the roots of her hair. She neither denied nor acknowledged the accusation.

After that, nobody mentioned the subject again. Things went back to normal. We busied ourselves with our own affairs while Mother spent the days in housework.

But one year later, Mother again raised the question with our elder sister.

It was on the eve of the lunar New Year. Our second sister and her husband were in Beijing on business. Our third sister, from the northwest, had also arrived for a visit. Once again, we girls got together. But on this particular

New Year's Eve, the customary air of joyous celebration was missing. Poor Mother, ever since raising the question, felt ashamed of herself. She dared not look us in the face.

At the New Year's Eve dinner table, Mother sat with downcast eyes, barely touching her food. Our elder brother-in-law, very kindhearted though spare of words, kept piling food into her bowl. Our second brother-in-law always had a ready flow of words; to break the embarrassing silence, he babbled about every subject under the sun, but to no effect. Suddenly he blurted out: "Little Sister, I'm told you've got yourself a boyfriend. Why don't you bring him over and let us have a look at him?" The words were barely out of his mouth before Little Sister jerked to her feet. Second Sister gave her husband a hard look. I was afraid that Little Sister was going to blurt out something outrageous, so I pulled her down to her seat and told her to remain silent.

I stole a look at Mother. She was sitting stonily, the food in front of her untouched. The embarrassment was unbearable. "Mom," I said, "let's take a turn in the courtyard."

When we were outside, Mother said: "Lan, you go back and enjoy yourself. I am a little dizzy from that wine. I think I'll lie down for a minute."

Back at the dinner table, the atmosphere was tense. Only our elder brother-in-law went on eating—eyes on his book. All the others sat in uneasy silence.

"Sit down," Elder Sister commanded me. "Mother says she wants to get herself an old man. Let's see what can be done about it." Silence.

Then Second Sister broke out. "What is she trying to do? She's living so well, and yet wants to marry some old fellow, a complete stranger! We'll be stuck with him and have to serve him like a parent! It's unnatural!"

"Yes," Elder Sister said, "I wonder if this is necessary. After all, she's over forty."

"So what if she's forty?" Little Sister exclaimed. "Can't you fall in love after forty? An elderly professor at our college got himself a cute little wife." She giggled.

Elder Sister rebuked her. "Your head is always full of nonsense." Then she turned to me. "What do you say, Sister Lan?" Meanwhile Little Sister was making faces, but she dared not reply.

I was confused. "Mother is to be pitied," I said lamely.

"Even now? Isn't that going too far?" Second Sister demanded.

"Mother says, all her life, nobody cared for her, nobody loved her. She's like a solitary ghost. My feeling is that—" I was very torn in my mind and searching for words.

Second Sister interrupted me. "So many children around her, and still no one to love her! All I can say is that she doesn't know how lucky she is." She looked to her husband for approval.

Her husband was smoking furiously. "This is a matter for you women," he said. "I can't add anything."

Elder Sister sighed. "It seems to me that poverty has its trials, of course, but good living also brings its own problems. When life is too easy . . ."

Second Sister broke in angrily. "Let me make this clear. If Mother is bringing in some old fellow to be our new parent, I wash my hands of this family."

"You're going too far," her husband exclaimed.

Third Sister, who had been sitting aside in silence, now broke in. "What a headache! Everything going along nicely and now this bother, straight out of the blue! Well, as the saying goes: 'The skies will rain, and women will marry.' If this is known in our native place, how people will laugh."

Little Sister, silent all this while, now burst out as if on the verge of a discovery. "Sister Lan, do you realize it— I'm the only Youth Leaguer here. All the rest of you are Communist party members. This is a serious meeting, momentous, I'd say. I'll go and tell Mother: the meeting has passed a unanimous resolution. Your application for permission to marry is turned down." She got to her feet.

"Shut up, you bigmouth." Elder Sister gave her a furious look.

Little Sister sat down, but kept appealing to everybody with her eyes. We all sat there dejectedly.

Our elder brother-in-law spoke slowly and deliberately. "As I see it, Mother has her reasons. Anyway, your elder sister is the authority in this family. I suggest she talk it over with your mother before making a decision."

And thus ended our meeting. After we broke up, I went to look for Mother. I discovered that she had been sitting in the next room. She was deadly pale and tears were swimming in her eyes. For the first time, I discovered that she had grown thin. Once again I saw in her the sorrowful mother of my childhood.

When she saw me, Mother got up and began to fumble over some work to hide her distress. She had heard our decision about her wishes. She did not question it. On the contrary, she seemed ashamed of herself for ever harboring such thoughts.

After that, Mother was more silent and timid than ever. She would slink about the house in her household chores, careful and deliberate in her every movement, as if afraid of giving offense to her daughters.

Soon after that, Mother said she wanted to go back to her third daughter in our native northwest. Elder Sister thought a change would be advisable, and thus Mother made ready to go.

Before leaving, Mother again let her hair grow and pinned it in a bun at the back of her head. Little Sister protested, but Mother explained. "Back at home, if people my age went around with short hair flying about, everybody would say they were shameless."

Still Little Sister objected. "Mother is so old-fashioned."

Mother put on the homemade coarse cotton jacket and trousers in which she had arrived. With a parcel in her hands, she was ready to go. We saw her off at the railway station. She sat in her seat in the car, looking, in turn, at us and at the bustling crowd. I pushed a bag of fruit into her lap, but she barely noticed it. My sisters bade her return soon. She answered mechanically, as if her mind was elsewhere. Finally the train pulled out. As Mother moved slowly out of view she looked at us fixedly; her eyes were full of hurt, shame, and perplexity.

After seeing Mother off, we walked home. Nobody spoke on the way. Elder Sister seemed lost in thought, while Little Sister was angry with her for letting Mother go. I looked at the road under my feet, then at the sky above. I couldn't forget Mother's last glance and the expression in her eyes. And I didn't know how to analyze my own feelings.

Later, with all the changes in our lives, neither Mother nor her daughters ever mentioned the matter again. As the years went by we daughters, at least, forgot it altogether.

After graduation, I was assigned to a factory in the northeast of the country. Little Sister and her husband volunteered for Sinkiang in the far west. Elder Sister was still in Beijing, Second Sister in the south, and Third Sister in our native northwest. We sisters were truly scattered over the four corners of the earth. Mother would divide her time between us, rushing about from one daughter to another, with her little parcel under her arm. Trains, buses, horse-drawn carts, and even pushcarts—it didn't matter what, as long as they took her to her daughters.

The nation was busy making iron in 1958, the year of the Great Leap Forward. Everywhere along the length and width of the country, fire and smoke were rising up to the skies. All the population was drawn into this twenty-four-hour-a-day frenzy. One day, just as I came back from another stint of iron making, mother turned up for a visit.

She was tired and dusty from travel. Her hair was gray white and her face tanned, and the wrinkles were deeply cut into her temples. But she was in good spirits and happy to see me.

One day, I managed to squeeze a minute away from the furnace and sat by Mother for a while. She smoothed my hair tenderly. I thought of Mother rushing about here and there for her daughters' sake, of our *resolution* over her *application*, and my heart ached. "Mother," I said guiltily, "we were too young to understand you. Now it seems . . ."

She let the tears flow and drip onto the back of my

hand. "What is the use of saying anything now? I have one foot in the grave. My life is over."

I could not say anything, only held her tightly. At the same time, I told myself: With the years, the emotions have withered away.

Mother washed and mended and busied herself setting my home in order. After that, she made it to remote Sinkiang to take care of Little Sister, who was going to give birth. And after that, she went back to Beijing to be with our elder sister and brother-in-law. Both of them had been implicated in the political campaign against rightist opportunists.

My elder sister had written to me at the time. She said:

Sister Lan,

Just when we most needed help, Mother arrived. She was such a comfort. She said, "The road of life is full of ups and downs, but we always make our way through." Her words gave us support. Life is so unpredictable. Who would have thought that we who are supposed to be tempered by the Revolution have never understood Mother. We have just made her work her fingers to the bone for us, and on top of that, we have made her share our worries and anxieties.

Lately, I often think back to our *resolution* over Mother's wish. I now feel that if Mother had married again, she would have done better than always slaving for her good-for-nothing daughters . . .

I read Elder Sister's letter over and over again, unable to sleep.

The time flew by, pursued by changes. I again lost touch with Mother, only hearing of her whereabouts from my sisters' letters.

Then, suddenly out of the blue, I got this telegram:

"Lan, mother died of sudden illness. Come back for funeral. Third Sister."

Everything went black before my eyes. I do not know how I got home. When I woke up, my pillow was soaking wet.

I do not remember how I got on the train, or anything of the journey. I always saw Mother in front of me, her kind face, her gentle smile, her hands that had caressed me—but she is gone forever.

Third Sister, dressed in deep mourning, was keeping her station by the body and sobbed out loud. Mother lay peacefully in the coffin, dressed in her burial clothes, as if resting after a long and arduous journey. I felt my heart was going to break at the sight.

Third Sister told me: "You know the scarcity of the last few years. Our sisters have all written to ask Mother to join them in the city. But she insisted on staying with us through these famine-ridden times. She couldn't bear to leave her little grandson. Enduring the hunger and fatigue from day to day . . ." Third Sister beat her breasts. "It is all my fault, I deserve to die. It's me and my child. We have caused Mother's death."

Yes, she was right. We daughters caused Mother's death. We made her work for us. We made her give up her whole life for us. I had always thought that after we overcame these bad times, I would make Mother stay with me. I would not let her rush about anymore. All this conjecture was futile. We would never see each other again.

The next day was the day of the burial. Uncle crossed mountains and plains to attend. He was dusty from head to foot. His hair was iron gray, but he was still strong and healthy. He knelt in front of Mother's coffin while the tears rained down. When the coffin was about to be closed, with trembling hands Uncle took out from within his breast little toy figures plaited out of grass—toy horses, toy deer, toy lambs. Softly he put them near Mother's pillow, to keep her eternal company, and to convey his everlasting remembrance.

Uncle watched as Mother's coffin was lowered. Then with his own hands, he piled the earth over her grave and planted a few willow saplings.

The years went by, but except for our third sister, none of us could visit Mother's grave. Third Sister wrote to say that Uncle, now completely white-haired, continued to visit Mother's grave regularly on the Festival of the Dead to bring her incense and offerings. Later on, in the ten years of turmoil, we were each in our own way swept up by the storm and struggled for sheer survival. It was only our Uncle who never forgot to commemorate our mother. Only he remembered to add new earth to her grave and plant willow saplings.

Mother had walked step by step down her bitter path in life. She had hoped for a new life, hoped to see her daughters grown, hoped for reunion, hoped for . . .

The new era had given her the beginnings of a new life and had kindled her hopes. She had her joys and her dreams.

Even at this moment, I feel as if I hear the stirring sounds of her song. Outwardly calm and resigned, Mother was in reality full of ardent yearnings. She must have been confident of being supported in her yearnings by her daughters, they being educated, and mindful of genuine values. But her ardor, so precious, so rare, was so short-lived; it was so rudely, so cruelly, so thoughtlessly trampled on.

It is true that a mother is always willing to sacrifice herself for her children, to give them all her love and hide her sorrows in her own breast. But what about the deplorable thoughts and actions of her children? How are they going to account for themselves, they who reckon themselves the enlightened generation?

Now I myself am over forty, just the age that Mother was during our first reunion after the Liberation. During the ten years of the Cultural Revolution, I was exiled into an isolated mountain region with my children, cut off from the rest of the world. At the time, how I had yearned for my husband, for others dear to me. I lost pleasure in life, was on the brink of suicide. Only then did I realize the emotional torment that Mother must have gone through.

In the middle of that protracted nightmare, when all values were overturned, I once got a letter from my little sister. Furiously, she denounced "this despicable trampling of people's most precious affections and hopes and beliefs." She added: "It makes my blood boil. . . ."

But I asked her in a reply smuggled out of my place of detention through a friend: "Little Sister, what you allude to is not, perhaps, a calamity inflicted from the outside. Perhaps its beginnings have been instilled in our blood?"

Lan, all her life Mother has had nobody to care for her, nobody to love her. She is all, all alone, like a solitary ghost . . . Mother's words still pierce my heart with their poignancy. They make me remember and think and dissect myself. And then I feel as if a dagger is driving itself into my heart.

Elder Sister and her husband, who have departed this world, cannot rethink the past. To them is lost forever the chance to repent and ask forgiveness at Mother's grave. But we who are living, do we not have an obligation to face life squarely, to see ourselves as we are, since life is still stretched before us?

Dearest Mother, you are selfless; living, your heart was filled with love for life and for your children. Now in the corridors of death, how you must yearn for the beauteous new life, for your erring children.

Dearest Mother, when the dawn lays its rosy tint upon my windowpanes and the warm winds of spring ruffle the meadows, I seem to hear your sweet, sad song. Your tender gaze seems fixed on me and my sisters, exhorting us to march on with steady footsteps on the road of life.

First published in Current Times (Dan Dai), *1982. Translated at the Rockefeller Study Center, Villa Serbelloni, Bellagio, May 30–June 2, 1990.*

THE TRAGEDY OF THE
WALNUT TREE

ZONG PU

Born in 1928 of a prestigious academic family, Zong Pu graduated from the English department of Qinghua University in 1951 and worked variously on the editorial staff of literary magazines and in literary research. As a writer of fiction, Zong Pu first made her mark with the short story "The Red Beans" (1957), which was attacked for its portrayal of a young woman's private emotions in conflict with revolutionary norms. Her other well-known works include "Melody in Dreams" (1978), about a disillusioned new generation emerging out of the Cultural Revolution. The novella The Everlasting Stone *(1980) and the short story "The Tragedy of the Walnut Tree" revolve around images of women who maintain dignity and integrity under insult and persecution. Other short stories—"Who Am I?" (1983), "A Head in the Marshes" (1985), and "The Shell Dwellers" (1981)—reflect Kafkaesque influences in the writer's effort to bring out the nightmarish quality of life. At present Zong Pu is working on a multivolume saga—*Ordeal. Heading South, *the first volume, is already published.*

A huge walnut tree. Tall it stands and generously it spreads out its rich foliage, sheltering the little courtyard beneath it. We still call it a courtyard, though the walls have collapsed and the open space has become a shortcut. For the last dozen years, people have been passing to and fro, each acting out his or her part in the drama of life. The walnut tree, however, is oblivious to mundane affairs. It simply grows there, fulfilling its office faithfully. With spring it sends forth tender buds; in summer it pours out a riot of green; in autumn its branches hang heavy with fruit; winter, indeed, strips it stark and bare, but the snow clinging to its branches provides a distinguished outline to the winter scene.

It is an evening in autumn. The walnut tree is laden with emerald-green walnuts glistening lusciously in the setting sun. Some branches hover near the window of the dwelling in the courtyard. If the tree could speak, it might address the mistress inside and beg her, for her own sake, to knock down all the walnuts hanging on the tree. Perhaps it *could* speak. Who knows?

Even if the walnut tree *did* address Liu Qingyi, she would not have been able to respond. For two days, she had been stricken with asthma. She reclined on her bed, gasping for breath. Because of this health problem, she had taken an early retirement from her office. But at home, she had not been idle. She worked on translations. She also volunteered as a typist, as there was no decent typewriter in the office. Her typing was impeccable. With the flood of people going abroad in the last few years, one practically had to line up for her service. Some people thought it a pity she wasted her talents on typing. "Why not take it easy, since you are retired?" they said.

But Qingyi felt that the tap-taps of her typewriter were signals bringing messages of the outside world. The pity was that with autumn, the messages had to stop. Racked with asthma, Qingyi always found autumn a terrible ordeal. And on top of it all, that walnut tree, inviting disaster.

The fact is, apart from her daughter, Ahyou, the walnut tree was Qingyi's best friend. Its mere presence had bolstered her through the last thirty years. It had witnessed all her loneliness and desolation, all the storms that had battered her in that time. Its leafy branches were spread over the little courtyard, often making a rustling sound. Qingyi loved listening to its soft murmur. She could hear in it all the endearing words of comfort that she yearned for.

In spite of the winds and storms raging round it, the walnut tree bore fruit every autumn without fail. If it could take a respite from this duty, it might have been better for everyone. The pity is, it knew too much, and it bore too much fruit. That is how many of life's problems are started.

Qingyi's daughter, Ahyou, finally got into a graduate studies program. She was buried in her books, with barely a minute to spare for her sick mother.

A victim of chronic ill health, Qingyi had learned to doctor herself. She had just gone through a bad spell and was now exhausted. She felt herself slowly sinking into slumber, all the creases of her being smoothing themselves out.

Swish—bang! A piece of flying brick crashed through the thick branches and landed on the ground, with a smothered sound of thunder. Qingyi bolted into wakefulness.

Swish—bang! Another brick. Then a rush of footsteps, apparently to snatch up the fallen walnuts.

There was a babble of masculine voices.

"That one's pretty big."

"That one belongs to me!"

"There're lots more up the tree!" Then *swish—bang*, another burst of thunder.

These outbreaks always unnerved Qingyi. She lifted herself from her reclining position and looked out the window. It was a big rectangular one-piece windowpane common to old-fashioned courtyard-style houses with spacious rooms. The inner half of the room was now walled off to accommodate other households. Qingyi's share of the room had become a mere strip, incongruously running the length of the window. From out of the window, Qingyi could see the branches of the walnut tree quivering under the stormy outburst created by the men.

Ahyou called this familiar scene "walnut fever." Who knew how many thousands of walnuts this big tree had brought forth in its time! Thirty years ago, when Qingyi first moved into this courtyard, it was already huge and flourishing, its trunk beyond a man's clasp. Before 1966, the walls of the courtyard were intact and there had never been any raid on the walnuts. During the ten years of turmoil, some people were busy making revolution; others were busy trying to save their own skins. Man-made disasters and the disintegration of families left people little time to hanker after the walnuts. Qingyi had occasionally been bothered by assaults on the tree, but at the time those were nothing compared with what she was suffering from other sources.

More recently, though, some people found their hands idle. And what was more fun than collecting a few walnuts for free? Others, though busy, could always find time for a snack of walnuts, which could be had by just striding across that gap in the wall and knocking them down from the tree. To Qingyi all this had become unbearable.

Qingyi could not bear the sight of the quivering tree; her eyes shifted slowly to the desk in front of the window and rested on an envelope. The oversized pale blue envelope was obviously of foreign origin; it stood against the penholder, coldly surveying the room.

Qingyi closed her eyes. She remembered that when she first came to look over the house with Jiali, he had immediately fallen in love with that walnut tree. He had said that the air around the tree was good for her asthma. Although the house was old and not well equipped, they had decided to move in at once. The house had belonged to Qingyi's maternal aunt and at her death had passed to Qingyi. For the first six months, it was Eden—those days beyond recall. At the time, Jiali had already secured a scholarship for studies abroad and was busy at his preparations.

The Liberation of the northern part of the mainland was imminent and Qingyi tried to persuade Jiali to stay. But he was afraid this was his last chance. They had also contemplated leaving together, but Qingyi had no scholarship. He suggested that they risk it—pack up and leave—but she was afraid of weighing him down. Under the walnut tree they had planned and hoped. And finally she had remained behind.

She had remained willingly. Staying on the land she

had trod from childhood gave her a sense of security, although she had never done anything for this land, she felt.

"Three years—it will pass so quickly," Jiali had reassured her. "I'll be back soon. The walnut tree is my witness," he added as a joke. Those words of his must have been engraved inside the rings of the tree.

Thirty years passed, but he had not returned.

Swish—bang! Poor walnut tree. The reverberation of this last assault shook even the envelope as it stood against the penholder.

When Jiali went away, Ahyou was not yet born. The day before he left, he had carelessly smashed one of a six-piece set of china. Qingyi felt as if he had done it on purpose and was very hurt. She had stood for a long time under the walnut tree, not wishing to reveal the pain written on her face. The branches of the walnut tree sweeping downward were like friendly arms giving her support.

She had held their month-old daughter and stood watching the fireworks in celebration of the founding of the People's Republic. The fireworks illumined the night, piercing the darkness with a constellation of sparkling lights, casting the walnut tree in a crimson glow. The country, racked by dissension and disaster, had finally found peace and stability.

She wrote to Jiali, urging him to return. She had never doubted that he would. But the years passed. Many others made their way back from the United States and Europe and settled on the homeland, but Jiali was not among them.

Thirty years passed—and still no Jiali. Instead this letter arrived, a letter that did not take her by surprise.

Swish—bang! Another brick. The leaves trembled on the branches and a few drifted to the ground.

The walnut tree. The steadfast walnut tree—witness to Qingyi's strange fate. There was a period when Ahyou settled in the Xishuanbanna national minorities area of Yunnan province on the southwest borders. Then Qingyi was all alone. She had only the tree to talk to, and no matter what she said, it seemed to answer her always with the same soft murmur. Once, after a specially boring session of self-castigation, Qingyi felt desperately lonely. She walked back and forth under the walnut tree, asking, "Are you coming back?" The question referred, of course, to her daughter, Ahyou.

Coming back! Coming back! The rustling leaves seemed to answer her as the sound receded slowly.

She asked again, lowering her voice "Are you coming back?" this time thinking of Jiali.

The rustling leaves replied. *Coming back, coming back.*

"And me—what's to become of me?" Qingyi held back the tears as they welled up. She had never imagined that the tree could give her such comfort.

It answered her again. *Caring for you, caring for you . . .* The soft sound caressed Qingyi. She had been swaying weakly and suddenly stood up straight.

From that day forward she voiced her fears and complaints to the tree, yearning to hear those words of comfort. Could a tree speak? She knew it was her own diseased imagination. *Caring for you, caring for you . . .*

Qingyi sighed. For the last few years, everything had taken a turn for the better. Who could have foreseen that this faithful friend of her lonely years would become a source of trouble to her?

"Aim! Shoot!" Voices were shouting outside. "That way!"

Qinqyi fixed her eyes on the window, waiting for the brick to land. Invariably, in the course of this routine, one of the bricks would smash the windowpane, leaving a gap. Before the piercing winds of winter came, she would have to plug the gap with a piece of newspaper.

As if satisfying her expectations, a brick flew through the branches and made straight for the window. Immediately there was a resounding crash and half of the windowpane lay in smithereens. Ironically, the brick itself always landed outside the window frame.

A hoot of laughter followed.

"Now we're in for it," said one vandal.

"So what!" another retorted. "There's only an old widow woman and her old maid of a daughter in there. What can they do?"

Others joined in with the same argument and a few more bricks followed.

Qingyi smiled bitterly. What could she do? Yes, indeed, what could she do even if she *wanted* to do something about it? She shrunk back further into her bed.

Suddenly there came the sound of a crash on the roof, then confused tramping over her head. They have climbed up the roof! Qingyi knew what that meant. Leakage. Begging for the repairman to come. Untold disasters. Even the deaf and the dumb could make a stand. She got up, ready to confront them.

Several branches and twigs lay on the ground beneath the walnut tree in a confused maze. A few lone walnuts that had escaped the looting hung forlornly on bare branches. The whole tree seem to be shaking pitifully. *I am useful, I can serve*, it seemed to be saying.

"Please leave," she said weakly.

"It's none of your business," one of the vandals shouted. A brick fell right next to her feet.

"Get down from my roof! Get out of here!" Qingyi was herself surprised at this sudden burst of anger. It seemed as if something was stuck in her throat. She had difficulty breathing, although the air was filled with the sweet scent of fresh walnuts. The words she shouted were barely above a hoarse whisper.

"Let's see who'll get out of here first! I'll see you leave feet foremost!" A young man jumped down from the roof and walked toward Qingyi menacingly, his face a mask of fury. "Remember your age, eh! Be careful!"

As Qingyi retreated before him she tripped against the doorway and fell. She felt herself suffocating and reached for the respirator.

Her plight excited another burst of derisive laughter. The young man cracked open a walnut and stuffed his mouth full of meat. "How fresh! How delicious!" he said in a singsong voice.

These people—how can they be so pitiful? Qingyi asked herself. But I am even more pitiful. I am but a lonely old widow and Ahyou an old maid. Where does this crowd come from? Why don't they take away the walnut tree— and that pale blue envelope, too—and leave me in peace! I can't bear this anymore.

She struggled out of bed again and inhaled at the respirator. Gradually her spirits calmed down.

"Just wait and see who's going to be kicked out first!" There was another outbreak and a few bricks flew about. Finally darkness began to descend and the racket died down. The voice of a man—the one with the venomous

face—let off a parting shot. "Be thankful for our patron-
age! We'll be back tomorrow!"

Silence. A chill stole in from the gap in the window.
The walnut tree was reflected in the remaining part of the
windowpane, its outlines distorted in the cracked glass. A
branch protruded through the gap, a few walnuts still
clinging to it. The green and tender walnuts could be seen
clearly in the gloaming.

The tree must be destroyed! The thought flashed through
Qingyi's mind, catching her by surprise.

The tree must be destroyed! Qingyi could not banish the
idea. The walnut tree was not to blame. It had stayed with
her through her loneliness. It was a true friend. It seemed
to be appealing to her: *I am useful! I can serve!*

Indeed, it had been useful. During those years of turmoil, when all normal human contacts were cut off, the
walnut tree had brought Qingyi the warmth of human relationships. People had come to her soliciting sprigs of
walnut as a last hope of life for their loved ones. (Eggs
boiled with sprigs of walnut was a cure for cancer, according to folklore.) The visitors would approach her timidly,
fearful that this act of theirs might in itself be another crime
charged against them.

Qingyi remembered the timid knocking, the words of
supplication. The walls of the courtyard had by then collapsed. People could easily have come and gone and helped
themselves to whatever they needed. She had always received them warmly, pointing out to them the tenderest
twigs, helping them to collect as much as they needed. She
had been so happy to be of use, happy to the point of tears.

But none of the people who had tried the walnut cure

had ever lived. As the news of their deaths reached her one by one Qingyi would sit in front of the window and gaze wistfully at the outline of the walnut tree. She felt that it, too, was sighing at its own helplessness.

But now she decided, she didn't want the walnut tree around. She didn't want to be disturbed. She wanted solitude. She sat up suddenly, snatched the pale blue envelope, and shoved it under her pillow.

"This won't do," she said aloud.

"What won't do?" asked Ahyou as she stepped into the room and approached her mother's bed. Her face was round, her eyes round, and her mouth a pouting bud. "It's the walnut fever again, isn't it?" She looked from her mother to the pillow and her eyes opened wide. "What's this, Mother?" One corner of the pillow was soaked in blood.

"Why? What happened?" Qingyi stretched out her hand and touched her forehead.

"Ah, I fell against the door. We had a quarrel."

Ahyou flushed with anger. "That's going too far. I'll deal with them." Actually she had no idea who the offenders were.

"Oh, don't," cried Qingyi. "These people have their own problems, too, you know."

Ahyou reflected for a moment. "Mother," she said at last, "we must get rid of the tree." It was the only rational solution to the predicament.

"You think so?" Qingyi did not want to admit that she had come to the same conclusion. "But the tree is not to blame."

"It is. Being valuable, it had wrongly chosen to grow up in our family. We do not have the power to protect it.

292

We can't even protect ourselves. We will never live to see the times when people will stop being mean and petty."

Qingyi gazed at Ahyou's round face. "Wrongly chosen to grow up in our family." How true! If this same tree had been patronized by royalty, it might have had a title conferred on it: Duke of Evergreen Shade or Supreme Commander of the Forests.

"If geometry interferes with man's interests, man will change that, too," Ahyou added. Dialectical materialism was one of the courses in Ahyou's graduate studies program.

Qingyi didn't care one way or another. Even if geometry could be changed, what was all this fuss over a tree? Qingyi looked out of the window. It was completely dark by now, but she could still make out the outline of the tree.

Ahyou muttered to herself as she climbed on the desk to patch the gap in the window with a piece of newspaper. All that was required, she remembered, was to carve out a ring on the bark around the trunk; the tree's supply of nutrition would be cut off—and the task completed.

Mother and daughter deliberated over it. Ahyou finally jumped down from the desk. She said she had to finish some work in the lab; after that, she would start work on the tree.

The way they discussed it, it was just like a conspiracy for murder, Qingyi thought to herself.

Ahyou laughed out loud. "Doesn't this sound like a murder plot?"

"What nonsense," Qingyi retorted.

Ahyou turned serious, looking out of the window, as if studying the tree. "Mother, didn't you once say that Mr.

Wang Jiali liked the tree? Well, cut it down so he'll never see it!" As a child, whenever she saw other kids with their fathers, she would think: my daddy is coming back soon and he will crack walnuts for me. After she grew up, she always alluded to that along-awaited father as *that Mr. Wang*. She bore the pain inside and knew that her mother, too, was carrying pain.

Qingyi felt that she had wronged her daughter by giving her such a father. Jiali was worse than having no father at all. Luckily, Ahyou did not count on any support other than her own studies. With that realization, Qingyi's heart felt at ease.

Ahyou muttered to herself. "If we don't act on our own, I'm afraid the only other way to get protection is to flaunt our overseas connections."

They had had to resort to various stratagems to stop the recurrent walnut fever. The walls to the courtyard had been repaired, but invariably torn down the next day. People were accustomed to taking this shortcut, and habits were hard to break. Mother and daughter had applied to the Neighborhood Committee for help, but the committee members had their hands full.

Ahyou was resolved. Only cutting down that tree would solve their problems. Besides, it would constitute revenge against Wang Jiali. Ahyou felt elated.

Before she left for her lab, she stood at her mother's bedside and tucked in her blanket. "That Mr. Wang Jiali," she said impulsively, "why doesn't he come back to visit? Is he afraid to? Is he ashamed? Can't he afford it? I saw in the English-language papers that he is going to Japan. Why doesn't he visit here?" After this outburst, Ahyou looked at her mother, unsure of her response.

"Do you want to see him?" Qingyi asked softly.

"No, of course not. I even want to get rid of his favorite tree."

"Let the past be forgotten." Qingyi smiled sweetly. "I repay everything I owe. I do not demand what is owed to me." This was Qingyi's philosophy of life. It was the philosophy of the weak, of course, for those without any incentive for struggle and strife.

Ahyou bent down and gave her mother a hug. "We rely on ourselves," she said softly, and turned to go. At the doorway, she added, "I've got the implements ready. I'll be back soon."

After Ahyou left, Qingyi closed her eyes and tried to get some rest. But she couldn't fall asleep. After a while, she groped for the letter under her pillow. It had arrived that morning. She had read it several times over. Wang Jiali had written to confess that he had wronged her. He knew the past was beyond repair, but he wanted to do something for her and Ahyou. He offered to support Ahyou for studies abroad, to be responsible for expenses.

Expenses? Preposterous! Qingyi thought. Is everything under the sun to be reckoned in terms of expenses? She had felt like a spirit shut up in a bottle, thrown to the bottom of the sea, cut off from all worldly contact. Her longing for news had been so agonizing that when it finally did come, she could not bear to face it. Anyway, she had known all along that news when it did come could only be bad news.

She deliberated whether or not to show the letter to Ahyou. The girl had the right to decide for herself. She had no right to hold back the message. As to herself, the past seemed like an unfinished piece of writing, torn up and burned. One could hardly pick up the ashes. Her real concern at present was the walnut tree. *Its* presence disturbed her peace.

The cut on her head caused her a dull pain. Ahyou had put some gauze over it and the strip of sticking plaster that held it in place adhered to the roots of her hair and also hurt. She put the letter on the stand near her bed. Her eyes wandered to the ax and the stool in the doorway. She wanted to do something to occupy her mind. Why not work at the tree? Ahyou would be so tired when she came back. Shakily Qingyi rose from bed, took up the tools, and ambled into the courtyard.

The moonlight was beautiful. The cold light of the moon filtered through the branches of the walnut tree, weaving a maze of light. The rich foliage formed a tentlike covering, irregular at the edges. The whole atmosphere was steeped in silence; not a leaf stirred.

Qingyi suddenly felt the blood coursing wildly within her body. This tree not only disturbed her peace; it had betrayed her. She put aside all doubts and uncertainties. One idea only occupied her: cut down that tree.

The ax was not as heavy as she thought, but the sound as it fell on the trunk was dull and heavy. Qingyi had to stop and catch her breath after every stroke. The reverberations of the strokes seemed to merge together into a plaintive cry. *Caring for you, caring for you.*

Qingyi stopped and looked around. There was not a whisper of wind. Every leaf was still. The notes of the cry recurred with every stroke of the ax, but Qingyi was unmoved. She kept on chopping. She felt somehow that she was striking at an empty crust. The trunk gave out a hollow sound that seemed to be asking: *Why are you hurting me?*

Qingyi looked at the tree closely. She had talked with it innumerable times, but of course she had known that the replies were just imaginary. Now the tree was literally speaking out loud. This tree, which had kept her company, had helped the ill and the dying, and conjured up so many disturbing memories, this tree was *really* speaking to her.

"Am I to blame?" it asked. The sound seemed to float from afar.

"You disturb my peace," Qingyi heard herself saying.

"I do not disturb you. You cannot deal with those who are really disturbing you, so you turn to the weak and defenseless. I am useful, I can serve. Don't you know that? Go and look up the *Book of Herbs*." The voice was close now, sorrowful but calm.

"I must strike you down precisely because you are useful. Because of your usefulness, these people come and make these disturbances." Qingyi found herself near tears. "There's nothing else I can do."

"I had hoped with you together. You also are weak." The walnut tree sighed. "Selfish and weak."

"I am just protecting myself. I am weak, therefore I must protect myself."

Qingyi suddenly became angry. Wasn't she entitled to some peace and quiet? Yes, the walnut tree was useful, but wasn't she herself useful, and wasn't Ahyou useful as well? Qingyi again took up the ax and slowly worked at the bark. Following every blow of the ax, the trunk began to bleed, though not profusely. The drops of blood sparkled in the moonlight.

What is that? Was it the blood of the tree? Qingyi stood up and inhaled at her respirator.

"These are my tears," a faint voice in the distance said, sorrowful but calm. "These are my tears."

Qingyi threw down the ax and tottered back to the house. She turned back for a last look and saw the tree bending, bending slowly toward the gap in the wall of the courtyard, tilting in slow motion, tilting until it finally collapsed without a sound. Its roots protruded from the ground, a tangled mass.

Because you are useful, but at the same time powerless, Qingyi thought to herself, *because you are but a tree . . .*

The moon shone on the fallen tree and the moundlike tangle of roots. It shone on Qingyi sitting at her desk, in front of the window.

Qingyi sat unmoving, taking no note of the time.

"Mother, the walnut tree has fallen." Ahyou exclaimed as she stepped into the room. "How strange!" Her round face was flushed, and she held a bunch of walnuts in her hand, each walnut round and plump and green, the same bunch that had poked though the gap in the window.

Ahyou placed the walnuts on the bedside table with a flush of victory. She plucked up the pale blue envelope. She read it through several times, stopped to think for a moment, then gave one look at her mother, whereupon she tore the letter into two. "We rely on ourselves, don't we, Mommy?" She hugged Qingyi's thin shoulders.

Qingyi opened the drawer of the desk. Both their salaries were kept there. She took out the money and started counting.

"What's that for, Mommy?" Ahyou leaned over and asked.

"To pay the fine." Qingyi lifted her head and smiled serenely. "We did not get permission from the Environmental Bureau to cut down the tree. We must pay the fine."

From The Bear's Paw, *Hundred Flowers Publishers, 1984. Translated in Beijing, 1988.*

GLOSSARY

Battalion During the Cultural Revolution, various contending factions named themselves after military units.

Big-character posters Once a person is denounced, he is attacked in big-character signs that are posted in public places.

Cultural Revolution Officially launched as the Great Proletarian Cultural Revolution in 1966, it was conceived as a campaign to wipe out all signs of revisionism and reversals to the capitalist road by appealing directly to the masses by Mao Zedong himself. After many disastrous twists and turns, it was effectively ended in 1976 with the death of Mao and the toppling of the Gang of Four (Jiang Qing, widow of Mao; Zhang Chunqiao, vice-premier; Yao Wenyuan, vice-premier; and Wang Hongwen, vice-chairman of the party). Now euphemistically alluded to as the "ten years of turmoil."

erguodou A strong white liquor.

fen One-tenth of a *jiao*.

Great Leap Forward A campaign in 1958–59 to vault into communism overnight by making pig iron in backyard furnaces and escalating agricultural production. The results were economic disaster and large numbers of deaths by famine.

hatted/unhatted The rightist political label, denoting an enemy category, as attached to a designated individual. The label can be removed after a period of thought reform, a practice popularly known as *unhatting*. Usually associated with the antirightist campaign of 1957, wherein those who answered the call to offer criticism and advice to the party during the Hundred Flowers movement ("let a hundred flowers bloom, let a hundred schools contend") were trapped as antiparty, antisocialist rightists and labeled accordingly.

jiao One-tenth of a *yuan*.

jin A measure of weight, equivalent to half a kilogram.

kang Rectangular, elevated platform bed, built of adobe, heated from within by a tunnel extending from stove in same or adjoining room.

li A measure of distance, equivalent to half a kilometer.

liang One-tenth of a *jin*.

PLA Abbreviation of the People's Liberation Army.

thirty-five legs Popular saying, referring to the set of furniture that the bridegroom is expected to provide. The growing number of legs signals the newlyweds' demand for more elaborate furniture.

yuan The basic monetary unit of *renminbi* (RMB). Official rate of exchange is about 5 RMB = \$1.

ABOUT THE TRANSLATOR

ZHU HONG, who has collected these stories and translated them into English, is a professor of Anglo-American literature at the Institute of Foreign Literature/Chinese Academy of Social Sciences in Beijing. Recognized in her own country for her writings on nineteenth-century fiction and literary interpretation, Zhu Hong has always been concerned with women's issues in China. This volume of translations will be followed by a critical study of Chinese/Anglo-American women writers.

Zhu Hong has traveled extensively abroad and has been a visiting fellow at the Harvard-Yenching Institute and the Bunting Institute of Radcliffe College in Cambridge, Massachusetts; the Humanities Research Centre at the Australian National University in Canberra; the University of Kent at Canterbury; the Rockefeller Study Center in Bellagio, Italy; and the National Center for the Humanities in North Carolina.

Zhu Hong embarked on this book of translations several years ago in the midst of many other commitments. It was finally at the Bunting Institute of Radcliffe College, with "a room of her own" and the support of the women's community there, that she was able to give the volume its final shape.

TITLES OF THE AVAILABLE PRESS
in order of publication

★Available in a Ballantine Mass Market Edition.

ARLISS, a novel by Llya Allen

THE CHINESE WESTERN: Short Fiction from Today's China, translated by Zhu Hong*

THE VOLUNTEERS, a novel by Moacyr Scliar

LOST SOULS, a novel by Anthony Schmitz

SEESAW MILLIONS, a novel by Janwillem van de Wetering

SWEET DIAMOND DUST, a novel by Rosario Ferré

SMOKEHOUSE JAM, a novel by Lloyd Little

THE ENGIMATIC EYE, short stories by Moacyr Scliar

THE WAY IT HAPPENS IN NOVELS, a novel by Kathleen O'Connor

THE FLAME FOREST, a novel by Michael Upchurch

FAMOUS QUESTIONS, a novel by Fanny Howe

SON OF TWO WORLDS, a novel by Haydn Middleton

WITHOUT A FARMHOUSE NEAR, a nonfiction by Deborah Rawson

THE RATTLESNAKE MASTER, a novel by Beaufort Cranford

BENEATH THE WATERS, a novel by Oswaldo França, Júnior

AN AVAILABLE MAN, a novel by Patric Kuh

THE HOLLOW DOLL (A Little Box of Japanese Shocks), by William Bohnaker

MAX AND THE CATS, a novel by Moacyr Scliar

FLIEGELMAN'S DESIRE, a novel by Lewis Buzbee

SLOW BURN, a novel by Sabina Murray

THE CARNAL PRAYER MAT, by Li Yu, translated by Patrick Hanon

THE MAN WHO WASN'T THERE, by Pat Barker

I WAS DORA SUAREZ, a mystery by Derek Raymond

LIVE FROM EARTH, a novel by Lance Olsen

THE CUTTER, a novel by Virgil Suarez

ONE SUMMER OUT WEST, a novel by Philippe Labro, translated by William R. Byron.

THE CHRIST OF THE BUTTERFLIES, a novel by Ardythe Ashley

CHINESE POETRY: Through the Words of the People, edited by Bonnie McCandless

IN SEARCH OF THE PERFECT RAVIOLI, a novel by Paul Mantee

SERENITY OF WHITENESS: Stories By and About Women in Contemporary China, selected and translated by Zhu Hong

*Available in a Ballantine Mass Market Edition.